DOCTOR WHO

AUTUMN MIST

DAVID A. McINTEE

D0880440

BBC

Published by BBC Worldwide Ltd,
Woodlands, 80 Wood Lane
London W12 0TT

First published 1999
Copyright © David A. McIntee 1999
The moral right of the author has been asserted

Original series broadcast on the BBC
Format © BBC 1963
Doctor Who and TARDIS are trademarks of the BBC

ISBN 0 563 55583 1
Imaging by Black Sheep, copyright © BBC 1999

Printed and bound in Great Britain by Mackays of Chatham
Cover printed by Belmont Press Ltd, Northampton

Acknowledgements this time to most everyone on the Authors' List, but especially Paul Leonard, Jon Blum, Peter Anghelides, Jac Rayner and Steve Cole. Maria for the German translations, and Lesley for digging out the poetry.

Also thanks to all those who've bought these ten Who books…

No great dependence is to be placed on the eagerness of young soldiers for action, for the prospect of fighting is agreeable to those who are strangers to it...

– Vegetius

Prologue

15 December 1944

Rapid fire passed over Wiesniewski's head with a ripping sound as he gasped for breath in the shelter of a fallen tree. From all around him the rest of the platoon returned fire. Not that their carbines would do any good against the machine guns in their small trio of pillboxes around the roadside bunker, but at least they'd discourage any Germans from venturing outside.

Wiesniewski doubted they would want to anyway: even without the gunfire their bunker would keep them sheltered from the heavy snow. With dusk falling, his snow-sodden uniform was beginning to stiffen, making his whole body look as if it had been frozen solid. Wiesniewski risked a look over the fallen trunk.

Cahill, Jonas and Dexter were lying amid their frosted blood in the hundred-foot strip of open ground that separated the edge of the woods from the Germans. Wade hadn't even got that far: he was still suspended on the barbed wire ten feet out from the trees.

As Wiesniewski fumbled for a new clip for his Thompson, someone pitched a grenade at the firing slit of the nearest pillbox, but the white ground was too wet for it to bounce on, and it exploded several yards short. The German guns didn't let up, and further bursts tore at the branches around Wiesniewski as Corporal Harris dived into cover beside him. 'Any luck from the other side of the trail?'

Harris shook his head. 'The road's mined, L.T. We'd never get round that way.'

'Damn.' Wade's blood had stopped dripping, Wiesniewski noticed absently, and had frozen into red icicles. It was a strange last impression to have of someone who was usually huddled closest round the fire. 'At least night's falling. Some Christmas, huh…?'

A dozen miles to the east, a small town nestled in the shelter of the various embankments and fortifications of the West Wall.

A trio of SdKfz 232 armoured command vehicles sped into the town square. They were eight-wheeled armoured cars, as self-contained as any tank, with a 20-mm cannon in the small turret. All three had peculiar antennae mounted on them, not unlike an indoor overhead clothes rack. One end was mounted over the turret, while the other was bolted to the rear of the vehicle.

'*Sturmbannführer*,' a man in the lead vehicle said, 'it's happening again.'

'Halt here,' the *Sturmbannführer* told the driver. He dropped from the turret into the cramped compartment in the centre of the vehicle. Where there would normally be ammunition, tools and paperwork stored, this 232 had a cluster of equipment that looked like radio and radar set-ups. Tiny green screens flickered with wave peaks. 'Where?'

'Difficult to tell,' the operator replied, 'but I think somewhere near Monschau.'

'Damn! We'll have to wait until the offensive has passed. Set up a command post here. We'll notify Wewelsburg that we have a potential capture here.'

The guns in the German bunker nest were still firing sporadically once night had fallen, but now they were nowhere near Wiesniewski. He had had a couple of the men string knives and spare helmets in the trees near the road. Their occasional clatter in the wind drew fire from the bunker, leaving the men free to move quietly elsewhere.

Wiesniewski, Harris and the others slipped around to the far side of the emplacements under cover of darkness, and were now crawling along under the barbed-wire perimeter. It reminded Wiesniewski a little of trying to sneak into the ballpark back in Pittsburgh, to see games without buying a ticket. Back then, the threat of a thick ear from one of the cops seemed almost as scary as the threat of death here.

Sweating despite the cold, Wiesniewski emerged from the last stretch of wire and started probing the muddy ground with a bayonet, searching for mines in his path. Behind him, Harris was silently making sure the rest of the men followed exactly in Wiesniewski's path.

It was a painfully slow crawl to the depression that marked the bunker's steel door, and Wiesniewski would have given a month's pay to be able to stand up and run at it. If he could have done so without being gunned down.

Gritting his teeth to stop them from chattering, Wiesniewski slowly cocked his Thompson, muffling the sound with his gloved hand. Harris and the other three men joined him. Anticipating his next wish, Harris took a grenade from his webbing. Wiesniewski nodded in agreement.

He then put his ear to the door, listening. He didn't want to find a bunch of gun muzzles pointed at him, if the occupants had heard him moving around. It might also help to try to judge how many men were in there.

'*Was werden die Amerikaner jetzt tun?*' a distinctly young voice was asking. '*Noch einmal angreifen, oder warten bis zur morgendëmmerung?*' Whatever that meant, the man's tone seemed relaxed enough. He hadn't been heard.

There was a rattle of cans, and Wiesniewski could imagine the ersatz coffee being poured. Even that would be better than nothing right now. '*Weder noch,*' a more weary voice replied. '*Sie werden sich unter dem schutz der dunkelheit zu ihren positionen zurückziehen.*'

'*Glauben sie, Herr Feldwebel?*' the first asked in a hopeful tone.

There was a sound of almost laughing, and a third voice joined in. '*Sie machen es genauso wie wir – sie fechten kleinere gefechte, um die neuankömmlinge ein bißchen pulver riechen zu lassen, bevor sie an wichtigere Fronten schicken. Wenn das ein ernsthafter angriff gewesen wäre, hätten sie Panzer mitgeschickt. Ich habe es ihnen ja schon gesagt: Hier passiert nie was ernstes.*'

Easier not to think of them as people if he couldn't understand them. Wiesniewski held up three fingers to Harris and gently tried the door handle. He doubted they would have locked the door on their side of the lines, since it would have trapped them if someone got a flame-thrower near enough to the firing slit.

He was right: the handle moved very gently. Hoping nobody inside had noticed, Wiesniewski mouthed 'now' to Harris, who pulled the pin on the grenade. Wiesniewski counted to three and tugged the door open. He ducked back as Harris tossed the grenade in.

The three Germans in the central room barely had time to start a yell before the grenade went off. Wiesniewski immediately ducked inside, spraying the room with gunfire.

There were three other doors inside, one for each pillbox, and Wiesniewski went straight for the one directly opposite. A German opened it just in time to catch a burst of fire.

There was more shooting from behind and to the sides as his men took the other two pillboxes, but Wiesniewski knew better than to divert his attention to them before securing his own target. He trusted his men not to let one of their targets get to him. The remaining two gunners in the pillbox had barely started to turn round before Wiesniewski shot them.

Only then did he look round to see how the others were doing.

Jansen had fallen, but Harris and the other two men had finished off the defenders. Wiesniewski grinned with relief, and nodded to Harris. 'Nice work, Joe.' He led the men back out of the bunker, glad to be away from the trapped smoke and smell of blood. 'OK, Joe, get back to the road and get a medical jeep up here. I'll set a couple of thermite charges in the bunker's ammo, just in case –'

Without warning, the harsh sound of machine-gun fire tore across the field. Wiesniewski dived to the ground instantly, catching Harris's freezing out of the corner of his eye. Across the field, a German half-track was heading down the road from behind their lines, a gunner firing from it.

He rolled to look for the others, but they were nowhere to be seen and Wiesniewski assumed they'd taken cover in the bunker. Only Harris was still with him, toppling slowly to the ground. 'Joe…'

The sound of the machine guns was slowing strangely, from the familiar maniacal chatter to a steady metronomic beat, like the ticking of an impossibly loud clock. At first Wiesniewski wasn't too concerned – he knew that time seemed to slow down sometimes when a guy was in mortal peril. No doubt the medics had some name for it or other.

Then he realised that his own ragged breathing still sounded normal and his heart was racing.

Wire jangled abruptly and Wiesniewski spun, firing wildly at the source. It was the barbed wire where Wade's corpse had hung. The wire was quivering like a bandsaw, but Wade wasn't there any more.

He instinctively looked for the bodies of the others in the open ground, and realised that Joe Harris wasn't there, either. Wiesniewski could have sworn he was dead – he had fallen right there… Could he have recovered enough to make it back to the bunker? Surely not without Wiesniewski hearing him…

Apart from the guns, there was no other sound. No birds, no footsteps, no voices. He could see flashes of mortar fire to the north, where another platoon was attacking a similar target, but they were unaccountably silent. The half-track was silent, too, and seemed to have stopped. He fired a burst at it, but nothing seemed to happen. The sound seemed like an insult to the forest.

He could sense something from the other direction, though. It wasn't a silence, but something beyond silence; it was, he supposed, the opposite of sound, where silence was merely the absence of it. Whatever it was, it was as noticeable as shots or screams would have been, and far more unnerving.

He turned to face the forest. Snow started to shake loose from the branches all around. Twigs broke soundlessly, and were carried on through the air. The forest closed in, black shadows grasping at the snow. Tiny breezes lifted snowflakes from the ground in an indistinct dance. The jagged shadows rippled and twisted, flitting around between the trees as if seeking shelter from the moonlight.

Skin crawling, Wiesniewski had the gut feeling that something was approaching. He cocked the Thompson and backtracked slowly, afraid to turn his back to whatever it was.

He wasn't afraid of the Germans, but so what? This wasn't them. He didn't know what it was, but he knew that much. And he knew also he was alone out here.

Alone as far as men were concerned, at least.

There were no soldiers, no bodies, but *something* was out here with him, and every animal instinct in his psyche told him that this was a war zone and he was an open target.

Something stirred the snow, but it wasn't a man. All around Wiesniewski, ripples of darkness rushed forward, and he screamed…

Chapter One
Greif

Fitz Kreiner was in the TARDIS's kitchen, trying to work out where the power for the microwave was coming from. An oven that looked like a TV and had no heating elements was weird enough, even before he had noticed that it worked without being plugged in.

Sam had originally told him that the TARDIS didn't have a kitchen: just a food machine. Fitz felt more comfortable slapping some scrambled eggs on toast into shape himself, if only because it gave his hands something to do when they wanted to be lighting up a cigarette. So he had found a kitchen.

The thing about it was, he wasn't sure whether Sam simply hadn't known that the kitchen was there, or whether the Doctor – or indeed the TARDIS itself – had created one for him.

It was, he had to admit, a hell of a kitchen. All he'd wanted was a little cubbyhole with a stove on which to heat a tin of something, but he got a cross between a medieval kitchen and Frankenstein's laboratory. Stone and wood, mingling with chrome and plastic. He kept meaning to take a look up the chimney that was over the open fireplace, to see where it went. Surely there couldn't be an opening out of the TARDIS there. Unfortunately, the log fire that burned therein never went out, even though it had never been stoked up as far as he knew.

The most important thing today was that Sam never came to the kitchen. He wasn't sure he really wanted to talk to her until he got some things worked out in his head – like, was the Sam he had slept with in San Francisco in *any way* the same

Sam who was with them now? Did she remember any of it – and, if so, what was she feeling about it? She'd been all sickly understanding to start with, but now she'd had time to think about it… Well, at least she hadn't hit him yet, so that was probably a positive sign.

For a moment he imagined himself as the jet-setting playboy to whom this kind of concern would never even occur. He wondered if the Doctor had *ever* been tempted over all his years of travels with pretty girls. Probably not, he decided. That would be too obvious, somehow.

The ground disappeared from under Wiesniewski's feet, and he plunged headlong into an abandoned foxhole, landing painfully. He gasped for breath, ready to set off again. His eyes darted frantically around, looking for any sign of that… whatever it was.

Something metallic jangled behind him and he rolled aside, grabbing for his gun. It wasn't there, and he wondered where he had left it.

Then he saw that the source of the noise was just a punctured ration can, hanging from a wire. The can's label proclaimed that it had once contained peaches from California. At least that meant he'd reached an American outpost.

He froze. What the hell was he doing back at an American line, anyway? He didn't remember running – just the darkness and its attendant silence rushing at him. Then nothing – nothing at all.

Now he was here.

Jesus, was he having blackouts now? He resolved not to mention that when he got back – much as he wanted to get back to the States, he didn't want it to be as a mental case. 'Get a grip,' he muttered to himself, taking several deep breaths. He'd been scared earlier. That was nothing new, of course: he'd been scared since he got to Europe, but this wasn't the ordinary fear of battle. He couldn't even remember what it was that had so frightened him.

Whatever he had been running from, it wasn't the Germans, surely. He remembered seeing a patrol show up, but it was some way away, and the Germans there had seemed scared, too. There had been something else; he was sure of it.

Unfortunately that was all he could be sure of. Anyway, how did he know it wasn't the Germans? Maybe they were testing some new weapon that messed with your head and made you see things. Some sort of gas, maybe. That made some sense, didn't it?

Yeah, that must be it. They'd tried some sort of new weapon on him and it had worked, hadn't it? Sent him running like a spooked colt. He repeated the thought to himself until it drowned out the unnerving protests from his subconscious. Now he just had to figure out where he was and get back to Company HQ.

The destination monitor was reading TEMPORAL ORBIT when Fitz reached the console room, cradling a cuppa. Sam was there, of course; she and the Doctor stuck so casually together that Fitz could almost imagine they'd been married for years.

The Doctor was in his shirtsleeves but still looked like he was ready to audition for a biopic of Oscar Wilde. His hair, a little longer than Fitz's, but a little curlier, was getting in the way as he hunched over an open panel on the central console. 'Something's not right…'

'How d'you mean?' Sam asked. She had shortish blonde hair again, and was wearing jeans and a PINKY AND THE BRAIN T-shirt. Whatever Pinky and the Brain was.

'I can't get the TARDIS away from Earth. Whatever destination I program, it keeps resetting back to Earth.' They looked up at the monitor, which remained frustratingly at the temporal-orbit setting.

'That's not the half of it,' Fitz said, noticing something on the mahogany console. He gingerly prodded the date readout. The revolving blocks, which normally indicated the day, month and year of arrival, were now blank. Fitz turned them over with a finger. 'Look. As if it isn't enough that something with only four sides could go up to ninety-nine…'

The Doctor came round to look. 'Four sides up to ninety-nine? That's just a function of the Heisenberg circuits. But I don't think they're supposed to go blank.' He sighed. 'I get the impression that nothing is going to help short of either invasive surgery –' Fitz blinked at the choice of term to describe repairs to a machine – 'or simply materialising back on Earth.'

'Materialise,' Sam suggested firmly. 'You remember what happened last time you started working on the TARDIS while in space…'

'I certainly never intended for us to be hauled off to Skaro. But you're right, of course,' he added with a smile. 'Materialisation it is.' The Doctor moved back to the relevant panel and operated some brass knobs and levers. The destination monitor responded by finally giving a reading, though it wasn't as much as could have been hoped for. '"Earth, Unknown Era". Not very helpful.'

Sam shook her head. 'You should have got a better OS for the TARDIS's systems. Was this one from a free CD on a magazine cover?'

'You know what they say about beggars not being choosers. The same holds true for thieves at times.' The Doctor threw a switch and a sky formed overhead. It wasn't any brighter than the usual shadows up there in that indeterminate ceiling. At least, Fitz supposed that logically there must be a ceiling, since the destination monitor and part of the time rotor were suspended from it. But whenever he tried to look at it his eyes just slid away, without registering what was really up there. For now, however, there were dimly lit clouds and snowflakes. Even though it was only an image of the weather outside, Fitz felt colder already.

'Winter!' the Doctor exclaimed. 'Excellent! Crisp snow, clear air, hot toddies…' As he enthused about winter wonders, he went over to retrieve a dark green velvet frock coat from a nearby stand. His sonic screwdriver and a few other oddments were on a table nearby, and he dropped them into the pockets, then looked down at his shoes. 'Hmm. No weather for the likes of you,' he muttered, kicking the loafers off. 'Sorry, but you'll just have to sit this one out.' He pulled a pair of knee-length boots from the cupboard. 'I suggest you wrap up warmly,' he called to Sam and Fitz. 'Don't want you to catch a chill. Oh, and be sure to cover your throat. That's very important when going from a warmer clime to a cooler one.'

'Did you get that from some ancient source of Time Lord wisdom?' Fitz asked.

'No, from David Niven, but it's still good advice.'

Sam was first out of the TARDIS, having found a thick woollen coat to wrap up in. As well as needing the coat for the cold, it also felt oddly comforting to be wrapped in something so enfolding and protective.

The TARDIS had materialised at one end of a bridge across a fast-flowing river. Though it was still dark, the broad valley they were in was illuminated by an eerie and unnatural glow from the clouds above. That shifting glow in turn reflected off the snow that covered the fields to either side. On the far side of the river, on a ridge line above, a darker mass was spread. Buildings, Sam thought – buildings without lights, backed by trees.

On this side of the river, the fields stretched away to some wooded slopes in the middle distance. Sam wasn't entirely sure, but there seemed to be some sort of buildings there, too.

They didn't look like houses, more like squat blockhouses or bunkers.

The fresh air was nice, if chilly, and Sam wandered off along the bridge. She peered down at the water below, but it was just a dark abyss. She imagined in daylight the view would've been quite pleasant, if only –

Sam shivered, feeling as if she were being watched. She had that weird feeling, as if someone had walked over her grave.

'The Evergreen Man,' a presence in the tree line opined to its neighbour. From their position they could observe the newcomers quite unseen, though it didn't stop the neighbour from feeling nervous about the possibility of being discovered.

'Is that what you call him?'

'It is who he is. What we call him matters little.'

'I suppose he is, at that… I never really looked at it that way.' Lots of other ways, but not that way. 'Couldn't we just go down now, and –'

'No. There are rules. Even we cannot flout them.'

'Even if the rules are wrong?'

'Who would judge whether they are? You? Me? Anyone who wishes?'

That was, unfortunately, an accurate point. It was still frustrating. 'Maybe somebody has to.'

'Perhaps. But not us. What happens, happens.'

'This looks groovy,' Fitz said, his voice less sarcastic than even he had expected. He had pulled on a brown leather jacket and some thick woollen gloves. 'Weird sky…'

The Doctor looked up from locking the TARDIS doors. 'Lights.' He had wrapped an old silk scarf round his throat, but otherwise didn't seem to mind the temperature.

'Lights?'

The Doctor nodded. 'Searchlights, I suppose. Someone's aiming them at the cloud cover from somewhere over there.' He pointed towards the trees. 'Maybe five or ten miles away, I should think. Quite a moving effect, isn't it?'

'To light up this area?'

'Presumably. I wonder why... Remind me to ask, when we meet someone. It might be a funfair... Or a mystery play, if it's Christmas. Haven't seen one of those in years.'

'A mystery play?'

'No, a Christmas.' The Doctor strolled off towards the bridge, looking up at the sky. 'Too much cloud cover to judge our position by the stars... From those trees I'd say we're in the northern hemisphere; Western Europe, or I'd be very surprised. This reminds me of the time I... Are you listening?'

Fitz wondered how the Doctor could be so relaxed in this weather. 'I dunno, really. I just saw a couple of brass monkeys carrying some welding gear home, and that's a bit of a distraction.'

'Oh. Well, I'm sure that's why man invented clothes instead.'

Sam wished for a moment that she had brought along the postcards her other self had left for her, after her experiences in San Francisco. She wasn't sure whether she'd like to read them in more privacy, away from the TARDIS, Fitz and the Doctor, or whether to tear them up and drop them in the river.

Some things were better left unsaid and unknown, and it was a painful truth that you usually didn't find out if they *were* better that way until it was too late.

Give Fitz his due, he hadn't pushed his luck by mentioning his liaisons with her other self. A few months ago he would have, but not now, and she was grateful for that. Intellectually, she knew she should probably talk to him about it to work things out, but people didn't always do what was right or best, did they? Not even her.

It was more comfortable to be absent-mindedly taking the opposite direction from Fitz, telling herself she was going to get a better view of the area from higher ground. More than anything, she needed more time to think.

Fitz glanced round to see that Sam had wandered off the other end of the bridge, and for a moment he considered following. No. He wasn't that stupid – not any more, anyway. All things considered, it'd be more sensible to follow the Doctor and let Sam have her space for a while. Women seemed to like that, Fitz thought.

'Look at this,' the Doctor was saying. 'Very interesting…' He had wandered over to a low concrete bunker set in a nearby bend in the river. He pushed at the clean metal door, and it swung open without resistance.

Fitz wasn't too impressed. 'It's just a pillbox.' Concrete walls, a few wooden stools, a small table. Nothing to write home about.

The Doctor was examining the plain walls with enthusiasm. 'But look there. The lamps are lit and there's ammunition ready, but no one's here.'

Fitz suddenly felt uneasy. Wartime. Fitz the Fritz. Laughing kids and fights. He was glad of the owners' absence. Thank heavens for small mercies. 'It must have been abandoned,' he said, affecting a casual tone. 'If this *is* wartime, perhaps the enemy's advanced past here.'

The Doctor shook his head, pacing around. 'No no no. Wouldn't an opposing force have taken this ammunition for itself?'

'Not if they use a different calibre.' Fitz gave himself a mental pat on the back.

'Then why not destroy it, so that the original owners can't steal it back? And, if it was simply abandoned, then why are there machine-gun mounts and ammunition, but no guns?'

8

'They must have taken them with them. Better that than leave them for the enemy to use.'

'Guns without ammunition aren't very useful. It'd make more sense to take the ammo and leave the guns, or take the guns and destroy the ammo. There's one explanation that makes sense. A supply stop.'

It was, Fitz supposed, rather inevitable. 'You mean someone will stop by to reload here?' And probably accuse himself and the Doctor of being spies, enemies, thieves or just bloody nuisances.

The Doctor nodded. 'German troops, too.'

'You can tell that from the dust and the footprints they've left behind, right?' Fitz crossed his arms and looked at the Doctor.

'Hmm. And the German writing on the ammunition boxes is a bit of a clue as well.'

'Hmm,' Fitz agreed, mock-thoughtfully. 'I think it's at this point that it might be a good idea to get back in the TARDIS and try again. I'm first-generation half-German and don't even speak the bloody lingo. I'd be shot as a traitor or a spy before you could say "ve haff vays of making you talk".'

'Not at all,' the Doctor said, breezily. 'Whatever language you speak, they'd hear it as perfect German.'

'Oh, yeah. The TARDIS again.' It didn't inspire that much confidence.

'She has her talents.'

'And her mood swings, in case you're forgetting. Do TARDISes get moody once a month?'

The Doctor seemed to consider this carefully. 'I shouldn't think so...' There was a distant rumbling from outside. 'I hope that isn't the weather changing. I'd take snow over rain any day of the week.' They went outside, where a few stray snowflakes were still drifting down.

'Look,' Fitz said, nodding towards the horizon where the

9

Doctor had said he thought the searchlights were. The sky was flickering and flashing, casting more brief patches of light on the clouds in that area. 'Something must be on fire.'

The Doctor's expression hardened. 'Back to the TARDIS. Sam!' he yelled across the river. 'Back to the TARDIS!'

'What?' Fitz asked, but already he heard the whistle that answered the question. 'Incoming!'

Sam's thoughts about Fitz, the Doctor and her other life were pushed aside in an instant as the Doctor's yell reached her. For a moment she was confused, but then made out the shrieking in the air. Fear gave her a hearty shove to start her running back down towards the bridge by the TARDIS. She had seen enough war movies to know what that sound represented.

She dived headlong into the snow as an explosion nearby showered her with earth. The dive saved her life, as the shrapnel passed too close over her back. She darted over and flung herself into the fresh crater as water fountained up from the river, soaking her.

She caught a brief frantic glimpse of the Doctor and Fitz turn and bolt back towards the bunker they had been looking at, but then buried her face in the cold earth as more blasts shook the world around her.

Chunks of stone from the side of the bridge burst away, splashing into the water. Just as she raised her head to see what the hell had happened, another shell screamed down, this time hitting the bridge square on.

The central arch lurched, torn apart in a cloud of dust and flying stone. Though the TARDIS had survived the blast, Sam's relief didn't last long. As she watched in horror, she realised that a chunk of the bridge several yards wide was crumbling.

Stone creaked and scraped, and the TARDIS listed alarmingly. With nothing to support it, the edge of the breach gave way, and the TARDIS toppled inexorably over the edge.

With almost as big a splash as the exploding shell, it crashed into the water, followed by still more pieces of stone.

The forest erupted with artillery fire – a deafening and primal cacophony. Wiesniewski was trapped, fenced in by exploding shells. Snow was falling again, but only from the higher branches as the trees shook.

Explosions were tearing the forest apart, as the air was filled with a storm of flying shards of wood laced with heated shrapnel.

Wiesniewski wasn't stupid enough to try to run, knowing that the shrapnel would cut him down. Instead he hugged the ground, praying that no shell would make it through the thick tree cover to land on top of him.

He tried to reassure himself by counting his blessings; at least this was something real and tangible to fear, unlike shadows in the mist.

Fitz was fervently wishing he could have been as sanguine about this as the various movie heroes would be. That would be better than fighting to retain bladder control. 'Sam!' the Doctor was calling from beside him, pacing around nervously. 'Sam?'

Though there was no answering call, Fitz was relieved to see Sam stumbling out of a crater and waving. The Doctor looked as if he was about to cry with relief. Maybe he was, for all Fitz knew. 'Half bloody deaf,' she shouted. 'Hang on a minute…'

A few jagged pieces of stone poked up above the surface of the river, but there was no sign of the TARDIS. They didn't even know how deep the water was here, and it was still too dark to see.

Fitz had an uncomfortable thought. 'Doctor, you don't think the TARDIS could have been –'

'Destroyed? No.' The Doctor moved up and down the path

by the bank, trying to get a good view. 'We just can't get to it.' He looked back at Sam. 'Can you hear me now?'

'Yeah, just about. How's the TARDIS?'

'She's fine, but we'll need some help to get her out of the river. I suppose we'll have to get on good terms with the engineering corps of one side or the other.' That didn't sound like a good idea to Fitz. He didn't fancy his chances of getting all pally with someone who'd just tried to bomb him flat.

'Which side?'

'That depends on which war this is!'

'You mean you don't know?'

'It's difficult to tell. When you're in the firing line, most modern wars are a bit like slasher movies: when you've seen one, you've seen them all.'

'That'd be funnier if I wasn't the blonde female separated from the others,' Sam retorted. 'You know what happens to them!' Fitz didn't, as it happened, but he could guess.

The Doctor merely looked vague and smiled reassuringly. He pointed downstream. 'We'll head that way and look for another road or bridge. Why don't you try the village, there? Somebody must know the nearest bridge.'

'Will do,' Sam called back. With a wave, she turned and started towards the village. Fitz looked around, wondering whether those responsible for the shelling were going to be coming to check on the results of their handiwork.

He looked back at the Doctor and shrugged. There wasn't much else he could do. 'Lead on, Macduff.'

'"*Lay* on,"' the Doctor said absently.

The streets of the little town were eerily silent when Sam got there. She could barely see where she was walking, either, as there were no lights on at all. She racked her brains, trying to remember whether other parts of Europe had blackouts in the war as well as Britain, but then decided that they did; it was common sense, really, wasn't it?

She didn't want to risk calling at one of the houses, but was able to find her way to a small inn on a corner of the town square. She knocked, trying to be both loud enough to wake the occupants, but quiet enough not to attract any other attention. There was no answer, though she couldn't tell whether the occupants were asleep, ignoring her or absent altogether.

Not wanting to push her luck, and feeling some sympathy for anyone who had to live in the firing line, Sam moved on along the street. A glimmer of light caught her eye at the end of the street and she realised it was a lamp showing through an open door.

She approached and knocked cautiously on the door. 'Hello? Anyone home?' There was no answer. Sam was reluctant to go nosing around in a stranger's house, but she was more reluctant to be trapped here, so she went in, closing the door behind her. There wasn't a sound from anywhere in the house, bar the ticking of a clock on the mantel. A half-eaten meal was on the table in the kitchen, but it was stone-cold. Nobody had been here for several hours at least, and they had left in a hurry.

Sam had no idea what had happened to the owners of this house, but she couldn't blame them for having fled. It was actually quite spooky, not just because the place was a ghost town, but because it reminded her so much of the news reports from Bosnia. It was a freaky feeling, as if she was in a picture and somehow divorced from herself. Almost as if she wasn't really here.

She still had that feeling from earlier, too: someone walking over her grave.

The feeling dissipated slightly when she saw a telephone in the corner of the living room. It was on a mahogany table beside a large armchair, and she got the impression that it was probably where the man of the house sat. Sexist, but, if this was the past, then true as well.

She lifted the receiver and rattled the phone a bit, but the line was as silent and dead as the rest of the village seemed to be.

Sam jumped as the door crashed open, and a man pointed a gun at her. There was a blur of drab-green uniforms as a couple of other men followed him in. 'Put the phone down, sister. Nice and slow.'

'It's dead,' Sam said numbly, trying to calm herself after the sudden shock. What the hell was going on here?

'Put it down or so are you.'

Sam did so, taking stock of the men. They seemed to be American soldiers, though with old uniforms, like the ones she'd seen in war movies on TV. At least that gave her a clue to the date: sometime in the last couple of years of World War Two.

The first man smiled faintly as he appraised her – bloody typical – and lowered his Tommy gun. Now she could make out the sergeant's stripes on his sleeve, too. 'A "please" wouldn't have killed you, would it?' she demanded, recovering.

His expression faltered. 'You're a Brit? Who were you trying to call?'

'Nobody yet. I was just trying to get an open line to find some help. Not only do I not know where I am, but our transport was knocked into the river when the shelling hit the bridge down there.' She gestured in the direction of the TARDIS.

The soldiers exchanged glances. 'You said "our". How many of you are there?'

'Two others: the Doctor and an orderly.' Best to try to make a favourable impression, even if it required a little white lie. 'We got separated when our transport broke down on the bridge, and they're on the other side of the river.'

14

The sergeant hesitated. 'Civilians. Hoo-rah. Charlie, get the field wire set up. I want a watch on the Losheim road.' He turned back to Sam. 'OK, so you say you're a Brit. What's your name?'

'Samantha Jones. Sam.'

He started to speak, then his eyes unfocused for a moment. 'Well, at least you're probably not a spy.'

'That makes a nice change,' she murmured. 'Usually people assume the opposite.' And it was a hell of a surprise that this guy didn't. She was grateful for it all the same. 'I'm flattered by your trust, Sergeant…?'

'Kovacs. Jeff Kovacs. And who said I trusted you?' His uniform was rumpled, of course, as were those of the other soldiers. But this sergeant gave off the subconscious impression that any and all clothes would look rumpled on him. He just wasn't meant to look respectable. Even his shaved head – surely the simplest of looks to maintain – had a shadow of stubble across it.

As well as the Tommy gun he carried he had a pistol belt. Sam just *knew* that it held a Colt .45 or something, not through recognising it, but because she instinctively knew he was the type of guy who would insist on a famous macho brand to make him feel more heroic. He was probably a complete tosser, then.

She sighed. Tosser or not, the presence of World War Two-era Allied troops in a European setting meant the alternative army to seek help from was the one full of Nazis. She imagined even the biggest tosser was preferable company to them.

'Well… um, Kovacs, I don't suppose you know where I could find someone able to get our transport out of the river?'

Kovacs seemed to gather his senses. 'Bold,' he said. 'If I did, I wouldn't tell you till you've been debriefed back at Company HQ. If your story checks out there, then they'll know the answer better than I would.'

'Cool,' Sam replied, with a confidence she didn't entirely feel.

One of the other soldiers, a bearded private, came in from the doorway. 'Sarge, there's a whole column of trucks and tank destroyers heading back toward Bucholz Station.'

'Theirs or ours, Charlie?'

'Ours. Looks like the 14th Cavalry.'

'You'd think if they couldn't warn us, they'd at least wave goodbye on their way past – show us some common decency.'

Sam shook her head, gritting her teeth in frustration. She looked out of the window, in case any of them misunderstood the look on her face and started thinking she was in favour of the enemy. The sky was beginning to lighten with approaching dawn. Under other circumstances the view outside might actually have been pleasant, but not with smoke among the trees, or ghostly movement on the road. Sam's eyes widened as she realised what she was seeing. 'Look!' she hissed to the soldiers.

Charlie and Kovacs peered out through the curtains. 'Paratroopers,' Kovacs murmured. 'Charlie, get on that field wire and raise some artillery fire on that column.'

'I'm trying, Sarge, but regiment says they can't give us any.'

'Can't give –' He snatched the field telephone from the other man. 'Gimme Russ,' Kovacs barked into the phone. 'Yeah… It's Kovacs. I need covering fire…' Sam couldn't hear what the person at the other end was saying, but she could take a guess from the rising colour of Kovacs's face. 'Listen, I don't give a damn how wide a front they're opening. All I know is I'm sitting in a rat hole in Lanzerath, with a goddam parachute division marching down the Losheim road. Now get me some fire – I don't care whether it's howitzers or mortars or goddam arrows – otherwise I might just give them a map to your billet before I get the hell out of here!'

He handed the radio back to Charlie and gestured to the nearest private. 'Get back to the dugout and pass the word for the guys to get their things together – we're bugging out under cover of the barrage. We'll fall back to Bucholz Station, and take the broad with us.' He turned to Sam before she could protest. 'Don't thank me yet, and keep the hell out of the way, OK?'

Thank him? He was practically abducting her, she thought. She could understand why, but she didn't like it.

'But the Doctor –' Sam began to protest.

'Look, lady,' Kovacs said, 'I got a responsibility to get these guys through this war in one piece, and I got half the German Army coming down that road to try to stop me. What I don't got is either the time or the inclination to send out search parties for stray civilians. If your friends are smart enough to keep their heads down, they might get through this. If not, then they're screwed, but I ain't gonna lose any sleep over it, and I ain't gonna lose any of my men over it, either. You got that?'

'Yes,' Sam said stiffly. 'I've got it.'

The Doctor and Fitz were whistling 'Colonel Bogey' and harmonising together as they walked down the road in search of another bridge. If he hadn't been getting shot at earlier, Fitz reckoned this would have been quite fun.

'You reckon Sam is all right up there?' Fitz asked.

'I've no idea,' the Doctor admitted, 'but I feel that she is. You get an instinct for danger after so long, and the village seemed quiet enough.'

'Nice line of bull,' Fitz said conversationally. 'Think you might convince somebody someday?'

'Until we find a bridge, there's not much else we can do than try to stay as optimistic as possible. Sam can take care of herself, the same as you can.'

'That's me: laughing at danger and not fazed by anything… Not very reassuring, is it?'

The Doctor looked sidelong at him without stopping.

'Wonderful,' he marvelled. 'Humans have such a great capacity for both selling themselves short and being overconfident. Sometimes I'm not sure how you keep things straight in your heads.'

'Sometimes we don't.' Fitz thought a little harder. 'Is that supposed to be an insult, or am I missing something?'

'You're missing something.' The Doctor suddenly halted and pulled Fitz to the hedge at the side of the road. 'Luckily *I* don't miss much. Listen.'

Fitz held his breath, which had seemed deafening after all that exertion, and could make out an engine approaching. 'Is that good or bad?'

'Let's wait and see.'

In a few moments, a jeep emerged out of the dawn half-light, with its headlights blacked out. Four American GIs were holding on as it bounced along the road. 'I'd call that good,' Fitz opined, and stepped out into the road, waving.

He heard a sigh from behind him. 'Haven't you heard of looking before you leap?'

'It's OK, they're Allied.'

'They don't know we are.'

Fitz's guts clenched as he realised what the Doctor meant, but it was too late. The jeep stopped beside them. 'Who are you?' the driver demanded. 'Don't you know this is a combat zone?' He didn't sound very American to Fitz. More like Australian or South African or something. Fitz knew that those nationalities served with the British Army in the war, but wasn't sure if they had also served in American regiments.

'We're just passing through,' the Doctor said hurriedly. Fitz had known him long enough to spot the looks that crossed his face, though he doubted the men in the jeep would have even noticed. 'When the shelling started, our transport was stuck on the bridge along there and now it's at the bottom of the river.' The GIs exchanged glances. 'We were just hoping to find another bridge so we can get up to the village there and meet a friend of ours.'

'A friend?' the driver asked.

The Doctor nodded. 'Man called Jochen. You know him?' What the hell was he talking about?

The driver grinned suddenly. 'Of course. You had me worried for a moment. So, the bridge is definitely down, then?'

'Very,' Fitz said firmly, not showing any sign of his puzzlement.

'Good.'

The Doctor nodded. 'Have the proper bridges been secured?'

'There's one about half a mile back that way. You can make contact there.'

'Thanks. Come on, Fitz, we have to be go–' There was a silent flash from above and Fitz looked up instinctively. A flare was drifting across the sky. He looked away, blinking green and purple spots from his eyes.

'They're Germans,' the Doctor muttered out of the corner of his mouth. 'Operation Greif; fifth columnists. You should be old enough to remember this from newsreels…'

'What?' Fitz gaped. There was no answer; the Doctor was already hurrying towards the jeep, only the faintest hint of a shadow preceding him, and Fitz thought he might be imagining even that. Fitz followed, his shadow stark and black against the snow.

A dozen or so Americans – real Americans? – were jogging out of the dimness. 'What the hell?' the jeep driver demanded. 'You tricked us!' He aimed his carbine at the Doctor, while the others started shooting at the approaching troops.

Fitz dived through the hedge, trying to get his head round what was going on. He could hear the Doctor shouting something, then the slippery ground underfoot gave way and he plunged into the freezing river.

Chapter Two
Call to Arms

Kovacs was lagging behind the main body of his platoon, making sure there weren't any stragglers. Three small support trucks were waiting for them on the road south of Lanzerath and he was dead set on getting to them before the Germans did. It wasn't that he much cared about his own skin, but it was his job to look after these guys.

And one girl, he reminded himself. Sam Jones was looking around frantically as they ran south, probably hoping that her friends would miraculously show up just in time to ride out with her. Kovacs knew they wouldn't, because he knew the world simply didn't work that way. Not in real life.

He had the nagging feeling that he should be more suspicious of her for some reason, but couldn't think why. He distinctly remembered being satisfied with her credentials. That made him frown – he couldn't remember what they were. Still, whatever, he supposed it must have been all right and proper.

Besides, he had more important things to think about right now. He caught a vague glimpse of Daniels helping Sam into one of the trucks, just before he reached the cab of another himself.

Kovacs hauled himself aboard. 'We all set?'

'Had to leave some of the equipment, but we're all here,' the private in the driver's seat answered.

'OK. Let's move.'

The sound of shooting drew Wiesniewski to alert. It didn't sound that far away and there was always the possibility that it was some of his men in a skirmish. Perhaps they had followed him.

His Tommy gun was gone, but at least he still had a pistol. Drawing it, Wiesniewski stumbled through the woods, towards the source of the sound. In a few moments he reached the edge of the trees and saw two groups of GIs facing off. He couldn't imagine why this would be the case until an oddly dressed civilian in a long dark-green frock coat pointed to the jeep and yelled something about the occupants being Germans.

The man in the green coat disarmed the driver, who was trying to shoot him, while another civilian fell into the river in the process of diving for cover.

The remaining three men from the jeep scattered, running for the woods. One of them almost ran straight into Wiesniewski. The GI raised his rifle, cursing in German. Wiesniewski was almost too stunned to shoot him. Almost.

The fake GI tumbled back down on to the road, his comrades ignoring him. The other soldiers, who Wiesniewski presumed were real Americans, pursued the three survivors into the woods.

'You OK, sir?' one of them paused to ask.

Wiesniewski nodded. 'I'm OK; you keep on after them.' The soldier followed the rest of his troop into the woods, while Wiesniewski came down on to the road and rested against the jeep.

'Thank you,' the civilian in the green coat said. He sounded English. 'You and your men were –'

Wiesniewski shook his head, trying to get his breath back. 'Not my men.' Which reminded him: where *were* his men?

'No? Well, thanks anyway.'

Wiesniewski waved the words aside. He was sure there was something very important he should be remembering. It would have to wait – there were more immediate problems at hand, like the thought of Germans in US uniforms. 'How did you know those guys were Germans?'

'Have you ever seen more than three GIs in a jeep?'

'Well, no, but I could imagine how it could happen...'

The guy in the green coat shrugged. 'The jeep also had blackout slits and none of them were wearing the same unit insignia. It's at times like this that I wish Fitz would think more carefully about what he sees. These things are quite well documented. Or will be,' he added, in response to Wiesniewski's blank look.

Wiesniewski was momentarily puzzled, but then remembered the civilian who had fallen into the river. 'I hope he can swim. I also hope you can drive.' He nodded towards the jeep 'Because you're going to have to.'

The strange civilian seemed to focus his mind back from some distant plane. 'I'm so sorry, I was miles away. What were you saying?'

'You have to drive,' Wiesniewski repeated. 'I sure as hell can't do it.' Not the way he felt; both from the throbbing pain in his head, and the sick sensation at having lost his men and his way. 'And you don't want to be around when they get here.'

'I had *two* friends with me, and now we're all separated. I have to find –'

Wiesniewski drew his pistol, and aimed it, in the loosest possible sense of the word, at this stranger. He didn't want to force this guy, but he had bigger things on his mind than a couple of lost civilians. 'Look, mister; I'm not asking you, I'm telling you. You *have* to drive.' Wiesniewski tried to put as much fire into his voice as he could, hoping it would distract the stranger from noticing how shaky the hand with the gun was.

The stranger sighed. 'Well, if you put it that way...' He abruptly twisted the gun out of Wiesniewski's grip, removed the magazine, then handed it back. 'If I was going to threaten someone at gunpoint, I think I'd at least take the safety catch off first.'

Wiesniewski tried not to let the strain show, but he couldn't do anything about the way the sky was tilting back and forth, or the ground trying to swallow him up.

The Doctor caught the lieutenant neatly. He grimaced. 'Oh… What am I supposed to do with you, hmm?'

'Leshy…' the officer mumbled. He was still no more than semiconscious, but something was clearly troubling him.

The Doctor leaned in closer. 'Leshy?'

'In mist… Leshy in mist…' The soldier fell silent again, his head lolling. Now the Doctor noticed that the back of the man's head was matted with dried blood. He looked over his shoulder to where the German impostors' jeep was sitting. With a sigh, the Doctor hoisted the unconscious man over his shoulder, and deposited him in the back of the jeep.

Then he rushed over to the riverbank, and carefully pushed through the hedge. He had no intention of duplicating Fitz's mistake in order to find him. By now, however, there was no sign of Fitz, and the river was flowing quite fast. He could be a mile downstream by now. There were plenty of logs and branches floating past, which had been knocked down by the fighting somewhere. There was no reason to assume that Fitz hadn't been able to grab one and use it for flotation.

Either he had been washed quite a way downstream, or he had drowned. The Doctor hoped it was the former, but he had enough sense to know that either way, there was no good he could do standing around here with a wounded man.

He returned to the jeep. If Fitz had managed to reach the shore, their best hope of meeting up would be to follow the road along the river as far as possible. If he hadn't found Fitz by the turning for Bullingen, he'd just have to come back and look later.

Something wet was hitting Wiesniewski's face, and, as his

mind cleared, he realised it was mud and dampness being churned up by the jeep he was in. The stranger in the velvet coat was driving, just on the right side of maniacally. He seemed to be enjoying it, and was singing to himself. The singing worried Wiesniewski more than anything else.

'What the...?'

'Welcome back to the land of the living,' the stranger said. He glanced at Wiesniewski and looked relieved. 'I was worried about you for a minute there.'

Wiesniewski put a hand to the back of his head and felt a field dressing there. He didn't even remember being injured, but he supposed it would explain a lot. There had been a lot of wood and stone flying around during the shelling and presumably a chunk had bounced off his skull. For once Wiesniewski was glad of what his mother had always called a hard head. 'Look, mister –'

'Doctor!'

'Doctor?' Well, that explained the field dressing, too. 'Where are we going, Dr...?'

'Just Doctor will do. Bullingen, as requested. I think. Hard to tell, since I don't actually know where we were, but it seems logical to head away from the Germans and hope for the best.'

'I thought you wanted to look for your friends.'

'I did, but they can look after themselves, you know. You've got a bad concussion that should be looked at in proper medical care. Besides, when you collapsed you said some interesting things. Right now *they're* probably more important.'

'Military things?' Wiesniewski asked guiltily.

'No. Not that it would have mattered if you did.' The Doctor held out a hand without taking his eyes off the road. 'John Smith, 55583. You can check from your headquarters if you really want to; drove an ambulance at El Alamein several lifetimes ago.'

'Lifetimes? I guess the war changes you, all right,' Wiesniewski agreed.

'That too.'

Dawn finally broke, as dull and grey as any prison wall in Fitz's imagination.

He wasn't sure how much further south he had drifted before the current lessened enough for him to climb back out of the water, but he had eventually reached a bridge that was still in one piece. That was more than could be said for the houses around it, many of which had holes in the walls and collapsed ceilings. He found himself hoping the occupants had had the good sense to bugger off when the shooting started last night – partly because he doubted they deserved to be caught in the shelling, and partly because he now needed to steal some dry clothes.

The main road through the town went straight over the bridge. As Fitz crossed it, shivering, he saw some American soldiers lounging around. There were a couple of Sherman tanks parked by a battered café, too. Fitz was tempted to ask them for help, but, after what had just happened, he wasn't sure they were genuine anyway.

All things considered, he felt, it would be best to just slip into an abandoned house and rifle their wardrobe. A sign nearby caught Fitz's eye. A tailor's shop. Dry, warm clothing. He almost whimpered.

He slipped down a narrow alley and found the tailor's door unlocked. It took only a few moments to confirm that the place was indeed empty. A fire was set in the living room of the small flat above, so Fitz lit it, and hung his leather jacket there to dry while he changed into slacks and shirt from the store below.

That done, he sat in front of the fire and wondered whether it would be able to warm him even if he sat in it.

* * *

The journey in the light truck was bumpy, to say the least. Sam was beginning to wonder if shock absorbers had actually been invented in this decade.

She considered such small but fundamental advancements in the modern age, and wondered, not for the first time, if she might find, when she got back to her own time, that things she had done in past eras had made things any better.

She had once read a story about someone who changed the whole course of human evolution by treading on a prehistoric butterfly, and thought about what it would be like to have ended famine or conflict in the nineties by the same method. She knew that hadn't happened, of course, but the part of her that was still a Coal Hill teenager continued to exercise its right to dream from time to time.

'You look troubled,' Charlie said from the driver's seat (she now knew his surname to be Daniels). He had apparently thought it would be more proper for her not to sit with the rest of the men. Sam had decided not to press the point, since the front seat was a damn sight more comfortable anyway.

'Just wondering whether stuff I've done has made a difference.'

'To the war?'

'To anything.'

Daniels artfully guided the truck into another pothole.

'I guess only you could know the answer to that. I dunno what you've –' Shattered glass and flying blood surrounded Sam, as machine-gun fire ripped through the cab. Daniels's body shielded Sam from the bullets, but she found herself yelling as the side of his head was torn away and fragments of the windscreen lacerated her face.

The truck skidded, overbalancing even more as the soldiers in the back were thrown around. Half blinded by cuts, and still catching her breath, Sam grabbed the steering wheel. She narrowly averted hitting a tree head on, but sideswiped it instead. The truck finally ground to a halt jammed between two trees in the roadside woods.

As Sam steadied her breathing, she could hear shooting from behind her. By the time she scrambled free of the truck's cab, it was all over. Half a dozen Germans were lying scattered between the truck and the road, and only three of the Americans were still standing.

More accurately, perhaps, they were leaning, on the truck or on trees, looking as stunned and shattered as Sam felt. No, worse, she reminded herself. The men killed in the truck were their friends, and she hadn't even known them.

She couldn't think of anything she could say to them.

Fitz had managed to find some bread, jam and a bottle of red wine that tasted like vinegar. It was better than nothing, so he drank it anyway, and somehow still managed to feel better for it.

From the window of the tailor's flat, he could see the Americans at work below. There seemed to be some cause for alarm among them, as the engines of the two Shermans rumbled into life. Fitz immediately got the urge to leave, but some of the Doctor's curiosity must have been rubbing off on him, as he craned his neck for a better view instead.

Whatever was happening, it all seemed to be on the other side of the bridge, and Fitz had to move through to a cramped bedroom to get a clearer view of that area.

Dark shapes were moving along the road on the far side, occasionally visible between the buildings – grey leviathans with caterpillar tracks and faded whitewash on their angular steel skins. Fitz recognised them vaguely as German tanks, but that was all he felt he needed to know. Pinning down the make and model was something he'd leave to the train-spotting brigade; all that mattered to Fitz was that they were something to stay the hell out of the way of.

There was a sudden roar of engine power from the German side. Fitz looked over, startled, and saw the very last thing he wanted to. Two Panthers, which he recognised from comics of his youth, were lumbering at speed towards the steel and concrete tank traps on the bridge, their machine guns blazing at the defenders. The Americans weren't staying put to be shot at, and returned fire, though small arms were useless against the Panthers' armour.

An antitank round from a gun positioned in the shelter of a small ornamental fountain in the town square hit the lead Panther, catching the front of its tracks. Several steel links were blasted away, and the track began to unfurl, as a second shell hit the gun mantelet on the front of the turret.

For a moment, Fitz thought the artillery men had managed to stop the Panther, but fifty tons of tank travelling at over thirty miles per hour had enough momentum to smash through the tank traps with a tremendous cacophony. Flames licking at the front of its turret, the Panther collided with one of the Shermans. With one track gone, and thus no longer able to travel in a straight line, the Panther swung around, its nose shunting into the side of a second Sherman.

As the two Shermans tried to disentangle themselves from the Panther that was now trapped between them, the second Panther negotiated the path the first had made through the tank traps. It crossed the bridge speedily and paused at the end, just long enough to blast a 75-mm round into the nearer Sherman.

The Sherman lurched and erupted in sparks and white smoke. As the smoke darkened, the turret arced through the air for several dozens of yards, propelled by the exploding fuel and shells within. Fitz's jaw dropped, amazed that such a heavy steel object could be flipped so far so easily. If he'd seen it in a film he would have laughed at how unrealistic it seemed.

The second Panther now gave covering fire while the crew of the first jumped down from their burning tank and took shelter. Small-arms fire erupted from a shopfront on the corner, and the Panther blasted it into a cloud of dust and rubble.

It revved up its engine, and pushed the burning hulk of its comrade off the road, keeping it between itself and the surviving Sherman.

Dan Bearclaw had no idea how he managed to work in all this noise and confusion, but he did. Somehow or other he was able to find a calm centre from which to aim the 57-mm antitank piece that he commanded.

Perhaps it was something to do with having three kids at home: if he could sleep through their running wild, then tuning out the cacophony of battle was no problem. Perhaps more miraculous was how the other two men in his crew were able to follow orders that they surely couldn't actually hear.

As he spun the wheels that traversed the gun, it occurred to Bearclaw that he could hit the stranded Panther again and kill its crew while they were exposed outside it. But what would be the point in wasting ammunition like that? They were most definitely out of the fight.

Besides, the other Panther was the greater threat. Already it was turning its gun towards their position by the fountain. 'Armour piercing!' Bearclaw called out. Someone slid the appropriate shell into the breach, and the gun fired.

It was too early, and the shell exploded into the wall at the edge of the bridge. 'Damn,' Bearclaw gasped. 'Run!'

The Panther fired and the ornamental fountain was ripped apart, the centrepiece statue of cavorting nymphs torn into dust.

Bearclaw slammed into the ground amid a shower of rubble

and rolled aside. With a tremendous crash, the mangled barrel of his antitank gun ploughed into the street a few yards to his left.

His ears ringing, Bearclaw groaned and looked for the rest of his crew. One was lying in a bloody pool a few yards away. The other had vanished entirely and Bearclaw had no idea whether he was buried under rubble or had taken off.

Under cover of the dust and stone fragments that were still hanging in the air, Bearclaw bolted. Nobody could say he hadn't done his part, and he wasn't about to stand up to Panzers while completely unarmed. If nothing else, he wanted to at least find a weapon.

If he should happen not to find one until he was in the clear, he wouldn't exactly be overcome with disappointment.

Fitz glanced back to the German side of the bridge, alerted by more metallic rumblings, and yells from below about 'Panzer fours'.

A column of about a dozen Panzers was advancing towards the bridge, their turrets swivelling from side to side as if to sniff out enemies. While a couple of them manoeuvred into position holding the far end, the lead tank led the others on to the bridge. Their turrets moved to cover the buildings flanking the American-held end of the bridge, and they began loosing pot shots into the riverbank buildings.

It finally dawned on Fitz that he too was in a riverbank building, and that it was close enough to the Americans for them to consider using it for cover. Stuffing his still-damp leather jacket into a bag, Fitz decided that legging it was definitely the better part of valour.

He left the way he had come in, and just in time. A shell tore off the upper corner of the building, raining pieces of wood and brick on him. The shock wave knocked Fitz down, and he rolled back to the riverbank at the very end of the bridge.

It was quite clear that the Americans were losing. Fitz sidled further down the muddy bank to the water's edge, hoping not to be noticed by the German troops that were crossing overhead in the Panzers' wake.

A dead soldier was there, his coal-scuttle helmet ripped open, just like the skull underneath. A disconnected pack of explosives was lying near his hand.

Searching for anything that would aid his survival, Fitz noticed that the corpse's outer clothing was a one-piece parasuit, worn over his normal uniform as camouflage. Fitz hastily pulled it off the body. So long as nobody asked to see a uniform underneath, it might suffice to disguise him well enough to get through this.

The shooting above was starting to die off and Fitz wondered if it was safe to emerge yet. When he started climbing back up the bank, an SS officer hailed him. 'You, there. Is the bridge mined?'

Fitz glanced around, then held up the pack that had been lying by the former owner of his parasuit. 'It was, but not any more.' Fitz sincerely hoped that the officer didn't mean he wanted the bridge mined.

'Good work.'

Fitz breathed a sigh of relief and carefully put the explosives down. 'Yeah,' he muttered to himself. Being trapped behind German lines in World War Two wasn't what he considered good work.

Bearclaw had found a jeep at the edge of town. There really was nothing more he could do here, unless it was stick around to get captured. At least if he got out now he could still fight again later.

So he took the jeep. It was actually quite relaxing to be driving again. He had rarely had the chance while on combat assignment, and it soothed him a little. He had been a trucker before the war and, though the jeep was much smaller, it was enough to relax him.

He was brought out of his reverie by the sight of a small group of people at a crossroads a couple of miles outside of town. Bearclaw braked the jeep as a couple of GIs flagged him down. They looked the worse for wear and had themselves clearly seen some action this morning. Oddly, there was a female civilian with them, wearing jeans and stuff rather than a dress.

'Need a ride, fellas?' he asked.

They all nodded. 'Are we glad to see you,' one of them said.

'What's happening? I thought we were the ones under attack…'

The GI shook his head. 'The whole front's under attack. There's a Parachute Division pushing down the Losheim road; Lanzerath and Bucholz Station have gone under…'

'Jeez. Who's the civilian?'

The GI shrugged. 'A Brit. Long story.'

'The name's Sam Jones,' the girl said. 'But he's right, it's a long story.'

'Well,' Bearclaw said, starting the now fully laden jeep, 'we got plenty of time before we hit Ligneuville.'

There was only sporadic shooting on the outskirts of town now, but things hadn't got any more peaceful as far as Fitz could tell.

Chain dogs, the German military police in the field, were directing traffic. Trucks and Hanomag half-tracks were disgorging troops and equipment to set up camp in the area, while the tanks weren't waiting.

A couple of Panzer IVs, and the damaged Panther, were stationed to watch what Fitz presumed were vital junctions. The rest of the Panzers were forming up and moving out. Since they weren't heading back the way they came, Fitz could only assume their attack wasn't finished yet, and they were moving on to their next targets for the day.

Fitz had scarcely realised that the sounds of the tanks' engines were fading – they were trundling away into the distance, after all. When his foot clipped a small pile of rubble, a few stones drifted down almost silently, and then he knew something was wrong.

He turned to look back at the end of the bridge. SS troops were clearing away bodies and setting up equipment, but there was something odd about it, Fitz thought. At first he thought his eyes were going funny, but then he realised that the light was fading in spite of the fact that it was still the middle of the day.

It wasn't actually getting darker: it was just becoming strangely fuzzy, as if neither light nor darkness really mattered. With a chill running down his back, he realised the troops indulging in hard work were moving slowly, unnaturally slowly.

Fitz was torn between wanting to run, in case something nasty happened, and wanting to go closer and see what the weirdness was about.

He almost jumped out of his skin when a hand grabbed his shoulder. He spun round, biting off a curse that could have got him shot, and found an officer looking almost as surprised as he was. 'What are you standing around for? Don't you have anything to do, or shall I give you something to do?'

Fitz glanced back towards the end of the bridge. Everything was normal again, or at least as normal as a street could be in the immediate aftermath of a battle. 'I thought I saw a flash in that window, sir,' he said, pointing to the nearest upstairs window across the road. 'Like the lens on a telescopic sight. It's probably nothing, but I was just about to go and check.'

The officer squinted up at the window, and nodded. 'Go ahead.' He turned away, immediately switching his attention to whatever he considered more important than Fitz's gawking.

Fitz was only too happy to oblige, though once he was inside the house he simply sat on the stairs and patted the pockets of the parasuit he had borrowed. He had hoped that there would have been cigarettes in one of them, as he could definitely use one after getting into this mess. Unfortunately he seemed to have looted the body of the only soldier in the war who didn't smoke. Bloody typical of his luck.

He grimaced at the thought of having taken coveralls from a corpse. But what else could he have done? Better to benefit from the dead than to join them, wasn't it?

But no matter how many times he told himself that, it didn't make him feel any better. What was he going to do? The Doctor and Sam weren't having as bad a time here as he was, he knew it. He'd just hope he'd see them again so he could tell them so.

Wiesniewski was glad to see the slightly more familiar surroundings of Bullingen. On each side of the road into the village was a small airstrip for spotter planes. Further up a side road, under the nearby trees, he could make out activity around the fuel dump that nestled there.

His first thought was to get to a company commander and call in his report, but then he noticed that the little spotter planes were beginning to start their engines. All of the ones on the 99th Artillery's airstrip were readying for takeoff at the same time, and that was odd. Wiesniewski hung on tightly, seeing explosions and smoke rising from the town centre. The sound of tank guns was clearly audible and he could make out five or six Panzers manoeuvring themselves across the railway lines at the junction on the far side of town.

There was some sort of activity on the far side of the 99th Division's airstrip, too, and Wiesniewski realised with a shock that it was gunfire. A group of half-tracks, led by a single

Panzer, were crossing the other road towards the airfield. As he watched, despairing of the hope of reaching safety and getting his act together, a bazooka round hit the tank with no visible effect.

'Uh oh,' the Doctor vocalised, as he was waved aside by men crewing a roadblock. He swung the jeep off the road, heading across a short scrubby area of field towards the 2nd Division's airfield.

Wiesniewski's expression hardened. Now he had something real and concrete to think about, and in a lot of ways it was a blessed relief.

Fitz had fallen asleep for a bit, much to his own surprise. Just like a real soldier, he supposed; he'd read tons of books that said they were able to sleep anywhere.

He ventured outside again, hoping for an opportunity to slip away without being noticed. Of course, he'd have to ditch the parasuit when he crossed the lines, but that was becoming an increasingly attractive idea anyway, in any conditions.

All the German troops seemed busy with whatever they were assigned to do, and for once Fitz was glad of that stereotyped image of efficiency. With any luck they'd assume he was on some important errand himself and not bother him. So long as he looked confident instead of furtive, he should be all right.

Hoisting the bag with his jacket over his shoulder, Fitz walked out into the street and headed back towards the main road.

It was easy. All he had to do was keep walking. 'You there,' someone called. 'Halt.' Fitz stiffened. He had no real reason to assume the call was directed at him, but he was used enough to his own luck that he just knew it was meant for him.

He stopped and turned to find an officer looking at him. 'Yes, sir?'

'Where's your weapon?'

Fitz groaned inwardly. He should have expected that a soldier without a gun might be suspect. 'It backfired, sir,' he replied quickly. 'I was just on my way to requisition a new one.'

'They're setting up a temporary quartermaster's in that bakery,' the officer said, peering at him closely, then pointing back towards the bridge. 'You can get one there.'

'Thank you, sir,' Fitz said dutifully, wishing he could tell the officer what to do with himself. Instead, he turned round, and walked back in the direction indicated. As he neared the erstwhile baker's shop, three eight-wheeled armoured cars rolled over the bridge at speed.

There was something unusual about these armoured cars. It wasn't that they were a type Fitz had never seen, since there were plenty of things here he had never seen before. It was, perhaps, the antennae mounted on top of them. He had seen the 'clothes-rack' type of antenna on some other vehicles during the day, but there was something far more sophisticated about the ones on these. They had much finer wire woven between the bars and a strange mounting that looked as if it could be used to alter the antenna's position, so as to focus on things better.

No doubt the Doctor would instantly recognise whatever they were for, but Fitz had to settle for that gut instinct.

He didn't recall speaking to anyone in the baker's shop, but he knew he must have done, because someone shoved a sub-machine-gun into his hand and made him sign for it. He sighed. Perhaps it was just as well he hadn't got out of town. Some instinct told him that the Doctor would want to know more about these mysteriously sophisticated vehicles if they met up again.

When they met up again.

Wiesniewski kept his head down as the Doctor weaved the

jeep through the hail of bullets. His head was throbbing as it was, each pulse draining a little more of his consciousness. 'We're trapped,' he called out.

'Never say die,' the Doctor said loudly. He guided the jeep on to the 2nd Division's airfield, heading for a couple of wounded men who were lying near an L5 spotter plane. 'Can you still walk?'

'Just about.' Actually he wasn't sure, but he wasn't about to say that. He'd shown enough weakness over the past twenty-four hours already.

'Good.' The jeep pulled up under the plane's wing. 'Help me get these men on board. It looks like they need help even more than you do, and we should be able to get the three of you out in the plane.'

Wiesniewski staggered out of the jeep without thinking. There were a lot more men than these two at risk from the advancing German armour, but even saving two would be better than none. Hell, even if they failed, at least it was better to go out trying, wasn't it?

The Doctor had quickly applied a pad to the first man's shoulder wound, and then lifted him bodily, with little apparent effort. Wiesniewski, on the other hand, pulled the man with the leg wound over to the door by his torso, so that the Doctor could lift him into the back of the plane. It was pretty cramped in there, and the men could still end up bleeding to death from the movement, but Wiesniewski didn't see much of a choice. They couldn't just leave them.

A neighbouring L5 was already starting its engine, under fire. 'Get in,' the Doctor told Wiesniewski. Wiesniewski staggered a little, but still managed to lift himself most of the way into the right-hand seat. The Doctor finished the job with a hearty shove, then boarded himself and pulled the door closed.

'Can you really fly one of these?' Wiesniewski asked belatedly.

'Let's find out!' the Doctor replied cheerily, starting the engine.

The fragile little plane turned, and now Wiesniewski could see a Panzer leading half a dozen half-tracks to block this airstrip. Most of the L5s were already burning on the ground and the other one that had got its engine started was hurtling towards the German armour.

The Doctor set their plane in motion, following its neighbour. Wiesniewski was afraid to look, knowing that they were both heading straight into the German fire. 'There's not enough runway for a takeoff!'

'Be positive,' the Doctor chided him. 'Too much negativity is… well, far too negative.'

The plane in front shuddered under the hail of gunfire, its wings tearing into shreds. Wiesniewski thought that was about as negative as it was possible to get, but it wasn't deterring the Doctor from his course, even when it exploded abruptly, scattering pieces of shrapnel across the German half-tracks. The engine and fuselage tumbled earthward, smashing into the nose of the half-track that had shot it down. Ammunition exploded within as the surviving troops leapt to safety. The explosion and the shrapnel, however, had blinded the Germans to the Doctor's plane.

It was too late for the Doctor to change his mind now. He pulled back on the stick. The half-tracks dropped away with a sickening lurch, but Wiesniewski could still hear gunfire, and was sure some of it was going through the wings and fuselage. To his amazement, however, the plane didn't start to plummet and soon the only sound was that of the engine.

'Told you so,' the Doctor said gently.

Wiesniewski shook his head wearily. 'Any idea where we're going?'

The Doctor tapped the glass on the fuel gauge. 'Not enough to reach the main Allied fields at Liège or Luxembourg City…

We could make Bastogne, but that's undoubtedly a major target for the Germans.'

'There are field medical facilities there,'Wiesniewski pointed out. Maybe it was his concussion, and maybe it was just light-headedness from the altitude, but he could feel himself drifting away. 'Those guys back there need treatment as early as possible. At least they might have a chance in Bastogne. If we run out of fuel and crash, then they're screwed. Of course, if we crash, we're all screwed.'

The Doctor nodded thoughtfully. 'All things considered, Bastogne looks to be our best bet.'

The Doctor banked the plane.

Fitz, against what he hoped wasn't his better judgement, had stayed on the sidelines of the German entrenchment. He had volunteered to try to repair a damaged radio, simply because it probably wouldn't lead to getting shot at. Besides, he had always enjoyed taking things apart and fiddling with them. Putting them back together, of course, was the trick.

He wasn't concentrating on it enough to do any good, but at least it made him look active, and thus unlikely to be disturbed by other German troops. And of course it gave his mind time to try to think of what to do next. Frustratingly, his mind seemed to be more interesting in screaming 'Jesus Christ!' and 'run!' over and over for the moment, but he was fairly sure that it would get itself in gear before too long.

It also gave him the opportunity to watch the crews of the new armoured cars. They seemed to be talking to just about everyone in turn, and Fitz was as pleased as he was dismayed to see the officer he had twice encountered point him out.

The officer beckoned him over, and Fitz went, hoping he wasn't shaking as much as he felt he was. 'Corporal, this is *Sturmbannführer* Leitz, assigned to special duties. He wishes to speak to everyone involved in the aftermath of the battle.'

Leitz looked at Fitz expectantly, and Fitz realised he was waiting for a Nazi salute. Fitz gave him one, the kids doing the same to him in the playground flashing into his mind. If they could only see him now… 'At ease, Corporal…?'

'Kreiner, sir,' Fitz answered in his best impression of the guards from *The Great Escape*.

'All right, Kreiner. The lieutenant here tells me you were here for the battle, and remained afterward.'

'That's correct, sir.'

'Have you seen any further American resistance?'

'No sir. I thought I saw a flash from a telescopic sight earlier, but it turned out to be a piece of a broken bedroom mirror.' If this guy wanted to believe this bull, that was fine with Fitz, but he reminded himself not to get cocky. This Leitz clearly wasn't stupid. There was something about his posture and the look in his eyes that proved that.

'Did you see anything… unusual, after the battle? Strange lights, perhaps?'

Fitz suddenly had a hunch. Something weird had happened on the street earlier and then these vehicles with weird antennae had turned up. It could be a coincidence, but he supposed he was beginning to develop an instinct for these things. 'You're looking for what caused the fuzziness?' He didn't want to say too much in case it helped them any. Just being around the SS made him nervous.

'Fuzziness? You *did* see something.'

'For a moment. Not light or darkness, but… something else.'

'For how long?'

'I'm not sure. There was…' He cleared his throat. 'A temporal anomaly.'

Now the *Sturmbannführer* regarded Fitz more closely and spoke. His expression was mild, but Fitz wasn't letting that fool him. 'Temporal anomaly. A curious phrase; what do you mean by it?'

'Exactly what I said. Time sort of… slowed down. People were moving… wrong.' The *Sturmbannführer* nodded and started to look away; obviously this was something he already knew about. That in itself interested Fitz, and he pressed on, feeling more than a little Doctorish. It was kind of fun; no wonder the Doctor behaved like this so often. 'There's nothing dense enough round here to cause relativistic effects, is there?' he asked, stringing together a few words he'd heard the Doctor use, that might make him sound as if he knew enough to be valuable.

The *Sturmbannführer* froze. 'No.' At least that told Fitz that the officer knew something about this. Or that he was trying to find out. He turned abruptly. 'Anyone driving to Lanzerath?'

One of the chain dogs indicated a Hanomag half-track and the *Sturmbannführer* turned back to Fitz. 'Go with them. A first aid station has been set up at the Café Scholzen; they'll fix that cut. I'll be there later tonight.'

Fitz saluted again. He wanted desperately to refuse, but what could he say? 'Sorry, mate, but I'd rather follow the Yanks and look for my time-travelling friends,' probably wouldn't cut it with the Nazis.

Jurgen Leitz watched Kreiner leave, knowing in his gut that there was something different about him. It wasn't that he was a spy for the Allies – at least he didn't think so – but he just wasn't Waffen SS material. He also seemed to know things that most ordinary men wouldn't even think about. He knew some of his peers would immediately haul the man in for interrogation, but what would be the point? He was one of their own side, after all, and news and rumour spread among soldiers even more quickly than VD.

The thing that seemed most odd was how casually he spoke of the event. Yes, that was it. He spoke with some familiarity. He would bear watching indeed. Leitz finally allowed a newly arriving presence to enter his thoughts and turned to the *Rottenführer* who had just returned from the lead armoured car. 'Yes, Farber?'

Farber gave a Nazi salute and an expression flushed with excitement. 'Sir, we have a prisoner.'

'A prisoner?'

'One of the special kind you wanted,' Farber said, barely above a whisper. 'The generators work, just as we hoped.' Leitz felt some of that excitement himself; this would look good on his reputation at Wewelsburg.

'Excellent. Where is it now?'

'On its way here, in a towed armoured car, with all the hatches sealed.'

Leitz nodded thoughtfully. 'All right. Set up the quarantine area in that field.' He indicated an expanse of open ground next to a barn. 'Have at least two generators running to be on the safe side and a third standing by, just in case.' That seemed efficient enough by anybody's standards. 'Arrange for guard duty, but make sure the guards know not to look inside.'

'Understood.'

Chapter Three
Slings and Arrows

Ray Garcia had been a real Latin charmer five years ago. Now he was just a baggy-eyed young man who looked permanently on the verge of toppling over from exhaustion. That was just his own diagnosis, from looking in the mirror. To others, he suspected, he probably just looked like death warmed up.

And he didn't remember ever being as charming as people assumed he had been. Charming people had social lives outside their jobs, which was something Garcia hadn't had for a very long time. It was less painful, overall, to live for the job in hand, if not very relaxing. He was lucky to sleep one night in a week, terrified of missing some important injury and losing a patient. Equally, he didn't want to screw up by being asleep on his feet, so he tried to doze at quieter moments, regardless of the time of day.

He had just about managed to grab a couple of hours' uncomfortable sleep on a small couch in his office, when there was a commotion from outside. The field hospital used to be a small hotel until a few months ago, but now the larger rooms were being used as wards and the old bar room had become an operating theatre. The reception area still fulfilled its original duty, though, and that was where the noise was coming from.

Groaning, Garcia rose, and went to the door of his office. It wasn't much of an office, either, being just a janitor's cubbyhole under the single worn staircase.

In the reception area, a man was arguing with one of the medical orderlies. He certainly wasn't a soldier and wore a dark-green, velvet frock coat, which, along with the curls of his shoulder-length hair, made him look like some wild outlandish figure.

For a moment, Garcia felt a flood of relief – he was obviously still asleep and dreaming. How else could Oscar Wilde be standing outside his office? Then the stranger's wide pale eyes looked straight at him, as if peering around right inside him, and he knew he wasn't dreaming.

'Ah, you must be in charge here, Captain,' the stranger said with a smile. 'I have three badly wounded men outside, who need urgent medical care.' He put an arm round Garcia's shoulder, steering him towards the front door as he continued urgently. 'Two have multiple bullet wounds, and the other has a bad concussion and hypothermia.'

'Hold it,' Garcia finally managed to say. 'Just who are you?'

'Oh, I *am* sorry, I'm forgetting my manners. I'm the Doctor.' He shook Garcia's hand with gusto.

'Of medicine?'

'Sometimes. I don't really like to get tied down to one science, you know. I've always found variety to be the spice of life.'

Garcia nodded in weary disbelief, but he found himself smiling anyway. 'Spice, huh? OK, bring your people in.'

The Hanomag pulled up in front of a battered building, the outer walls of which were chipped and marked with bullet holes. Someone had hung a swastika flag above the door, all but covering the sign proclaiming this was the Café Scholzen.

Fitz tried not to look too nervous as he climbed out of the half-track. After all, he wanted to look like someone who was supposed to be here. He caught a glimpse of his reflection in a window and shivered slightly. If his father were alive to see him in an SS parasuit… well. He wouldn't exactly be made up.

The sight did remind him of one thing, though: from the outside, he looked like a card-carrying member of the so-called master race. How hard a role could that be to play?

It was an odd thing, he'd noticed, that the more corrupt and evil a regime was, in his experience anyway, the better fashion sense it seemed to have. Why *was* that? Maybe there was some sort of natural law that said every race of bad guys in the universe had to have at least one positive attribute in their nastiness, however small. Take the Ruin, for instance. Probably wonderful to their mums.

He had to restrain the urge to put on a very cod-German accent. In the muddy streets that met at this crossroads, SS troopers were setting up defensive positions, just in case – unloading supplies, directing traffic. It was a pretty busy area.

Inside, an SS *Standartenführer* was trying to spread out a map on a dresser, but it kept rolling back up. Visibly annoyed, he took bayonets from two of the soldiers and speared it to the wall with them. As he did so, a group of men in parachutists' jumpsuits and rimless helmets came in. 'Colonel von Hofman.' The *Standartenführer* acknowledged their leader with a salute. 'Where the hell have you been?'

'Fighting.' He pointed to a spot on the map. 'These woods seem to be heavily fortified. The roads are mined and scattered fire from pillboxes is holding us up. It's impossible to attack under those conditions.'

'*Seem* to be heavily fortified? Have you personally reconnoitred the American positions?'

'My battalion commander for that area has made a full report,' he said, gesturing to one of his men.

'Then *you* made the reconnaissance?' the *Standartenführer* asked.

The paratrooper shook his head. 'Captain Grauman –'

The *Standartenführer* thrust a telephone into the paratroop commander's hand. 'Call him.'

Fitz didn't know who any of these people were, but the *Standartenführer* was very annoyed at something, and he was glad he wasn't in any of the other soldiers' shoes.

The soldier did so. 'Captain Graumann –'

The *Standartenführer* grabbed the phone back. 'Graumann, this is Lt-Colonel Peiper. I'm told you surveyed the American positions?' He listened carefully to the response, clearly irritated by the answers he was getting. 'Then,' Peiper said pointedly, 'you haven't personally seen any American resistance at all?'

He paused to listen to another response. 'That's what I thought.' He banged down the phone and glared at von Hofman and his battalion commander. They had the good sense not to say anything incriminating or inflammatory. Either that or they were speechless with fear, and Fitz couldn't blame them.

Peiper rounded on the battalion commander. 'You're relieved of duty, for incompetence. You could at least have checked on the enemy positions yourself. You,' he said to von Hofman, 'will second his men to my direct command. And don't say a damn word – I don't want any more excuses for your incompetence. Now both of you get out of my sight!'

The paratroop officers retreated hastily, and the *Standartenführer* snarled and kicked over a chair. He turned to one of his aides. 'Get two Panthers up front. I'll lead the paras in half-tracks behind them, flanked with whatever Panzers we can spare. Let me know when they're assembled.' He stalked out, muttering something under his breath. Fitz doubted it was very complimentary towards the paratroops. The men almost collided with Leitz on his way out, but didn't say anything; doubtless, Leitz outranked him in his own branch of the military.

Now that they were indoors, Fitz got a better look at Leitz. He was a harried-looking *Sturmbannführer*. Though he was meticulously clean-shaven, Fitz got the impression that he'd skipped a few meals too many. He looked like the sort of man who was just in too damn much of a rush to bother with trivialities like eating. It'd probably get him killed someday, Fitz theorised, and probably just as well.

'Ah, Kreiner. I've been looking for you.'

That put Fitz on alert. 'You have? Sir?'

Leitz nodded. 'You seem to have done good work back there. I need good men. I'm having you transferred to my unit. Farber will be round soon with your assignment for guard duty.'

Fitz wasn't sure how to respond to that. 'Thank you, sir,' seemed appropriate to blend in.

Leitz sat beside Fitz and passed him a mug of particularly vile ersatz coffee. 'Unlike some officers, I like to know a little about my subordinates. Where are you from?'

'Leipzig,' Fitz replied easily. At least, that was where his father had come from before leaving Germany.

Leitz took that in. 'I'm from Bremen, myself. Still, we're all pretty far from home, eh?'

'Very,' Fitz agreed, with great feeling.

Leitz frowned. 'Your accent is a little strange... One of Skorzeny's?'

Fitz shrugged as casually as he could. 'Yeah,' he agreed, hoping that this 'Skorzeny' was a good thing or person to be associated with in the eyes of the German military. 'I'm half British,' he explained. 'On my mother's side.'

'Interesting,' Leitz murmured. 'Didn't that cause you any problems?'

Fitz shook his head. 'She died a long time ago.'

'Ah... Well, so long as it doesn't interfere with your duties. It's not as if you were half Jewish, is it?' He rose. 'You may as well stay here until you're assigned a billet. When Farber comes with your assignment, you'll have guard duty tonight.' He turned and left.

Fitz snapped a hurried salute.

'*Jawohl*,' he said as Leitz turned and went back through the door, then added 'mein Obergruppennazibollocks...'

If all this wasn't so terrifying it'd be damn funny.

In the cramped office, Wiesniewski had been repeating to Garcia the tale he had already told the Doctor. 'I don't even remember how I got here,' Wiesniewski finished. 'One minute I was in combat, the next I was in a foxhole.'

'And what was it you saw in between?' the Doctor asked. 'Can you remember?'

'I didn't see anything. Maybe a couple of deer watching me…'

'Deer?' Garcia echoed. 'You must have been seeing things. Or that mist was thicker than you thought.'

'Mist?'

The Doctor turned back to Wiesniewski. 'You're forgetting it, aren't you? You're forgetting that a mist rose, and you saw something in it that frightened you.'

Wiesniewski looked blank for a moment, then astonished. 'The mist, yes! How the hell could I forget that? And there was… something.'

'Deer, naturally,' Garcia suggested drily, tying off the last stitch to a cut in Wiesniewski's scalp.

Wiesniewski started to nod, but then caught himself. 'It can't have been. Not on two legs…'

The Doctor smiled suddenly. 'Now that's some useful information.'

'It is?' Garcia asked. For the life of him, he couldn't see how a vague story about mist and deer from a possible deserter could be in any way informative.

'Well, it informs us that his perceptions have been tampered with, and quite expertly, too. Someone doesn't want him to remember something he saw.'

'Like a couple of out-of-place deer? Not exactly a big secret worth covering up, surely?'

The Doctor shook his head. 'The deer aren't real. I'd guess

they're a cover memory, implanted to take the place of something else – something more… worrying.'

'Like the Germans?' Garcia asked. Germans didn't really worry Garcia: he was of the opinion that people really were alike all over. He led the Doctor outside the little operating area. 'He's probably just repressing some really bad experience. Losing his squad would certainly qualify, I should think.'

'Depends who he lost them to, doesn't it?' the Doctor replied. 'In any case, he's left me with plenty to think about. Tell me: where can I find a staff officer who might be able to authorise equipment issues?'

Garcia thought. The current ranking officer, Middleton, had reportedly been ordered to pull back; and there was some talk of McAuliffe having come to visit him. 'There are some changes due at the top, so I'd guess Colonel Lewis would be your best bet.'

'Lewis?'

'In charge of I and R. Intelligence and Reconnaissance,' Garcia added in response to the Doctor's polite raised eyebrow. 'He's got a headquarters set up in the old police headquarters here. God knows why, but he seems to like it there.'

'Good for interrogating prisoners, I imagine.'

Garcia shrugged. 'You'd think so, but the weird thing is that his own private office is in one of the old cells.'

'That is odd,' the Doctor agreed, brightly. 'It probably says something profoundly worrying about his psychological state.'

'Well, I wouldn't know. I like illnesses I can see. And can see I've fixed up.'

'There's always going to be something just out of view.' For a moment the Doctor's features clouded over and he looked much older. Then he affected to shrug the moment off. 'I don't suppose you could show me the way? To Lewis I mean.'

'Sure. Wait just one moment.'

Garcia walked back to the cubbyhole and put his head round the door. 'Think you can make it to one of the wards?' he asked Wiesniewski; then, without waiting for an answer, 'Twelve hours' complete rest. That's an order.' He went back to the Doctor. 'OK. Let's go.'

The walk would give him a chance to find out just who this stranger was.

Bearclaw had started quietly humming an old song under his breath, since there was little more to do while their jeep was stuck in a traffic jam of US Army trucks. Sam seemed like a nice girl, if a little too tomboyish for his taste.

'This your first time out of the States?' she asked.

He nodded, then corrected himself. 'Well, I been up to Canada and down to Mexico a couple of times. That isn't really the same thing, though, is it?'

'It's better than nothing.'

'How about you? You travel a lot, or just because of the war?'

Sam laughed. 'Oh, I travel a lot. I've been to a lot of places you've never heard of, and some you wouldn't want to.'

'Ever been to the States?'

'A couple of times. DC and San Francisco.'

'Never been to DC myself.' Didn't sound very interesting, to be honest. Sure it was the nation's capital, but it sounded rather lifeless to him. 'Frisco's nice; I been there.'

'Sightseeing?'

He shook his head, as much to clear away the irritation that came with being stuck in such a damn slow-moving column. 'Delivering stuff. Driving a truck.' He'd have been as quick to walk. In fact two dog-faces passing his jeep were overtaking him. Some asshole screwed up at the front of the column, no doubt. 'Always like to get home, though.'

'Married?'

'Yep. Three kids. Who nearly, but not quite, piss me off as much as sitting on my ass in a line like this.' He realised she was looking at him warily and felt strangely hurt. It was probably best to keep quiet, make a little conversation and let things take their course. But Bearclaw hated that. He was cold, tired, scared half out of his wits and just wanted to get home. And some fool up ahead was keeping him that way.

He thumped the steering wheel in frustration. 'Dammit, move!' He'd barely finished the short bark when he realised Sam had jumped half out of her skin. Poor kid was probably more screwed up out here than he was, and all he did was go and act like a thug...

In a lot of ways, that just made him more angry. At himself, this time. 'Sorry. I just...'

'Yeah, I know. It's us Brits who enjoy queueing, isn't it?'

He smiled sheepishly. 'I guess so.'

Suddenly there was an explosion of gunfire, and everyone in the jeep looked around fearfully. At the rear of the column the sound of gunfire was deafening, but the body of the column blocked any view of what was going on.

'What's happening?' Bearclaw asked.

Sam pointed up at the cloudy sky, where a tiny shape was puttering along. 'Could they be shooting at that doodlebug?'

'I don't think so...' Bearclaw said slowly. Men were jumping out of the trucks ahead and shooting towards the east with their rifles. He stepped half out of the jeep, so that he could see past the trucks ahead. 'Oh, damn! Get out! Get out now!'

'What?' Sam asked blankly. Instead of answering, Bearclaw swung her bodily out of the jeep and dropped to the ground beside her.

Sam still had no idea what the problem was as she hit the

ground, but it was clear that something very bad was happening. Some way ahead the first few trucks in the column were burning. A huge tank was sitting, blocking the road. Eastward, more tanks, supported by half-tracks and infantry, were advancing across the snowy field from the parallel road half a mile away. The tanks were raking the column with machine-gun fire and picking off individual trucks with shellfire.

Men were leaping for cover in the roadside ditches, or at least ducking behind their trucks. One man plunged silently headlong into a stream; it was impossible to tell whether he was alive or dead.

Sam ducked as the nearby catering truck took a direct hit and exploded, scattering flaming wreckage over the road and several other trucks. As if it was the crack of a starting pistol, Sam took off as fast as her legs would carry her. Bearclaw followed, guiding her away from the vulnerable targets on the road. 'Get into cover!' he yelled.

Sam and Bearclaw leapt headlong into the ditch as the jeep erupted in flames behind them.

Her heart pounding frantically, Sam looked for a way out, catching only fragmented glimpses of the running figures and falling bodies around her. Something dug into her shoulder, and she was halfway towards fighting back when she realised it was Bearclaw trying to attract her attention. 'Look,' he said, pointing.

Another American soldier was waving at them from the corner of the Café Bodarwe, an inn at the crossroads a couple of hundred yards away. 'Come on,' she said. 'If we're quick, we might not be noticed.'

'That's what I thought,' he agreed. Sam took several deep breaths and then she and Bearclaw dashed across the open ground to the back wall of the café. They stumbled to a halt once they were sheltered from the firing, and Sam noticed a couple of other GIs following their lead.

To Sam's horror, she could already hear German voices and shooting from inside the café. 'Too late,' she muttered. 'Where the hell else is there?'

One of the men who had followed her answered. 'What about in there?' He nodded towards a little woodshed at the back of the café. Sam knew the wooden walls would offer no protection if a tank fired at the shed, but at least it would hide them from view.

They all piled inside and for a surreal moment Sam was reminded of playing hide and seek in the allotments at home. There was an old double-barrelled shotgun propped against the wall, and Sam grabbed it. The hammers were stiff under her thumb, but moved eventually. They had just cocked into place when the first German soldier kicked the door open.

The SS trooper froze, evidently realising that, even if he tried to dodge, the spread from the shotgun would at least wound him. He was young, Sam noticed, and he held his rifle just as awkwardly as she held the shotgun.

'Shoot him,' Bearclaw urged hoarsely. 'Shoot the bastard, now!'

Sam's finger tightened on one of the triggers. What else could she do? This was a life-or-death situation, and hadn't she killed before to save herself?

But this guy… he looked as scared as she felt. Hell, he was even younger than she was, by the looks of him; he should be at university or messing around with his mates, not trying to take over the world. How was she supposed to kill him?

She knew the answer before she thought of the question. She couldn't. All she could do was lower the gun and feel the looks of the others upon her.

Standartenführer Jochen Peiper was now merely simmering after his earlier rage against the battalion commander in the

Café Scholzen, as he questioned a prisoner at the foot of a shallow hill. Several of his half-tracks had been damaged by mines left by the Americans, but no matter. They were easily repaired.

As he had suspected, there was no actual resistance as such, and, despite the paratroops' tales of *stiff* resistance, he had broken through from Lanzerath to Honsfeld without so much as firing a single shot.

The paratroops had been an elite force in the original blitzkrieg, he remembered, but they had obviously gone soft. His own forces tempered his anger, though, performing perfectly, as far as he could tell.

Or so he thought until the sounds of shooting and explosions attracted his attention to the traffic jam at the crossroads at Baugnez. Leaving an aide to keep an eye on the prisoner, he took the jeep that had been captured along with the American, and drove back up the hill to see what was going on. A King Tiger had brought an American column to a halt, thoroughly blocking the Ligneuville road with burning trucks.

'Cease fire!' he yelled. Some units were still shooting, and he sent out a runner with instructions to shoot the gunners if that was what it took. After a few minutes, the firing finally died away.

Peiper clenched his fists in frustration as he regarded the column of burning and shattered vehicles. 'Idiots,' he growled at the tank commanders. 'Those beautiful trucks, which we need so badly, all shot up...' Beyond and in between the wrecked trucks American soldiers were beginning to emerge from the ditches, their hands raised.

SS troops began to herd them away from the wreckage, snatching rings and watches from their prisoners. Even gloves and hats were quickly appropriated and anyone who protested was clubbed down.

Peiper, meanwhile, gathered the unit commanders together. 'This is no time for hanging around wasting time on the fleeing. I want that road cleared for our Panzers immediately. You understand?'

A chorus of agreement satisfied him and he climbed aboard a Hanomag. 'Remember – clear the road!'

The half-track drove off.

'I'm sorry, Doctor,' Colonel Allen Lewis said, almost sincerely, 'but there's nothing I can do. We're falling back throughout this sector, in the hope of digging in at the most vital points. I certainly don't have any men or equipment spare to go looking for stray civilians.'

The Doctor leaned forward, looking strangely at home in the pale tiled cell that Lewis had adopted as his office. 'They're not stray civilians, Colonel. They're my friends and my assistants –'

'And as such I'm sure they've been very valuable to the war effort. Montgomery's headquarters said good things about you when I called them, and I've no doubt that applies to your friends too. But –'

'You called about me?' the Doctor asked, surprised. 'Already?'

Lewis nodded. 'Combining your service number from Lieutenant Wiesniewski when he telephoned to report his arrival, and the encounter with a…' Lewis looked at a handwritten sheet through half-moon spectacles. 'Sam Jones, who one of our units encountered –'

'Sam?' The Doctor was clearly delighted. 'That's wonderful news! What did she say?'

Lewis sat back. 'It seems she made contact with a Sergeant Kovacs as he was pulling out of Lanzerath. He put her on one of the unit's vehicles. So far he's made it back, but her truck hasn't.'

'Oh, no…' The Doctor jumped up. 'Do they know what happened to it?'

'Could be nothing. There are logjams on every road coming off the Skyline Drive. They could have run into advancing Germans or they could just be in a queue waiting to get here.'

'I'd like to go out there and see for myself,' said the Doctor, shuffling from foot to foot, full of jittery energy. 'If this Kovacs of yours can tell me where he last saw Sam…'

Lewis enjoyed being calm and superior, but he didn't like not being listened to. 'I told you once already: I can't spare the men or the equipment.'

'A motorcycle, then –'

'No. The way things are going, I want to know where I can find anybody I need at any given time, and that includes you. Garcia tells me you did a good job keeping those three guys in one piece. They wouldn't have made it without you. Perhaps Garcia can use you.' Lewis smiled faintly, recognising from the Doctor's pained expression where his weakness lay. 'Or perhaps you'd prefer some men to die for lack of treatment?'

The Doctor's eyes flashed with anger and Lewis found himself almost recoiling.

'That's hardly fair,' the Doctor said very quietly.

'It's also true, though, isn't it? If you put finding your friends above helping those wounded men, you wouldn't be here today.'

The Doctor scowled. 'I came here because I also need some engineering equipment to recover my vehicle…'

Lewis smiled, drily. 'I see. That, too, is more important than your friends?'

'All right,' the Doctor said finally. 'But I help on my own terms.'

'Your choice,' Lewis agreed, magnanimous in victory.

'Yes, it is. And I advise you to remember that.' With a flurry of coat-tails the Doctor was gone.

Lewis sat back and lit a small cigar. He felt calmer now that a potential problem had been dealt with. He recognised the strength in the Doctor's eyes, but seeing his own urbane and calm image in the small shaving mirror on the desk had focused him, reminded him that he *was* urbane and calm. He could deal with this. He always could.

Be indispensable was the first lesson he had learned at West Point; and the biggest part of that was never letting the strain get to you. Or, if it did, then hiding it.

'Did you hear all that?' he asked of the empty air.

'Yes,' a cheerful voice said beside his ear, even though there was no one there to speak it. 'It's exactly who we thought.'

'He looks different than you described.'

'Not to me. You humans are so limited in your perceptions, it's almost an insult to us.' Was Lewis imagining the tremor of madness in the voice? Perhaps even his friend was feeling the strain.

'I could take that as an insult to humanity,' Lewis replied. 'That would be very irresponsible, wouldn't it? We outnumber you massively, if we decided to take action for the insult.'

'Numbers mean nothing, little man, however provoked the majority might feel. We could cut off half the human race, if we so chose.'

Fitz had been on guard duty for what seemed like hours. He hoped desperately that no one would attack the village, not just for fear of a skirmish, but because he had no idea whether it would be morally right of him to sound any alarm. He'd much rather go off and have a quiet smoke on his own – if he could have bummed some cigarettes off someone – and maybe a little nose around.

He was guarding one side of a field just on the fringe of town. At the centre of the group of antenna-covered armoured cars was Leitz's mobile headquarters. A large truck had been converted into some kind of armoured command post, and a number of large tents had been put up all around.

The largest tent had an odd sheen to it and Fitz saw that it had steel and copper woven into the material. He couldn't think why, unless it was maybe for heating. But there was no insulation, so the tent would burn down if the wire was heated.

There was a sound from inside – a strange and atonal cry. It was as if someone was playing a dirge with an out-of-tune pipe. It wasn't mechanical, though. It felt to him like a living creature in pain.

Fitz's immediate instinct was to back off and forget about it. But it was so bizarre and so heartfelt that he couldn't. It was also so close to the command truck that he couldn't really just walk over without being noticed.

Fitz was in something of a quandary. The Germans had accepted him as one of their men at face value, so theoretically he could simply walk straight out of here. But he knew that people would wonder where he was going – and he didn't have an answer to give them.

Worse still, he was very aware that if they decided he was an enemy, wearing their uniform, he would be shot out of hand rather than sent to a POW camp. All things considered, it looked like being best to sit tight for now.

When Sam was a little girl she used to be as excited by snow as the Doctor had been when they'd landed. But right now there was no getting around the feeling that winter was death. It was as cold as a morgue freezer, and the white patches of snow dotting the fields now seemed more like bone showing through rotting skin.

The SS troops had marched all their prisoners from the convoy about a hundred yards along the road south of the crossroads and café. As they moved, they punctuated the orders with rough pushes from gun butts.

By now the prisoners had been lined up in eight ragged rows in a field, about sixty feet from the roadside. The men in front of Sam tried to jostle backward, and she couldn't blame them – she imagined the only way she could feel more terrified was if she were straight in the firing line of those two tanks that had remained by the roadside when the others began to move on. 'What are they doing?'

Bearclaw shrugged. 'I guess they don't have the facilities to guard us here. They must be waiting for some trucks to pick us up.'

Sam was relieved, although she didn't exactly relish the idea of spending time in a POW camp. She hoped that, having seen *The Great Escape* a few times on boring Bank Holidays, she would have some idea of what to expect. All things considered, it could be worse. Shot at dawn, all that stuff.

All things considered, she corrected herself, she still expected to be rescued by the Doctor, or escape on her own, before things came anywhere close to that.

The weird moaning from the tent had been getting to Fitz all day. He had also noticed that none of the other SS troops would go near it, and that made him wonder.

Fitz had heard all manner of horror stories about Nazi atrocities; he'd seen the newsreel film of the liberation of the death camps, and other stuff he didn't like to think about. What could be so nasty that the Nazi elite wanted nothing to do with it?

What, he asked himself, would the Doctor do? Well, he'd go and see what the bloody noise was for a start. Of course, he'd also have some bit of handy knowledge about what sort of thing made noises like that and how to handle the situation. Fitz supposed that, when you'd been doing this stuff for a thousand years or so, you'd pretty much have some sort of precedent set for just about everything.

Making a mental note to tell himself that he had 'told himself so' when it all went pear-shaped, Fitz walked over to the marquee as unobtrusively as possible.

The tent was supported with posts that seemed to be cast of pig iron. Two small petrol-powered generators were puttering to themselves on either side, but all the tables were unoccupied.

At the heart of the structure, four more posts formed the corners of a cage, made of iron again. It seemed an awful length to go to to hold a prisoner of war, Fitz thought.

Then he saw the cage's occupant, which was curled up in a ball on the floor, obviously in pain. Correction, he thought, it looked as if it had gone past pain and into total shock. He couldn't see much of it, and he began to wonder if his sight was going. The prisoner was blurred and shapeless, yet the bars around it were clear enough.

After a moment, Fitz realised two things. First, that the prisoner was the one that was weird, and not his eyesight; and, secondly, that travelling through time and space was beginning to desensitise him to things being deeply strange and unsettling. He wasn't sure if that was good or bad yet, but had the nasty suspicion that he'd find out soon enough if it was bad.

Major Poetschke, who was proud to serve the Fatherland as commander of the 1st SS Panzer Battalion, trotted over to the Panzer IVs. As well as the 75-mm main gun, the tanks also had two machine guns: one beside the driver and one beside the main gun. He was gratified to see that these two had also been fitted with more mobile MG42s on a ring around the commander's hatch, as a concession to defending against aircraft.

Several of the tank crewmen had dismounted already. Though the weather was cold, at least they had a chance to stretch their legs. A couple of them passed him with pistols in their hands, to help guard the prisoners. They were new men, of course; some of them probably had never even seen an American yet, but all knew of the devastation that US bombers were wreaking on German cities.

Everyone had lost friends or relatives in the bombing, and would like nothing better than to give the Allies a taste of their own medicine. True, the Luftwaffe had bombed Britain earlier in the war, but that was different to him; that was just to try to persuade the British. Now the Americans were trying to exterminate the German nation outright.

There were rules of war that were supposed to prevent such things, but they seemed to count for naught these days. Of course, there were also rules about the treatment of prisoners. But if the Allies could break rules – and he had been told about the atrocities perpetrated upon helpless German prisoners – then perhaps they had lost their right to be protected by those rules.

Besides, none of the lawmakers of those rules were here.

Yes, here was a chance to give the grieving men what they must need. Poetschke clambered up onto the hull of the nearest Mk IV. 'Open fire,' he said to the commander.

The tank commander grinned, and disappeared down into the turret. He reappeared a moment later, less cheerful. 'We can't; not from this angle. The gun won't depress far enough.'

'Does it matter how it's done?'

The tank commander hesitated, then called out 'Private Fleps!' One of the tank crew whom Poetschke had passed looked round from where he was taunting an American lieutenant. 'Do it.'

Sam saw something in the tank crewman's eyes when he turned back. She wasn't sure what it was, but she could tell something had changed.

'Oh, sweet Jesus.'

'What?' Bearclaw asked.

She swallowed hard. 'I just remembered what happened to Richard Attenborough and Gordon Jackson,' she said.

'What?'

'Never mind…' But it wasn't the memory that terrified her. It was the looks in the SS men's eyes.

She knew she was already starting to open her mouth to shout or yell at the prisoners to move, but her voice was coming so slowly and the SS man's arm was coming up faster, putting his pistol to the forehead of the nearest American soldier.

For a sickeningly teasing moment, Sam tried to convince herself it was all a bluff. But then the SS man pulled the trigger, the bullet snapping the American's head back. Like a stack of dominoes, the men behind stumbled back as the body fell over.

Then the sound of the gunshot broke the spell that had seemed to slow down time. The prisoners were shouting – some in fear and some in anger – and trying to push away.

'Stand still,' an officer shouted, probably thinking the disruption among the prisoners would spook the Germans into thinking this was a breakout attempt. 'Don't provoke more –' A couple of men pushed past a frozen Sam as the SS man turned and shot a man with a Red Cross armband.

They seemed to be shooting at random – or were they picking on disruptive prisoners? Sam regretted not being able to hear what the men at the tank had said to each other.

'Kill them all!' a German voice shouted from the direction of the two tanks. Immediately, the tanks' machine guns burst into life, hosing the rows of screaming prisoners with gunfire.

All around Sam, men tumbled to the ground, or broke and ran, or dived for cover behind comrades who had been cut down in the first volley. Sam was scarcely able to think through the screams and the gunfire, her mind refusing to process the information it was getting.

Bullets darted across the field in buzzing shoals. Bodies paused for barely perceptible moments before falling. Cordite and blood stung her nostrils, and suddenly something exploded low in her back and in her thigh.

For a moment Sam was still watching the more alert prisoners bolt for the tree line, then her legs gave way and the churned mud rose to meet her.

Sam's senses were jumbled. She couldn't feel anything. Maybe it was her wounds, and maybe it was just her brain trying to turn away from as much of the carnage as it could.

Men ran and trucks circled the field, but none of the movement seemed real. Proper. They were there and they were blurred, then they were gone. All the time the guns were a mechanical heartbeat, pumping blood out of bodies instead of through them.

Sam had been to a lot of places, but she had never really been to hell before.

It was getting dark by the time the Doctor and Garcia returned to the hotel. 'Look,' Garcia was saying. 'I know Lewis can be a bit of an idiot, but for what it's worth I appreciate the help. Even if I understand why you'd rather be out finding your friends.'

The Doctor shook his head. 'That's all right. There's something else going on here, anyway, that I want to look into.'

'Wiesniewski's story?'

'Yes. I don't think he was either imagining things, or gassed by the Germans as he seems to believe.'

Garcia had to admit it was a hell of a weird story Wiesniewski had told them, and weirder still when he seemed to forget it so quickly. But Garcia hadn't really given it much thought. People wounded in battle reported a lot of strange things: ghosts, religious experiences, you name it. None of it made much of an impression on Garcia any more. 'Then what *do* you think?' he asked.

'I don't know yet.' The Doctor held the hotel door open for Garcia. The reception lounge was full of walking wounded, back in uniform, but still bandaged here and there. Most of the serious cases had been evacuated back to safer ground, and the hospital was now showing a quick turnover of lesser wounds. Those men would stay to man the defences, if Garcia was any judge of most of their characters.

Nevertheless, there were still a few serious cases in private rooms upstairs. Burns cases, or those with internal bleeding. The ones who weren't able to be moved along bumpy roads. 'It's time I was doing my rounds. You're welcome to come along, but I wouldn't blame you if you'd rather not see any more injuries today.'

'I *am* the Doctor,' the Doctor reminded him gently.

Garcia shrugged.

They went upstairs and checked on a couple of patients. The first two were doing fine. They were still too ill to be driven out, but Garcia reckoned they would live, barring accidents. 'This one's more borderline,' he told the Doctor at the next door. 'Massive burns. Frankly I'm surprised he's lasted this long. Still, that he has suggests that maybe he's got what it takes to make it all the way.' He opened the door.

'He certainly seems to have gone *some* way,' the Doctor said mildly.

Garcia blinked. The bed was neatly made, but empty.

'What the hell?' Garcia looked at the sheets, while the Doctor went over and tried the window. It didn't budge, and the sheets were neatly pressed and clean. It didn't look like anyone had slept in them recently, let alone a badly injured burns case.

Garcia rubbed at his eyes, half asleep. He didn't even want to risk blinking in case his eyes refused to open again. 'It's nothing. Happens all the time.'

The Doctor had produced a tin mug of hot coffee from somewhere, though Garcia was sure he couldn't have gone out of the room to get it. He took it gratefully anyway as the Doctor spoke.

'"Nothing" can't happen all the time. If I had people disappearing on me all the time, I'd be worried.'

'I don't mean literally disappearing. At least, I don't think I do... It's just the way things are in the Army. SNAFU, you know. Men discharge themselves to get back to their units, or swap papers to get home, and by the time anybody figures out what's what the whole mess of paperwork is just too screwed up to get straight. Probably he died and somebody took the body out without being patient enough to go through channels.'

He sat down and looked through at the ward. 'The only weird thing is that the bed's been made. A burial detail wouldn't stop to do that. And one of my staff would have told me if anyone had come up to change the sheets.'

'Weird is my business,' the Doctor said cheerily. 'What was this man's condition? You said something about fifty-fifty.' For some reason, he was tapping the walls.

'This guy had been in a Ronson.'

'Ronson?'

'A Sherman. Very quick and easy to light up. Anyway, he'd been in one that took a round to the side. He got clear, but was covered in third-degree burns. Trust me on this: he'll be lucky to walk after six months in traction and rehab. I guess somebody came by to take him out for shipping home, but I just can't see how they did it without my noticing.' A thought struck him, and he put down the mug. 'Jesus, I must be having blackouts.'

'I don't think you are. But I do think we should talk to Lieutenant Wiesniewski.'

'What would he know about this?'

'Nothing,' the Doctor admitted. 'But he lost some bodies, too.'

'Well, you can wait till morning. Garcia rubbed his eyes and stood back up. 'I said twelve hours' complete rest for him, and I meant it.'

The shooting seemed to have lasted all day, but according to Sam's watch it had been only about a quarter of an hour.

A constant stream of vehicles had rumbled along the road. Far from stopping to help the wounded, plenty of occupants of passing half-tracks had fired a few bursts into the bodies in the field.

Tears had been squeezed out of her eyes by the pain, though she had now gone beyond that into a burning numbness. Was it the wounds sapping her life away, or the cold? She thought of the man with the Red Cross armband. He could've helped me, she thought. Now I'm going to die. I'll probably end up on a cenotaph or something. One of those poppies on Remembrance Sunday will be for me. I wonder if the Doctor and Fitz will ever find my name on some memorial or other. Or Mum and Dad.

No, they won't put my name anywhere. I don't belong here. I'm no one. Suddenly, panic stabbed at her. I shouldn't be here, she thought. This is all wrong. I can't die in World War Two, it's stupid.

But it was too cold for the feeling to last for long. Soon it, too, began to freeze like the rest of her body, the urgency bleeding out of her into the ground beneath that must already be sodden with her blood.

She was feeling detached now. It was as if her whole body had succumbed to the constant buzz of a raging toothache. She'd give anything for it to go away… anything for comfort.

She heard German voices somewhere towards the road, but didn't dare look round to see what they were doing. Out of the corner of her eye, she saw men in black SS coveralls moving through the field, stopping occasionally to examine a body here and there.

There was a sudden shot from somewhere out of vision and Sam tried not to start. If they thought she was dead they would leave her alone. Then maybe she could move, get away. Or maybe someone would find her.

What was left of her.

Several more shots came over the next few minutes. 'Does anyone need help?' a voice was calling. 'Put up your hand if you need medical attention.' Sam felt hope stir, tried to raise her hand, but was too weak and too cold. To one side, she saw a wounded man raise his arm.

The would-be Samaritan laughed and shot him in the head. Sam was too weak even to cry over it. Why was she still conscious, anyway? What was she supposed to do now?

This was mad. This was an outrage. She wanted out. This just wasn't bloody fair.

The Doctor paced around the little courtyard at the back of the makeshift hospital, scribbling notes on a little pad. He didn't really need to do that while thinking, but it felt and looked more practical. It would set people's minds at ease.

On the pad, he had been drawing little patterns – ones that linked Sweden and San Francisco with the Ardennes. More accurately, he was drawing things that would hopefully make sense as some kind of pattern.

There were always patterns in things. He considered asking one of the humans to try, since they had an innate talent for this sort of thing. But if he did that then he'd be at a loose end while waiting, and that was the last thing he wanted.

Why had the TARDIS brought them here? To punish him for allowing the things that had happened to her in Sweden and San Francisco? Giving him a taste of his own medicine perhaps? Or maybe he was thinking too theatrically – always a fault of his. It was all just chance. The TARDIS loved Earth, as he did. *Because* he did, he told himself.

He could feel the TARDIS out there, smug and secure even under rubble at the bottom of a river. She never grieved for herself. Maybe at the time, she would feel pain, or outrage, but never for long. Like him, she bounced back. She *kept* bouncing back. Just like him.

'I must stop imagining things,' he muttered. 'I'll be talking to myself next.'

He still hadn't heard any more of Fitz or Sam. He knew they could look after themselves, but it didn't stop him needing to take care of them. To watch over them more, to –

Strange that he should think this way, he thought, then realised that he wasn't. The TARDIS's telepathic circuits were operating at an increased level. He could feel them trying to spark an alert in his brain. Something was going wrong somewhere.

'A penny for them?' The Doctor looked round – it was Garcia.

'Just wondering where my friends are, and whether they're all right.'

'You look more like you've seen a ghost.'

'More like a premonition.'

The silence was strange after the hours of constant noise. Sam's tears had frozen to her face and the numbing pain was all that was left to concentrate on. Darkness was falling – she wasn't sure if that was real or just her senses failing – and there were fewer moans or gunshots.

The frosted grass beside her crunched under boots, and she sensed someone bending down. A foot rolled her over, though she didn't really feel it. Two Germans were looming over her. 'You want help?' one of them asked.

In spite of herself, Sam nodded weakly. They could see she

was alive. There was no point in playing possum. There was always a chance.

The two men exchanged unpleasant smiles and one of them bent to help her up. 'We can help each other,' he said. 'The boy here's still a virgin – you can help him with that, eh?' The Germans laughed, and Sam just stared at them.

'Or perhaps not…' the German said. He had noticed her wounds now. 'Sorry, kid,' he said to his comrade. 'I don't think she's got what it takes left.'

Sam hoped against hope that this meant they would leave her. *There's always a chance.* Even so, she was about to tell them what they could do with themselves, since really it was all she could do, when her words froze in her throat. The German pressed the muzzle of his pistol against her breastbone.

She didn't register the sound of the shot, or the flash that scorched her chest, as he pulled the trigger. She didn't register anything.

She tried to take another breath, but couldn't. There was nothing in her. Nothing in the world. You're dead, she told herself, but it seemed ridiculous, a hollow word, more nothing.

Chapter Four
The Oz Factor

Leitz lit up a cigarette as they sat on the flank of his armoured car, poring over the plans and rota that Farber had drawn up for protecting his prisoner. 'Your precautions seem adequate,' he told Farber. 'I'm sure they'll be pleased at Wewelsburg.'

'The important thing is to be pleased here. If your prisoner escapes, you'll be hard put to catch another one.'

'Not necessarily,' Leitz argued lightly. 'With the new 232s, and the experience we've had with this one, it should be child's play to repeat it.' His features hardened slightly. 'But we won't have to, will we?'

Farber shook his head.

'All right, you can turn in now. I'll see you at dawn.'

Farber nodded sharply, and saluted before leaving. One of the old school, Leitz reflected. Reliable, not a thug like most of his men, and smart enough to see which way the political winds were blowing.

Leitz winced as another volley of shells was fired at the American positions from the other side of town. War would be a lot more pleasant, he reflected, if it could be done quietly.

He walked back to his armoured car, ignoring the distant gunfire and the flashes on the horizon. He had kept the bottle of schnapps his vehicle had been issued with before the attack. Most of the men who had had bottles handed out drank theirs around their cooking fires the night before they went into action, but Leitz felt more comfortable with the idea of drinking to celebrate. Going into battle drunk was always a bad idea, and he was sure they had lost more men than they should because of the alcohol.

So long as none of those losses were his men, he didn't really care. It wasn't as if this offensive would win the war, whatever the rank and file thought. It would inflict some pain on the enemy, and delay them so that some plans could be made by those with foresight. That was all, really.

However, it had given him this opportunity to research some of his theories, albeit in ways he'd previously never considered. For that, he was grateful. Leitz grinned to himself, wishing he could speak of this to someone – to anyone. It would be worth it just to get it off his chest.

He knew that wasn't possible, at least not if he didn't want to get his head off his shoulders as well. Things had changed over the last five years, and not for the better. It wasn't just the strategic developments, but the personal things. When he had first ridden into France in one of Kleist's tanks in 1940, the pay had been good and the home leave was generous. Nowadays the pay was useless and the home leave was something to be avoided, since the billets were better than a bombed-out house and dead relatives.

He paused at the hatch set between the middle wheels of his 232 and gave the dark marquee a habitual glance. He froze, then. Something was moving in the shadows, emerging from the tent. For an awful moment, Leitz thought that his prisoner might be escaping and foresaw a short life-span on the Eastern Front for himself.

As his eyes adjusted, he saw that it was one of the SS Infantry, in a winter camouflage overall. It looked like that man he'd spoken to earlier: Kreiner, wasn't it?

Leitz smiled to himself. He hadn't thought Kreiner could resist poking his nose in. He approached Kreiner silently, having put out his cigarette. 'Everything quiet?'

Kreiner jumped. 'I – Er, I mean, yes, sir.'

'I saw you coming out of the tent.'

'I thought I heard a noise,' Kreiner said.

Leitz decided that the man was trying to bullshit him.

Everyone in the village could hear a noise from the tent.

'And was it saboteurs?' Leitz asked drily.

'No… To be honest I thought maybe the prisoner was escaping. It's probably keeping half the town awake.'

Leitz was slightly mollified. Perhaps he was going to be honest after all. 'I think it just makes that noise to annoy us. Tell me, have you ever seen anyone like our prisoner before?'

'No,' Kreiner answered, and this time Leitz knew he was being completely truthful. 'It was dark in there anyway – I'd be hard put to say what he looked like.'

'He's a mystery man. You seem to enjoy mysteries, Kreiner?'

Kreiner paused. 'Sometimes.'

'Curiosity may kill cats, but I also find a use for it. Now that you've seen my prisoner, I hope you understand why I ask you to join my unit permanently.'

'Because I have an enquiring mind?'

'Because if you refuse I will have you shot. My project is of the most secret nature. You might say I am investigating the abilities of…' Leitz broke off and gave a staccato laugh. 'Well, of Light and Dark Elves, if you will. I suppose that is as good a code-name as any.'

Kreiner didn't react except to widen his eyes a little. 'And you're telling me this?'

Leitz nodded. 'I've been watching you today, and you seem intelligent and curious. You are also quite well educated by the sound of things. So I would rather recruit you than kill you.'

Kreiner smiled nervously. 'Works for me.'

'Good. If it makes you feel better, this will help the war effort.' They both looked up, and listened to the distant hum of aircraft far overhead. 'Damned Allied bombers….Barbarians murdering our children in their homes.'

'As the Luftwaffe did in 1940… If the British can take it, why can't we?'

Leitz found himself laughing briefly. 'You have a point there, Corporal. But every man has his degree of hypocrisy.'

Night was falling quickly, and the temperature plummeting even faster. At least, Bearclaw assumed night was falling, as the light was fading, though to be honest it didn't really seem to be getting dark. It was more as if the light was being replaced by some opposite force...

Who wouldn't be spooked in a place like this? he asked himself. It was nothing. Bearclaw carefully crawled over to where the girl, Sam, had fallen. She was dead all right; her skin cold, no pulse... He was going to kill some Kraut for that, he promised silently. Bad enough that they shot the rest of these guys, but civilian girls? Some things could be forgiven only with the shedding of blood.

The girl's eyes wouldn't close because they were already frosted over, so he put a handkerchief across her face. The handkerchief fluttered from the shaking of his hand, and it was neither cold, nor fear, nor weakness that caused it. He moved away, sadly, to check on some of the other GIs.

Suddenly, there was something like a noise from behind him and he turned round. Except it wasn't a real noise: it was sort of... musical. A tinkling sound. It seemed to be coming from the area where Sam and a couple of other men were lightly blanketed with fresh snow. Maybe one of them was still alive after all...

There was a faint light hovering around some of the bodies, casting an eerie glow as touches of mist rose from the ground. Bearclaw shivered in spite of himself. Was he imagining things, or were there really tiny glowing light sources circling a few inches above the bodies?

It was getting harder to tell as the mist thickened. He could almost make out humanoid shapes within; it was as if the lights were reflecting off parts of limbs. But there was no one there. Suddenly, the lights gathered around Sam's body and the mist swirled around it. Bearclaw resisted the urge to yell at them, because that would bring more Germans. They winked out, and Sam's corpse was gone too. Only the mist remained, desolately thinning and fading.

Bearclaw blinked. What the hell was that? He scuttled over to where Sam's body had been – and her outline in the new snow was all that was left.

Bearclaw blinked several times, looking around. She couldn't have got up and left, and there had been no one to carry her away. He shuddered again, and a word came unbidden into his mind: Kachinas.

Cloud people. He snorted. There had been a little mist, to be sure, but hardly a cloud, and surely no people. Yet someone had moved Sam's body.

He stood there for some time, silent. He hadn't even been able to keep her safe after death.

What sort of man was he to let these things happen, and stay alive himself?

'…There's no way he could have got off that wire himself, or anyone could have taken him, so quickly. It's physically impossible.' Wiesniewski was sipping a morning orange juice, while the Doctor played with a stethoscope.

Garcia agreed with the Doctor's judgement that Wiesniewski's tale was interesting, but it was hardly rational. 'A body vanished in the space of a moment?'

'That's right.' Wiesniewski spread his hands. 'I know it's crazy, and probably just a mix-up in all the confusion, but I'd swear to that on a bible.'

'You'll have to forgive me if I jump to fairly paranoid conclusions,' the Doctor said, 'but I can't help seeing a connection here. Two bodies literally vanish into thin air while someone's back is turned. No one could have carried them, and they couldn't have walked away…' He shook his head. 'Too much of a coincidence to be a coincidence.'

'Bodies vanish and go undiscovered all the time,' Garcia protested.

'Not from hospitals,' the Doctor countered, then seemed to think twice. 'Well, except under some pretty exceptional circumstances,' he added.

'Then what happened to them?'

'I don't know. But I will; I promise you that.'

'You haven't even got anything to go on.'

'Ah, but I have. The Oz Factor.'

Garcia's mind went blank in a failed attempt to understand that. 'The what?'

'The sudden silence and disassociation from the environment. It's a phenomenon that some experts on this matter call the "Oz Factor". There are very precise sets of experiences that follow it, and so that's my starting point.'

Garcia had finally managed to get away from the little hotel/hospital to have dinner at one of the few remaining restaurants that were still open. Naturally it catered only to the officers, and the place was staffed by the Army's catering service, serving army food, but the atmosphere was more convivial.

Here he could relax over breakfast, getting a quiet hour or so away from the hustle and bustle, and the screams that even morphine couldn't stop some men from making. The coffee was good too.

As he sat, trying both to relax and wake up – he didn't think about how much of a contradiction that was – he caught a glimpse of a uniform in the kitchen. The kitchen staff were from the Catering Corps, but they generally wore coveralls or chefs' aprons. Garcia could have sworn he just saw a combat uniform, wrapped around a stubble-headed bulldog of a man.

Curious, he switched seats, to get a slightly better view. He saw that he was right: there was a sergeant in there, counting out money. Garcia knew he should probably keep his nose out of it, but he was also sure that the sergeant was very much out of place there. Which most likely meant he had an illicit reason for being there.

Garcia drained his coffee, his tiredness momentarily forgotten. He left the little restaurant and found a narrow alley that came out into a back street along which was the back door. Piles of trash had built up around the door, but he could still see the sergeant when he left.

Not even having the common grace to look around furtively, the sergeant marched off in the opposite direction. Garcia followed quietly, suddenly awake and alert at the mystery. Perhaps a change really was as good as a rest.

Wiesniewski was feeling a lot better than he had the previous day. He was sitting alone in the little room where they'd treated him. As an officer, he'd been given the little luxury, though as a combat veteran he didn't really need or even want it.

He had written down the memories of his experience, in case he forgot again. The thought of going nuts was totally creepy, and he felt reading and rereading the note, knowing the experience was there in black and white, would help him rest easier. And anyway, there were others who had believed him.

As if on cue, the Doctor came back into the room.

'I was hoping I'd see you again,' Wiesniewski said. 'I think in all the rush since we met, I forgot to say thanks. And to say sorry that Lewis didn't let you go find your friends.'

'I'll find them.' The Doctor shuffled his feet, looking a little embarrassed at the attention. 'You're off to a new assignment?'

Wiesniewski nodded. 'Desk job at Lewis's place. They want

to check me out, I suppose, after I lost my squad.' He understood why they didn't trust him with a combat assignment, but it still hurt to be considered suspect. He was as much disappointed not to be able to prove himself again, as he was relieved to be out of the firing line for a time.

'I think it's pretty clear that wasn't your fault.'

Wiesniewski shrugged. 'It's the way things work.'

The Doctor regarded him for a moment, then handed him his tie. 'You'll need that for an office job. Actually, I wanted to see you before you left. To ask for your help with something.'

'Go ahead, shoot.'

'I want you to keep an ear out for any stories similar to yours among the troops here.'

'You mean weird mists, bodies vanishing…?'

'Yes, yes, I mean exactly that. I strongly suspect that you're not the only one to experience this sort of thing, and if I'm going to get to the bottom of it I'll need some idea of how widespread it is, and how long it's been going on.'

Wiesniewski nodded. Perhaps it would throw some light on what happened to him. If it had happened to others, then he could be sure he wasn't just going crazy. 'I doubt there'll be any formal reports…' He himself certainly wouldn't put the weirder elements in a formal report. That would cause too much trouble with his superiors.

'That doesn't matter.' The Doctor smiled. 'Rumours and chat are all I need to go on.'

Bearclaw had been staggering along for hours. He even managed to stow away on the back of a truck for a short while, though it had hurt like hell when he jumped back out.

He had no idea where he was this morning, but he figured that if he kept heading west he'd hit some American lines eventually.

He didn't feel cold any more, and instead just wanted to go

to sleep. In spite of the tremendous urge to stop and rest, he forced himself to carry on through the fields. He had been brought up in the mountains of the southwest's Four Corners area, and knew that he was feeling the symptoms of hypothermia and exposure. He also knew that, if he gave in to the urge to sleep, he would never wake up.

Ordinarily, even he wouldn't have the strength to keep going, but the sounds of shooting in his ears and the look on Sam's face that hovered in his eyes drove him on. What had happened back there at the Baugnez crossroads had to be reported, and avenged. He had no idea whether anybody else made it out. It was down to him.

His wife would think him crazy for taking on so much responsibility, but he had no doubt she would also love him for his stubbornness. She was like that. His kids would approve too. They all thought their dad was a hero.

Yeah, right. Being a hero just meant fate had screwed you over and you'd survived it. But you couldn't survive it every time. All the heroes he knew were dead.

He realised that the landscape hadn't moved in several minutes, and finally came to the conclusion that he had fallen over without even realising it. He hoped he wasn't asleep. If he was he must be dead already, and he didn't like the thought of spending eternity feeling like this.

His legs hurt like hell as he stood, and didn't ease up any when he got going again.

If nothing else, the overload of pain from that drowned out the pain when he stumbled and fell again. He must be falling asleep, he decided, as he was dreaming. He dreamed of faces hovering around him and hands lifting him into the air. Then he was floating, his whole body numb.

Weary before he even began the new day's duties, Garcia returned to the former hotel and checked the incomings and outgoings at reception. While he had been out following that sergeant, two men had died and another five been brought in from the line.

He felt guilty, even though he knew those men would have died even if he had been at their bedside the whole time.

The sergeant he had followed had indulged in some pretty strange behaviour. He had visited several local shopkeepers, then gone and retired to a room in the local brothel. Garcia found it somewhat offensive that a brothel was considered so vital as to be allowed to stay open, but he wasn't going to make waves about it. He indulged himself a wry smile. Well, if it gave the men an incentive to get out of his hospital…

He would think about this curious sergeant's activities later, and then make a decision. He knew where to find the man when he was ready.

At this rate he wouldn't have enough room for all the wounded coming in. Still, some of the men taking the beds would be dead soon enough. Garcia shook his head. He knew that you lost people sometimes, no matter what you did; but they still all took a piece of him with them. Making a note to check on the newcomers first, he went to his office to pick up a white coat.

Garcia paused in the doorway. The Doctor was sitting at the desk, with only a small table lamp illuminating the room. He was holding one hand under the light, scrutinising it closely, with an unreadable expression on his usually clear features. Garcia wondered what he was doing – checking for shell shocks, maybe? Seeing whether his hand remained steady, or was getting shaky…?

Then he realised that the Doctor's eyes weren't quite focused on the hand, but the desk beneath. It looked as if he was making shadow animals with his fingers, but there was something not quite right…

The Doctor stood up, giving an apologetic smile that was too rushed to be entirely genuine, in Garcia's opinion. 'Sorry, I didn't realise you'd be coming in at this hour.'

'I sleep here.' He refined the statement. 'At least, I sleep here for about half an hour between operations.'

'Not a much of a nine-to-five job, this war business, is it?'

'I wouldn't know: I've never really worked that way.' He was quite proud of that fact actually. He enjoyed feeling just a little different from others. Not much, just a little. It was, perhaps, more interesting.

'What did you do before all this?' the Doctor asked.

'Much the same,' Garcia said with a shrug, 'but under better conditions. I was a surgical intern at LA County until I got drafted. At least I had skills too valuable to make me a GI. How about you? What's your profession?'

'Me? I take stands. Oh, and cheat Death, of course.'

'Cheat Death, huh? Interesting profession.'

'Oh, no. Making things Right is my profession. Cheating Death's just a sort of hobby… But I seem to be rather talented at it.'

Garcia nodded absently. 'The problem with cheating Death is that he's a sore loser at the best of times.'

'Yes,' the Doctor agreed mildly, 'she is.'

'She? The trick cyclists have probably got a word for that sort of association. Probably start asking nonsense about your mother.'

The Doctor sniffed. 'I'm afraid they'd only get nonsense back, then. I don't imagine they'd believe the truth even if I was in the mood to tell it.'

'That bad, huh?'

Emil Metz tried without success to stop his boots from making any noise as his patrol moved through the woods near a reported American position on the Schnee Eifel. The whole ridge of the Eifel ran for miles and should be cleared of

Americans by now, but there was always the chance that a small group had been overlooked or cut off.

While he still got scared from time to time, the ease with which their forces had advanced made him feel quite proud to be part of the German army.

Although he was a paratrooper, he had never had to jump out of an aircraft. He was glad of that. Facing enemy fire was one thing, but the thought of plummeting to Earth through miles of open air was just too scary. He would never have signed up for the paratroopers in the old days, when they did still jump. Come to that, he would never have signed up for them if he had realised how far their elite image had fallen.

Not only were they the butt of the Infantry and SS jokes, but of the quartermasters' too. Metz's Schmeisser had a broken firing pin when he was issued with it, and there were no replacements. He had had to wait for somebody to get killed, then take their gun.

It was quite a pleasant day, in spite of the snowy mud and the cold. The air was sharp and clean, and he remembered playing in woods just like this when he was a boy. He was thinking about those days more and more. He hoped there wouldn't be any fighting for the unit today; it would spoil the atmosphere of peace around here.

'Listen,' their corporal said. Everyone paused, straining their ears, just as Metz did.

'I don't hear anything,' Metz said. And what was wrong with that? Nothing, as far as he was concerned. Like he said, a peaceful atmosphere.

'Exactly,' the corporal muttered. 'No birdsong, no sounds of battle from the front… Not even our own footsteps.'

Metz looked down, stepping on to a twig. He heard it crack. Then he noticed the others moving their feet, but heard nothing. That was very strange. He saw himself as a boy in the woods looking round, wide-eyed. Then a sound did come.

Metz swallowed nervously, cursed, cocked his gun. It was a low, persistent hum, like something trying to force its way through the air.

It wasn't coming from above, but from all around. Everyone in the patrol was looking for the source, evidently as nervous as Metz suddenly felt. He didn't see anything and turned back towards the others. He didn't see them any more either – a grey wall of mist was rising to obscure them. Between that and the hum, it was almost as if the snow was being melted to steam on a griddle. Despite that, it all still lay on the ground unchanged.

The humming suddenly ended, splintering into a chorus of low animal sounds, but like no animal Metz had ever heard before. They came from different directions and he had no idea which way to move.

When the gunfire started, it was both inevitable and shocking. Metz spun round to face its source, trying to work out what was being shot at.

Then something black coalesced out of the mist, and Metz never saw whatever his target was. He never saw anything again.

Garcia ran down the stairs at the same time as the Doctor emerged from the little office. A jeep had pulled up outside, with a casualty found in a small area of no-man's-land, suffering from exposure.

The men who had found him carried him up to a room with a fire in it, having wrapped him in their topcoats for the trip back. 'He should be OK. They caught him in time. He'll need to be kept warm, given something hot to drink, but that should be about all.'

'And the blood?' one of the men asked.

'Seems to be someone else's. Aside from some cuts and bruising from some hard falls, he's pretty much unharmed.'

While Garcia escorted the men out of the door, the Doctor checked the new patient's dog tags. 'Daniel Bearclaw.'

At the sound of his name, Bearclaw's eyes flicked open, staring but not seeing, if Garcia was any judge. The GI grabbed the Doctor's wrist. 'Nayenezgani,' he said in a tone of wonderment. 'Nayenezgani, and Kachinas. I saw the Kachinas. Examining the dead... They were examining the dead...' His face contorted. 'Murdering Nazi bastards!' He slipped away again, as if exhausted by the effort of his last shout.

'Best to let him sleep it off while we patch up those cuts,' Garcia suggested.

The Doctor absently handed him a needle and some suture thread. 'You heard what he said, though?'

Garcia nodded. 'Didn't understand a word of it, mind you, but I heard.'

'Kachinas,' the Doctor murmured softly. 'In Hopi mythology, the "cloud people". Yet Nayenezgani is a Navajo word...'

'And what does it mean?' Not that it was likely to be important.

'It means he seems to recognise me.'

'You've met before?'

'Not personally, no. Unless it was in my future, of course.'

'Wha-'

'But actually the really important part of his story was the part about the Kachinas examining the bodies of the dead.'

Garcia hadn't been the least bit surprised by that part of Bearclaw's tale. 'Yes... It definitely helps prove how near death he was. Between the shock and the temperatures out there, I'd have been more worried if he hadn't had a few hallucinations.'

'A few hallucinations,' the Doctor echoed. He smiled faintly. 'No no no. Whatever injuries he's sustained, I think they may have caused him to see something real... What if he'd fallen into an altered state of consciousness, his brain flooded with emergency chemicals? That's as likely to open new neural pathways as to shut off the usual ones.'

Colonel Lewis walked into Wiesniewski's office without knocking. 'Lieutenant.'

Wiesniewski stood, saluting. 'Sir.'

'At ease.' Lewis watched Wiesniewski thoughtfully. 'I just wanted to welcome you to the unit. I know it can't be easy for a combat man to take on a desk job.'

Wiesniewski looked quite sanguine about it. 'I pledged to do my duty, sir, whatever that might be.'

Lewis nodded. 'Glad to hear it.' Both he and his nebulous companion would be glad to hear it, in fact. He resisted the urge to look towards where his partner would be.

'There is one thing, though. I've been hearing some odd rumours lately. Nonsense stories about… I dunno, ghosts or phantoms. Bodysnatchers.'

Wiesniewski looked uncomfortable. 'People under combat conditions are also under a lot of stress –'

Lewis grinned broadly. 'Correct. I'm glad you agree with us. With me. I don't want to look like a martinet, but I'd like these stories to stop. They're just spooking people, and it's bad for morale.'

'I'm afraid we can't stop people from thinking about what they… think they saw.'

'I'll settle for stopping them talking about it. I want it known that if someone really wants to get it off their chest, they can write it up in a confidential report. If not, then they should keep it to themselves. If I hear any man gossiping about such nonsense, there's always the chance that he will be written off as a Section Eight at best. Possibly court-martialled for cowardice, if he's just trying to get home on a Section Eight rap. You'll see to that?'

'Yes, sir, I will.'

'Good. I'm glad we understand each other. Carry on.' Lewis left Wiesniewski to his work. In reality, of course, the person most afraid was Lewis himself; he knew that. He was afraid of things getting out of hand, and out of his personal control.

He didn't mind any of the things that were happening, so long as he was in charge. And whatever his partner might think, he *was* in charge.

Bearclaw could hardly believe his luck. When he had felt himself lifted into the air, his brain had never entertained the possibility that it was a jeep crew lifting him on to their jeep. He had his priorities in his mind when he awoke and had insisted on dictating a report on the massacre he had escaped.

A nurse was taking it down. Maybe it wasn't the sort of revenge he had hoped for, but at least he was doing something towards it. The more people who knew, the more chance that somebody would do something.

There were others listening too; Garcia, and Nayene– The Doctor, he corrected himself. Apparently those two had worked on him when he'd been brought in. He wouldn't forget that.

'They shot forty or fifty of our guys. Some civilians too; the café owner, the English girl we'd picked up…'

'English girl?' the Doctor asked. 'What English girl?'

'She said her name was… Sam, yeah, that's it. Samantha something.'

'Jones?' the Doctor whispered, his face pale.

'That's right.' Bearclaw paused. 'Someone you know?'

'Yes.' The Doctor just stared at him. His mouth kept opening and clc··g, but no words would come for a good few minutes. Then, finally, desperately, he managed, 'Are you sure she –'

Bearclaw nodded sadly. 'I'm sorry. She was hit at least twice ·· the back. When the Krauts were going round finishing people off, two of them picked her up. I think they wanted to… Well, they weren't planning to help much. Anyway, I guess they decided she wasn't good enough, so one of them –' Bearclaw held two fingers in a gun gesture and put them to the centre of the Doctor's chest – 'put a gun right to her like this and pulled the trigger.' He let his hand fall back against the pillow. 'You don't survive a wound like that.'

The next morning – at least he hoped it was only the next morning, and he hadn't slept for a full day or more – Jeff Kovacs was wakened by a knocking at the door to his room in the brothel. It was decorated horribly, full of red velvet, but it was comfortable. He had the room indefinitely, for services rendered. He had his pick of the girls, for free, too, though still only by the hour.

'Go to hell,' he groaned back at the knocking. 'I got a three-day pass, so come back when it's over.'

'Open the damn door or I'll have it revoked right now.'

Goddam officers, Kovacs thought. He pulled the door open, not bothering to put on anything over his shorts and vest. The man standing outside looked like he had caught a whiff of something stinking. Which he probably had. 'This room ain't free, sir. Not my decision, but the management's.'

'I didn't want a room. I wanted to speak to you, Kovacs.'

'I ain't for sale. If you're that desperate, there's a house round the corner.' He leaned casually against the door frame. He'd seen this guy around. Garcia, that was it, from the hospital.

'I was thinking of the scam you're running,' Garcia said. 'Pay-offs at the officers' restaurant, you know? Trips to see certain local shopkeepers – you deliver, they pay you off.'

'OK, OK,' Kovacs protested. 'Not so loud…'

'Then tell me what exactly you were doing there.'

Kovacs grimaced, looking around the corridor, then pulled

Garcia inside and closed the door. 'I was just fulfilling a little deal with the local hoteliers, that's all.'

'Deal?'

Kovacs sighed. 'Look, you know what the catering service is like, don't you? For a company of two hundred men, they bring in enough food for two hundred and fifty. Then, when you count guys who get killed or wounded and shipped back behind the lines, there's maybe only a hundred and fifty to feed at any one time. And what do they do with the extra?'

Kovacs watched the man think it over. Garcia was probably about to say that the extra food would be redistributed among the troops or held over for later use.

'I'll tell you what they do with it,' Kovacs said. 'They throw it in the trash. The whole lot – a hundred extra meals a day, at least.'

Garcia looked horrified. 'But... But that food could be... It shouldn't be wasted!'

Kovacs smiled. 'Exactly, sir. That's what I been doing, see. I sell the extra to the local hotels and cafés just behind the lines. In return I get free booze, free nights in the local whorehouse – no waiting in line, either – and a little retirement fund. I'm telling you – sir – it's wide open. Now, I know this ain't exactly legit, but at least this way it's helping out some of the civilians the Krauts have starved, instead of just going in the trash to feed the rats.'

Garcia was glaring at him. 'And I'm supposed to agree with that?'

Kovacs sized the man up. 'You'd be letting a lot of people starve if you don't. Hey, let me sweeten the pill a little. You're a hard-working man, a good man, I know you. You help me out, I can help make things a little more... comfortable for you. I can cut you in for a piece. You can take it in cash if you want, but something else can always be arranged. A case of Scotch a week... free time with a couple of hookers, whatever you want. Your call.'

Garcia looked down at his shoes, and Kovacs tried not to smile. Garcia was biting, he knew it. 'You know I should turn you in,' Garcia said quietly.

Kovacs shrugged. 'Sure. And if you do, then I go to the stockade, which won't exactly break my heart, seeing as I'll be out of the line that way. And like I say, the extra rations will go back to being dumped in the trash, where they ain't no good to anybody.'

'All right,' Garcia said. 'I'll turn a blind eye to this... for now, anyway. But I'll want something in return.'

'Just name it, partner.' Kovacs smiled, relishing Garcia's discomfort and waiting expectantly to hear the price.

Garcia turned and walked away. 'I don't know yet. But when I do I know where to find you.'

The Doctor held a bandage he'd just removed from a wounded man for changing. Death. It was so random, yet so inevitable. This was bound to happen sooner or later, he told himself. How lightly he took death in the run of things. He'd seen so much, and never so much as blinked. And now Sam...

He threw the bandage aside. 'Time to go and find them myself.'

Garcia was coming into reception as the Doctor passed through, but the Time Lord took no notice. Instead, he made his way through the kitchen to a small courtyard outside. Perhaps he could make contact with the TARDIS's telepathic circuits out here.

'Lost friends and lost souls,' he murmured to himself.

'Evergreen Man,' a voice said. There was a hint of music, not just in the voice, but accompanying it, at the very edge of hearing. The Doctor turned, looking to see who had spoken.

91

There was no one else in the little courtyard. Something was changing, however. The sky was strangely unfocused, and the shadows that crossed the buildings bore no relationship to the light around them.

'Do you have only human eyes? Can you not see me?'

He turned again, realising that the voice was coming from under the tree in the corner. There was a slight shadow there – not deep enough or dark enough to hide a person, but that was definitely where it came from. As the Doctor watched, a small and feminine figure stepped out from behind the tree that could never have concealed her.

She had a slender waist, but wide hips. Her cheeks were also wide, and her chin narrowed to a point. The rest of her unearthly features shifted and changed constantly, and the Doctor found her quite beautiful. Her shining hair, parted in the middle and curling inward over her shoulders, was red yet pale, the whitest of gold.

She was wearing the greenest green, like the grass on the other side of the fence, and sheer enough to display every muscle under the skin. Bells sewn into the material tinkled softly, though the sound didn't seem to travel very far at all. It certainly didn't attract anyone's attention from within the building.

'Hello,' the Doctor said politely. 'I'm the Doctor, and to be honest I'm feeling more blue than green right now. How can I help you?'

'I came to ask the same question of you. You spoke of lost friends a moment ago. Perhaps I can find them for you.'

The Doctor glanced sadly at the ground. 'Sometimes that's not possible.'

'Everything's possible, to the imaginative.' She approached, silent and barefoot, heedless of the cold. 'Friends are important.'

'Who are you?' he asked.

She smiled, stroking his hair. 'An old friend, who would not see you suffer in silence.' She cocked her head, and slid an arm around his waist.

'I'm sure I would have remembered you...'

'Are you? It appears otherwise.' Suddenly her lips were on his, her tongue gently courting his.

He stepped back hurriedly, looking somewhat puzzled. 'That's not right, is it?' he murmured to himself. 'And yet it doesn't seem terribly wrong...' He turned, taking quick, nervous paces back towards the gate. She was in front of him when he got there.

'Come along, and perhaps we'll find your other friends.'

She stepped forward and vanished. The Doctor could still hear the faint musical tinkling of bells in the air. She left it behind like human women might leave a waft of perfume.

In spite of himself, the Doctor found himself following her. Hope, he realised, that she might be able to help him. As it did so often, hope was moving him automatically.

But, instead of the Bastogne side street, he found a quite different landscape outside the gate.

He was in a wooded glade, filled with vibrantly coloured leaves in spite of the season. Through the trees, he could glimpse white walls and golden domes. A city of some kind, woven throughout the forest. Dark patches on the walls slunk away from the eye, and the Doctor had an uncomfortable feeling of recognition, though he couldn't say why.

She was waiting for him there, and this time her dress seemed appropriate for the surroundings. 'I almost feared you would not come.'

'Who are you?' he asked again.

'A traveller, like yourself. A seeker of knowledge.' She touched his cheek with one finger, and he was unaccountably speechless. 'A philosopher, if you like.'

'And an old friend?'

'Better than that.' She stepped out of her dress.

The Doctor focused on her eyes, which didn't shift or change. 'My friends –'

'Will still be there.' She fell into his arms, and he found himself holding her to stop her from falling. She insinuated herself into his embrace, pressing herself against him. 'Later.'

Chapter Five
The Undiscovered Country

Garcia had followed the Doctor through to the kitchen, and was standing in the doorway. 'Doctor!' he bellowed. If the man was *anywhere* in the city, he had to have heard that. Garcia was rewarded with the sound of a thud to his left. He hurried out into the little courtyard, and saw the Doctor leaning against the little tree there, looking dazed.

'Are you all right?'

The Doctor dusted himself off and nodded. 'I think so… How long was I gone?'

'Gone? Gone where? I followed you out just a moment ago.'

The Doctor frowned, then took a hold of Garcia's arm to look at his wristwatch. 'No elapsed objective time at all…' He knelt by the foot of the tree, running his fingertips over the footprints there. As far as Garcia could tell, there were only the Doctor's own prints. 'No sign of anyone else being here, either.'

'Was someone here?'

'Maybe. Or maybe not. I think it was probably wholly subjective, but I can't see it being imaginary.'

Garcia didn't like the way this conversation was going. 'You sound like you're trying to say you had a vision.'

'You could call her that.'

Garcia smiled indulgently. At least that was better than talk about spook lights and mist. 'You've been in the field too long, like the rest of us.'

The Doctor grabbed Garcia's arms. 'No. Don't you see? It was definitely a related phenomenon to what Wiesniewski and the others in there saw. It can't have been a coincidence.'

'And I thought you were a man of knowledge,' Garcia said, not unkindly.

'The world asks a high price for knowledge, Captain. When you live long enough to start learning how it works, it takes away those things you hold dearest, as payment. In the end, when you've lost enough, then you lose the ability to even feel loss. And that's the biggest loss of all.'

Garcia shivered. The Doctor didn't sound like he was quoting something he'd heard second-hand. 'And what can you do about it?'

The Doctor squinted into the distance, as if trying to read words written in the chilly air. 'Try to keep ahead of the world, by holding on to what you hold dear, and finding new things to care about when you can't.'

Wiesniewski was passing Lewis's office on his way to the water cooler beyond. He hated being down here in the cell area. He imagined someone locking the door, trapping him here, denying him the chance to ever see his baby daughter. He wondered whether she had inherited his eyes or her mother's.

Lewis seemed to be in a good mood, whoever he was talking to. The acoustics down here were annoying, Wiesniewski had quickly discovered. You could always tell when someone was talking, but could never make out what was being said. Instead it just grated on the nerves and interfered with concentration.

He let his eyes wander sideways as he passed, vaguely curious to see who was visiting. But there was no one else in the room. Wiesniewski paused in midstep at that realisation.

Lewis was leaning back, his long legs up on the table, his tanned face in repose as he enjoyed a cigar. His eyes were closed, even though he was still talking. 'I still need map co-ordinates. It's the way things are done here.'

Wiesniewski didn't hear a reply, but Lewis evidently did, as he sighed heavily. 'It doesn't work that way. We learned that last October, back in Philadelphia. Precision is what we need.'

Wiesniewski shivered. And this was the man asking him to keep disturbing thoughts to himself.

'Neither of us care about what Leitz has done,' Lewis said, agreeing with some unheard speech. 'So why bring it up? They're still playing catch-up, and you know it.'

Wiesniewski couldn't say why, but he got the distinct impression that it wasn't just Lewis losing it – there really was someone or something with him. It just wasn't anything he could see or hear.

He knew how dumb the idea was. In fact it was downright crazy. But, call him paranoid, he was sure of it all the same: Lewis really was talking to someone who wasn't there. Suddenly, Wiesniewski wasn't so keen on fetching some water, even though his mouth was drier than ever. Instead he stepped carefully back the way he had come. He may not have been able to see Lewis's silent partner, but he didn't want to take a chance on whether or not the reverse was also true.

Bearclaw had been issued with some clean fatigues and was about ready to see if he could find some officer from his own battalion to report to. He wanted to get back out in the field, even though the field was closing around Bastogne. If he waited much longer, there wouldn't be an outside to get to.

He left his room, feeling weakened, but generally healthy. Once he got some good food – some hope round here, but he could dream, wouldn't he? – into his stomach, he'd be fighting fit.

He paused at the top of the stairs, as three figures passed across his peripheral vision. He turned to look at them, wondering how they could have got past him without his hearing them.

They seemed to be surgeons, or at least they wore what looked like surgical gowns. Bearclaw's vision was out of focus all of a sudden, so he couldn't swear to that. He was still surprised that they were so quiet. His eyes flicked over to a clock on the landing. It was silent, too, and the pendulum was hovering to one side, apparently in defiance of gravity.

Confused, and a little dazed by his inconsistent vision, he turned back to the surgeons. The hems of their gowns wafted silently over the floor, but Bearclaw couldn't make out any boots or shoes under the gap. They seemed to have no feet at all.

One of the figures started to turn, and Bearclaw ducked back round the corner, instinctively knowing that if he caught their eyes he would be lost. There was no further sound, other than the drawn-out beat of his own heart, urging him to risk taking another look.

Like in a dream, like when you were a kid and you did something you shouldn't just 'cause you were told not to, he eventually found himself looking round the corner.

There was no one there.

Seizing his chance, Bearclaw darted over to the stairs, and went to look for the Doctor. Another word flashed through his head with that thought – Nayenezgani. He shook his head to clear it.

Leitz and Farber were out for a constitutional stroll, looking infuriatingly well rested to Fitz. His body was a mass of cricks and stitches from trying to sleep lying against an armoured car's wheel after his shift was over.

More than anything else, the uncomfortable night had convinced Fitz that he had learned enough to pass on to the Doctor. He wanted to be back in a real bed, somewhere utterly unreal. He thought back wistfully to some of the far-flung places he'd visited with Sam and the Doctor, before the TARDIS had got so hooked on dropping them all in it in a variety of crap Earth locations.

First chance he got, he decided, he would have a go at

helping the prisoner. Quite frankly, it would serve Leitz right for putting Fitz to such trouble. He grinned at the thought. Putting one over on the smarmy bastard would be worth the effort.

And after that, he would leg it as fast as he could.

Fitz went into the café to scrounge some food and drink before his great escape, completely oblivious of the thin tendrils of mist that were creeping around the corner at the end of the street.

Unlike a normal fog, this mist stayed low to the ground, wispy fingers wrapping themselves around stone and wood as if to pull its main body along.

Instead of rising invisibly from the ground, it was approaching with stealth.

'Doctor,' Bearclaw called.

'Yes?' Garcia and the Doctor answered together. 'Sorry,' the Doctor said.

'What is it, Bearclaw?' Garcia asked.

'There's something both of you should see upstairs.' Garcia and the Doctor exchanged glances, then followed Bearclaw up to the corridor that linked all the tiny wards. 'The clock's started again,' he noted.

'Had it stopped?' the Doctor asked urgently.

'Yeah, but the weird thing is the pendulum was up at one side.'

'Excellent!' the Doctor enthused. 'I was rather expecting something like this.'

So much for being all cut up about the blonde, Bearclaw thought. Still, how many friends had *he* lost? War did that to you.

Garcia kept pace with the Doctor as Bearclaw led them along to a room at one end. 'There were three men... Well, they looked kind of like three men, anyway. They came in here. There was something weird about them. It was like there was nothing under their gowns.'

'You mean they were naked?' Garcia asked, raising an eyebrow.

'No, I mean there was nothing in the gap between the hems of their gowns and the floor. No feet, no legs, nothing.'

'Ghosts?' Garcia scoffed.

'Not ghosts,' the Doctor whispered. He had opened the door a crack, and was peeping through the gap. 'Look at this.'

Garcia joined him, but Bearclaw hung back. 'I'd rather not. Not again.'

Garcia saw four occupied beds crammed into the tiny room. Three figures in green robes were clustered round the bed occupied by, if Garcia recalled correctly, a man who had a fractured skull. They looked pretty much like surgical nurses to him, though he didn't recall any being slated for duty in here today.

Garcia was about to go in and ask the three nurses whether they needed his help, but the Doctor stayed him with an arm across his chest. 'Shh. Watch.'

'What do you mean "watch"? They might need some –' Garcia's voice faded, as he realised there was something odd about the trio. They were all a little on the short side, for one thing. Their postures were odd, too: poised like ballet dancers, but effortlessly so.

Abruptly, their bodies suddenly stretched and narrowed into flickers of light, which danced around each other for a moment before vanishing. Then they were gone, and so was the wounded man who had been in the bed.

Garcia rushed over, prodding the still-warm bedclothes. 'What the hell!' He looked at the Doctor. 'We'd better raise the alarm –'

'About what?'

The Doctor was shaking his head. 'Were those Germans?'

'Hell no… I dunno. What was that thing with the lights, and…?'

The Doctor drew him aside with a hand on his shoulder. Evidently he didn't want to disturb any of the other patients. 'I'm not sure. It could've been a transmat energy discharge, I suppose, but –'

'A what? What are you talking about?'

'A means to travel long distances instantaneously. But it just didn't seem right… I wonder whose side they're on.'

Garcia grabbed the Doctor's arm; he was determined not to let go until he got a straight answer. 'A few minutes ago you said you were expecting something like this. You know more than you're telling.'

The Doctor looked suddenly shifty. 'Everybody knows more than they tell. You know what you had for breakfast yesterday, or your mother's favourite food, or what books you read in school. Why would you mention any of them unless you felt them worth telling?'

Bearclaw nodded. 'Come on, Doctor. I wanna hear who those people were.'

The Doctor thrust his hands in his pockets. 'I'm not sure. There is a possibility, but that can't be right… Surely they must be extinct by now…'

She felt as if she had been falling for hours, yet couldn't really say in which direction she was travelling. It was actually quite relaxing to float along through the shadows as the tunnel swished by. She thought it was a shaft or tunnel, anyway. She couldn't actually see the walls, but it somehow gave the impression of being a circular tunnel.

She thought it was odd that she didn't feel afraid, and wondered why not. She knew that ordinarily she should be terrified by something like this. But no matter how much she tried to feel fear – or any other emotion – she couldn't.

Ahead, there was an orange speck, like a sun setting far off in the distance. She wondered if that was why she felt so calm – maybe she wasn't really moving and this was just some sort of tunnel vision. Concussion or something. It was growing larger, though; one of them was approaching the other, though she couldn't tell which.

It wasn't just a sunset… There was a golden light within the orange, and silver within that… Before she had a chance to think about it, or perhaps as a result of thinking about it, it had grown larger, surrounded her and swallowed her up.

The lighting was so bright that she couldn't even tell whether she was indoors or outside. But the brightness didn't hurt her eyes. Whoever had set this up knew their stuff. It was clean, clinical. Some kind of hospital, maybe… I've been abducted. Aliens. 'No weird stuff.'

'The only thing weird around here, young lady, is you.'

She took a sharp breath, bracing herself for the pain she expected to come. It never did, and she relaxed. Perhaps her nervous system had just packed in… She was *sure* there ought to be pain: getting shot at point-blank range and lying in a snowy field had to hurt, didn't it?

Apparently not, as far as her body was concerned.

Anyway, she didn't think she was lying down, now, though she didn't seem to be standing either. It was more like being suspended in the air, without being able to feel whatever was holding her up. She didn't feel anything under her feet, but she sensed movement of some kind when she made a walking motion with them.

In front of her, silvery images danced in a strange nonlight. There was a baby among them, and little girl, and other figures more familiar. They were her. Somehow they were all her, and somehow she was seeing them both one at a time and all at once. It made her head spin, seeing all these figures of herself without even knowing who she was.

Maybe that was the point, she thought, as memory hit her like a punch. Now she remembered. Terrific.

Her name was Samantha Angeline Jones, and she was dead.

Leitz was busy transcribing all the data he had gathered from observations of his prisoner, ready for transmission to his superiors at Wewelsburg. Some judicious editing was necessary, of course: he wanted to make sure he held something back for later, just in case.

He was sure the Inner Circle who met there would much rather be conducting this research in the castle itself, but there seemed to be some geographical limitations at work. This was the only place where good specimens were currently to be found.

So much the better for him.

Leitz had started the war as a fervent Nazi. He was well educated, and knew that joining the SS was a political expediency to work his way up faster than his peers. Now he had almost *carte blanche* to research exactly as he pleased.

Even the prospect of execution for failure didn't bother him now. He had held back enough material as insurance to be certain that he could simply lie and get away with it. If all else failed, he was sure some other nation would consider his researches worth keeping him alive for.

There was a sudden crash of firing outside. Leitz leapt to his feet as gunfire erupted in the fields. Surely the Americans hadn't gathered forces for a counterattack so quickly? Or could it be...?

He snatched up a Schmeisser and dashed out of his command truck into what the British called a 'peasouper' of a fog. He was sure there had been no hint of it earlier.

There were screams and shots from the streets all around. Something black and indistinct flashed past and Leitz fired instinctively, but it was gone immediately, with no sign of whether he had hit it.

Concerned, he headed towards the source of most of the noise.

It wasn't so much like experiencing memories as watching them from afar. Or watching a movie of them. It was a lot more creepy than that, though, as each image sparked a memory of a physical sensation, or an emotion.

She tried to turn away, but, no matter which way she faced, the visions were still in front of her.

Although she recognised herself, and recognised many of the images that flashed past her, there were others that were simply… wrong. Like someone had borrowed her body and told her about it after putting it to their own use. This had to be a trick. Yes, that was it. This was some kind of trick.

Or a nightmare, she supposed. Did people dream when they were unconscious – or when they were dead – like they did when they were asleep?

With that thought, light flared around her.

Sam shifted slightly, and the side of her face came out of the light. She blinked, feeling a smooth hard surface under her back. The light above seemed to be some kind of beam, shining down on her from the ceiling. A lamp? Like in an operating theatre? Then she'd been right, hadn't she. What had they…?

She moved aside, to see out of the light. The ceiling around the light source was smooth and earthy, perhaps of stone. It was puzzling, but at least it was definitely a physical place. Maybe she wasn't dead. Maybe.

She seemed to be lying on some kind of stone altar or sarcophagus. Gingerly, in case the movement would make her giddy, she swung herself into a sitting position.

She felt no ill effects, and stood, the stone floor smooth

against her feet. Sam looked down at herself. Something was very odd. She'd expected to find herself undressed, somehow, but there was an irregular area of pure white skin between her breasts, and another on her hip and on her thigh. She touched the white area of her chest. The feeling from that area of skin was perfectly normal, but her fingertips sent a different report. It just wasn't quite right. This skin was much finer and smoother than any human skin had a right to be, she thought, different even from the perfection she'd been given by the Nanites back on Bel. That was as close as she could come to rationalising the difference.

The white patches precisely marked the wounds she had sustained, and she shivered at the memory. She thought a bit more: surely that couldn't be right? It certainly wasn't scar tissue, which you might expect to form over such wounds… No entry or exit holes, no bleeding…

But then you'd also expect to be dead after being shot in the heart at point-blank range and left in a field for the snow to bury you.

Wouldn't you?

Fitz had stumbled over a corpse as soon as he emerged from the Café Scholzen. In spite of the sounds of gunfire, this body hadn't been shot: it was an SS trooper with scratches on his face, and eyes bulging with terror.

Whatever had attacked the man hadn't been deterred by his gun, and if his expression was anything to go by Fitz wasn't in a hurry to meet it. It somehow seemed natural to automatically think of the thing as an 'it' rather than a person. A person couldn't have done this.

A shot boomed, and Fitz heard the most bizarre and unnatural howl of his life in return. Something flashed past him on its way to the soldier who had fired; all he got was a jumbled impression of unpleasant chitin and legs that were too angular and spindly for comfort. Then it and the man were gone, leaving only an insane gurgling scream and the smell of blood hanging in the damp air.

Sod this for a game of soldiers, Fitz thought. Time for his hastily planned, and barely thought-out, great escape.

Sam had found some clothes hanging on the wall. They were light unisex trousers and shirt, but – surely not a coincidence – in exactly her size. Despite not trusting anything here, she put them on. She couldn't remember feeling more utterly vulnerable.

As she explored the room, she began to wonder if she was inside a pyramid or something. The place had that sort of look about it. There was a dark doorway on one wall, and Sam had no choice but to go through it. It was the only visible exit.

The tunnel led down and along, finally emerging on to a causeway of dressed stone. Now Sam got the first real chance to see that, to put it mildly, she wasn't in Kansas any more.

The rock that it was carved from was smooth and cool to the touch. In fact it was quite pleasant and comfortable. Eventually the causeway moved out of the rock into clear sunlight, and Sam turned to look back.

The tunnel had been cut into a large mesa, set in a huge circular lake, the waters far more blue than she'd ever seen in nature, at least on Earth. There were buildings on top; she had a vague impression of pillars and golden domes, too, though she couldn't make them out really clearly.

The causeway descended across the lake to a wide expanse of rolling green hills. Even from here, she could make out flower meadows, and forests straight out of a Disney cartoon.

At the very edge of the horizon were jagged mountain peaks, almost lost in a fine haze. She squinted, wishing she had a pair of binoculars or something. The haze was odd, like rainbows merging together – or some kind of energy field set up around an artificial environment.

Resisting the obvious conclusion (though she could see the *Sunday Sport* headline now – ALIEN AFTERLIFE STOLE MY SOUL!) and with nowhere else to go, she continued down to the lake shore. Sam froze, as a creature loped into view and crouched almost within touching distance. Whatever it was, it didn't look like anything she would expect to find in any artist's impression of heaven.

The face had a sharpness to it, from forehead to chin. The jaw swept back from the chin in a very triangular shape, and the crown of the white-haired head was strangely flattened. It looked to Sam not unlike the effect you might get by shaving the face of a cat. Jewel-like eyes looked into hers. And, like a cat, she could imagine this creature capable of cruelty both playful and innate. The rest of it seemed humanoid enough, though it may have had a more alien muscle structure under its velvet and leather clothes.

It straightened, and she realised the crouch wasn't a sign of hostile intent, but just its legs absorbing the impact of dropping from above. 'Forgive me,' it said. 'I did not mean to alarm you.' Its mouth was moving as if singing, and strange lights seemed to be flicking just beyond her vision, but at least she heard its voice in English.

'Welcome,' it said.

Fitz ducked into the tent – and quickly reversed course. The guard was staying on duty, despite the fuss outside. Fitz hurried over to a small workbench where equipment for maintaining the tent and generators was kept. Unnoticed, he selected a large spanner from a toolbox there, then returned to the tent, this time more openly. The guard turned, raising his gun, anxiously, but then relaxed. 'What's going on?' he asked.

'I'm here to relieve you,' Fitz said, ignoring the guard's concern. 'There's some hot food waiting back in the café.'

The guard looked relieved at the thought that all the commotion wouldn't cheat him of his dinner, but he didn't move. 'Thanks, but Leitz is a stickler for details. You're new, but you'll learn.' He turned away, as if about to speak to the prisoner, and Fitz lunged forward.

Fitz hit him in the back of the neck with the spanner, and the guard dropped. 'There's a lesson for you,' he muttered.

He hopped over the unconscious body, and switched off both the generators, afraid that the bars were probably electrified or something. Next he opened the cage. Sam would be proud of me, he thought. Go free, strange thing. The prisoner didn't move. Fitz stood in the doorway, wondering if he was too late and it was dead.

It must have realised it was being watched, because it suddenly moved, two slitted eyes looking right into Fitz. Before Fitz even realised it was about to move, the prisoner had uncoiled and was almost nose to nose with him.

Fitz bit off a yell and tried to pull himself together, reminding himself that it was the people *outside* the cage he ought to be frightened of.

Now that the prisoner was so close, Fitz found he could see clearly again. It was a man, lean and stringy, with piercing green eyes and flowing red hair. 'Help me,' he asked softly. 'Free me.'

Fitz stepped back, but had recovered enough to stay facing the prisoner. 'That was the general idea. But Jeez, did you scare me!' Fitz put out a hand to help the red-haired man up. From the way he was acting, Fitz was prepared to have to put a lot of physical effort into moving him, and as a result almost overbalanced; the man couldn't weigh more than a couple of stone, despite seeming perfectly healthy.

Fitz helped the man out of the tent. The noise of battle was getting closer, and men were running around with weapons, trying to find a target. Hopefully, wearing the same uniform as them should disqualify him from being it, Fitz thought.

He really needed to find a vehicle of some sort, but there didn't seem to be any handy. Even the armoured cars had rumbled off somewhere. Luckily none of the men milling around seemed interested in bothering Fitz or his new charge. He couldn't blame them – he'd be a bit single minded if someone was shooting at him too.

There were a couple of motorcycles leaning against the side of a house further down, but those were no good. His new friend was hardly in a state to ride pillion.

Several men grouped together and ran off to the east of town, armed and ready. That was enough reason for Fitz to head west. Walking as fast as possible, they dodged running men, and occasional Kubelwagens, but Fitz knew that sooner or later someone would stop and ask why they were going the wrong way.

That guard would probably wake up soon, too. Or not at all; Fitz was no expert at judging how to precisely render people unconscious for limited times.

Ahead a motorcycle and sidecar was bumping towards them. Fitz saw that his luck must be on the up; the bike had a rider, but no one in the sidecar. Fitz thought about waving the rider to halt, but that would mean awkward questions, and in any case the guy didn't look like he was in the mood to stop. So, instead, Fitz stepped up to the side of the road, removed his helmet, and hit the rider in the face with it as he went past.

The rider was catapulted back out of the saddle, and the bike spun off to the side, grinding to a halt. Fitz considered himself bloody lucky that it hadn't just swung around and run into him. Fitz neither knew nor cared whether there was any ammunition for the machine gun that was mounted on the sidecar. So long as the engine worked, he'd be happy.

The red-haired man groaned loudly as Fitz helped him into the sidecar. Fitz winced, expecting an immediate reply by way of klaxons and gunfire. He wasn't disappointed.

As if a spell had been broken, the other troops nearby noticed what he was up to, and seemed to think it wasn't the right behaviour. That was the impression Fitz got from their shouts, and the shots that escorted him and his newfound friend out of town.

Leitz had found the source of the noise, and immediately wished he hadn't. Men were shooting at shadows all right, but these shadows turned out to be alive. They were indistinct, and every one seemed to have different limbs or different claws and fangs, but they were all hostile, as well as being apparently indestructible.

It was as if the bullets went harmlessly through without damaging their flesh. If they had any flesh.

Even face-on, a whole magazine from Leitz's Schmeisser didn't stop the quadrupedal nightmare that had loomed out of the fog at him. He couldn't describe it all, as his brain seemed to refuse to accept parts of it, but it was fast, chitinous and razor-sharp. It was a combination of every phobia rolled into one furious beast.

Leitz screamed, a noise that split the mist, before he suddenly realised that he was alone again. The creature was gone.

He wished it was so easy to make its breath vanish from his nostrils, or to drive it from his vision when he closed his eyes. But outside of his head, in the real world, it had gone.

Leitz fell painfully into a sitting position, his legs just too shaky to support him any more. He still wanted to scream. He wanted to scream until he passed out, then wake up safe in the knowledge that it had all been a terrible nightmare.

Instead, he drew his knees up to his chest and hugged them,

hyperventilating. After this, he thought, nothing the Circle at Wewelsburg said or threatened would ever frighten him again. He laughed, nervously, and the sound seemed ludicrously out of place.

Leitz wondered for a moment if he'd gone mad. The creatures had been awful, terrible… He wished he *could* have dismissed them as fancy, but, no, the deaths of his men were real enough. So why hadn't they finished the job? Of course – a stickler for efficiency himself, he should've realised – that depended on what their job was.

They weren't there to kill him, or even to slaughter randomly. They had been moving in a distinct pattern, and killing only those who got in their way. A search pattern? Yes, of course, that was it. They were searching for something or someone as alien and unnatural as themselves. He stood, unsteadily. His prisoner. They must be a related species.

That still begged the question of why they had stopped, instead of going straight through him as they had gone through the other men. Logically, the circumstances must have changed. The prisoner had been set free.

Again he laughed. The creature may as well have killed him, after all.

Farber found him a moment later. 'Are you all right, sir?'

'Yes,' replied Leitz, flatly.

'There's been some trouble at the camp –'

'Don't bother,' Leitz snapped. 'The prisoner has gone?'

Farber nodded, surprised. 'A few minutes ago. How did –'

'A logical conclusion. What happened?'

'It was that corporal, Kreiner. He knocked out the guard and stole a motorcycle and sidecar. They could be halfway to Brussels by now.'

Leitz rose stiffly to his feet and nodded, grimly. 'Of course. Kreiner.'

* * *

Sam let the being walk her around the edge of the lake. She was both surprised and relieved to see that they were not alone.

From all around, men were appearing. Not alien and uncomfortable like the being who accompanied her, but as human as she was. They were in different uniforms, both German and American, and maybe others, too, by the look of them. A couple of faces she recognised from the massacre that had done for her. They had been shot too.

An army of the dead, she thought with a shiver. 'So this is Mictlan, is it?'

'Mictlan?'

'You can't fool me. The Doctor warned me about how the Celestis take those on the brink of death to Mictlan to persuade them to enter their service. Well, forget it. No way.'

The being tinkled with laughter. 'This is not Mictlan. Mictlan is but a shadow of this realm. Oh, it's true that there are celestial beings who act as you describe. It's also true that, given your relationship with the Evergreen Man, they were probably looking for you. But we found you first, and saved you.'

'Found me?'

'You were on the path,' the being told her. 'What humans call dead, yes.'

Sam felt herself shiver at its words. 'My heart had stopped?'

'Your heart was destroyed. Reduced to cold meat. But not irreparable, Samanthajones.'

'You seem to have the advantage of me. Who are you, anyway?'

'I am –' it sang, not in discernible words, but a clear and brief harmony, even though it was from the throat of a single being. At the same time, there was a strange ripple, as if Sam's eyes were momentarily blurred, and she felt a hint of an emotion she couldn't recognise. She realised that all those things were part of its – his – name. They must have pretty impressive-looking birth certificates round here.

'I don't think I can quite manage that,' Sam admitted. 'Though a bit of it sounded like…' She paused, feeling a little ridiculous. 'Galastel?'

The being blinked, one ear twitching slightly. 'It does not matter. I have had many names. You may call me that if it makes you feel more comfortable.'

Fitz kept looking over his shoulder as he drove along, desperate to put as much distance as possible between himself and Leitz, preferably in a vaguely western direction.

'Stop, please,' the man he had rescued begged. He sounded hurt, and Fitz wondered what he was supposed to do about it. He could talk like Dr Kildare to please the ladies, but he certainly couldn't treat an injury.

'If you're hurt, we have to get you medical help.'

'No. It burns.'

'What does?'

'This carriage.'

Fitz pulled the bike into the side of the snowy road. Perhaps some part of the bike was overheating. Or perhaps it was the metal itself. It was a metal cage that kept him in pain, after all…

The red-haired man stumbled out of the sidecar. 'Thank you. I will be fine soon. You should go now.'

Fitz shook his head, enjoying the chance to be a hero now that they were somewhat safer. 'Saving the world's my business, even if it's only one person at a time. Besides, there's not just the Jerries to worry about – there are weird creatures out there, slaughtering people.'

'No longer,' the man said, shaking his head in a funny kind of manner, Fitz noted. 'The Black Dogs will have been recalled now that I am free.'

'Recalled? By who?'

'By the rest of my clan. They will be concerned for me. I command a whole regiment.'

Fitz wondered what he meant by that, but didn't have time to speculate further, as a Kubelwagen suddenly came into sight further up the road, the noise of gunfire carrying with the growl of its engine. Bullets started spanging off the bike.

'We'd better go into the woods,' Fitz said. 'The car can't follow us there.'

He helped the man up, still amazed at his lightness. There was something odd about his ears too: they weren't small and round, like human ears, but carved into flowing points. A bit like Tom's in the *Tom and Jerry* cartoons.

Galastel had led Sam to a large boat, or perhaps a small ship, further round the lake shore. It had a single triangular sail, like an Arab *dhow*. 'We should board. It will be quicker to cross the lake to reach our destination than to go around.'

'Across the Styx?' Sam presumed. She still couldn't believe she wasn't really dead. If she was, then it wasn't bloody fair. And it wasn't fair that she couldn't say goodbye to all the people who mattered. All the people who deserved a goodbye from her: the Doctor, Fitz, her parents, her old friends from home.

She sighed and walked to the edge of the deck, Galastel by her side, as the vessel cast off. She looked down into the waters through which the ship was passing. They were crystal clear, and looked very inviting. It would be so relaxing to go for a swim in there... But where were the fish? Such clear waters surely ought to be full of them.

Something was moving around there, though. It was hard to tell how deep the water was; perhaps it was just something very small moving through the vegetation that grew on the bottom. Even the silt down there was pure white. Sam frowned. The silt was as white as snow. And the vegetation looked a little like…

A feeling of unreality washed over her and she swayed, kept upright only by her grip on the wooden rail. The movement down there was… men. Tiny men and tiny tanks, moving through tiny snowbound trees at the bottom of a lake.

Fitz and his new-found friend ran through the woods as quietly as they could. Fitz felt a bit cheesed off that he seemed to be feeling the strain a lot more than the other guy. He could have sworn that the man's feet weren't touching the ground most of the time.

The Germans pursuing them were not being so careful, and so a lot more direct. Fitz wished that he had hung on to the gun he'd been issued.

By now, they had reached a small clearing, with a natural rocky mound at its centre. Fitz saw that a startling change had occurred: the red-haired man now seemed more like a golden figure, almost flying around the tree trunks, his eyes blazing. He was shrinking too. 'What the hell?'

'Nothing to do with hell,' the man said, grinning. 'We can make the big small, and the small big, as you see. Now come quickly. I can take you to a safer place than this.

Fitz stared at him, feeling sick. 'What are you saying?'

The figure seemed mildly irritated. 'That my world can harbour you, human.'

'Your world?' Fitz stumbled backward, a dozen folk tales and Tolkienesque visions rushing irrationally through his head. 'Forget it. You're not… I mean, you must be…'

Even as Fitz continued to withdraw, the man dissolved into a vague cluster of lights, then flickered out of existence.

Forgetting caution, his strength renewed by fear, Fitz ran on twice as fast as before.

Chapter Six
Commonwealth Games

Wiesniewski had come to find the Doctor after his shift at Lewis's HQ had finished, and was surprised to discover him now walking through the streets in the direction of the former police station – with a baffled Garcia and Bearclaw exchanging glances as they followed in his wake. 'Leshy and Kachinas, Leshy and Kachinas, Leshy and Kachinas…' he was muttering over and over again.

'Leshy', he thought. There was a word he hadn't heard since he was a child, when his grandmother would tell him stories before bedtime. It was a little unnerving to hear it chanted like a mantra by someone like the Doctor. He had no idea what Kachinas were; perhaps the Doctor was confused. 'Are you feeling OK?' Wiesniewski asked.

'I am, yes, but I'm not so sure if the world is.' Before Garcia could translate his own baffled look into a question, the Doctor continued. 'You heard what he said. What both of them said. Leshy and Kachinas.'

'Well, yeah, but what does that have to –'

'The Leshy are a feature of Polish folklore.' Wiesniewski nodded confirmation as the Doctor continued. 'Woodland elementals. Kachinas belong to Hopi myth. It's an awful coincidence, isn't it, that two people from such different cultural backgrounds would have folklore-related experiences in the same area at similar times?'

'Not really,' countered Garcia. 'They were both under severe stress, acting on instinct. Their upbringing is bound to get involved in colouring their perceptions under those circumstances.'

'Yes!' the Doctor exclaimed. 'That's it exactly.' He was

beaming. Garcia didn't follow at all. The Doctor sighed. 'Both these men saw something that they could relate to only by their folk history. And I'd bet you my shirt that the Germans are having similar experiences.'

'I think so, too,' Wiesniewski agreed. The others looked at him. 'I had a very interesting conversation with Colonel Lewis. He wants to clamp down on people talking about the sort of experiences we're discussing here. He says that, if anyone is really keen to say something, they should make out an official report to him.'

'He wants people to talk nonsense to him, but not to each other?' Bearclaw echoed.

'Very interesting,' the Doctor murmured. 'We were just on our way to see him. I'll give him nonsense...'

'I'd be careful if I was you, Doctor,' Wiesniewski warned. 'This is going to sound crazy... Oh, what the hell! Lewis was talking to someone this morning. Someone who wasn't there.'

'What?' said Garcia.

'You mean he's going nuts?' Bearclaw suggested.

'I dunno... Maybe *I* am. I didn't see or hear anyone else there, but... I could feel something. Like there was someone or something really there.' He shook his head, knowing how unbelievable it sounded, but relieved to have said it out loud. Let other people decide if he was crazy or not, he was sick of worrying about it.

'Did he call his visitor by any name?' the Doctor asked.

Wiesniewski couldn't believe he was being taken seriously. 'Not that I heard.'

'What were they discussing?'

'I don't know. I only heard one side of part of a conversation. He said something about learning something last year in Philly. And something about lights being behind.'

'There was some light left behind when those fake nurses disappeared,' Garcia pointed out. 'And Bearclaw saw lights at the –'

'Yes,' said the Doctor, cutting him off. 'Filly? A horse?'

'Philadelphia,' Wiesniewski supplied.

'Philadelphia…' The Doctor suddenly grabbed Wiesniewski by the shoulders, and for a moment the lieutenant was afraid that the Doctor was going to kiss him. 'You're a genius!' The Doctor beamed, looking as energised as if someone had plugged him into the mains. 'That explains quite a bit.'

Garcia nodded, wearily. 'I don't suppose you'd care to share?'

'I'm not really sure I should,' said the Doctor, indignantly. 'It's all still classified at this time, and I could get in terrible trouble for saying the wrong thing.' He carried straight on, but then Garcia had worked out by now that the Doctor didn't exactly care much for the rules.

'Well, basically, in October last year there was a top-secret experiment that didn't go entirely to plan. Trying to make a ship and its crew invisible within an electromagnetic field, you know the sort of thing. If Lewis was part of that, then it's possible he's trying to start up a variation on that experiment here. And if that's right, it would help explain a lot of the phenomena here.'

'You mean he's causing it?' asked Wiesniewski.

'No, not exactly. It would take tremendous power to do it with the crude methods available to Lewis, and he couldn't keep that a secret. But it does mean that he had the same help then as now; and it means I know how that help is getting around without being noticed by all and sundry. Phasing technology, and almost certainly electrical in nature.'

'I have no idea what that means,' said Garcia, sighing.

'Good! No one in this decade should know what that means.' He stopped in the middle of the street, as air-raid sirens began to sound. 'Ah. I wondered how long before we had one of those…' He spun on his heel. 'Come on! Back to the hospital; the patients are going to need care when they're moved to the shelters.'

* * *

Leitz saluted the handful of fighter-bombers that flew over Lanzerath on their way to put Bastogne under siege. Right now, he wished he could be up there with them, soaring above the land, looking down at this mess from on high…

As a boy, he had dreamed of being a pilot. Still, pity the man, someone had once told him, who fulfils all his dreams. Then, like Alexander, he would have no more worlds to conquer, and no more reason to live.

Or to die, he reminded himself.

Leitz lowered his eyes to look straight ahead as he entered the Café Scholzen. Everyone was rather nervously avoiding his gaze, and he knew immediately that there had been some communication from Wewelsburg.

'Well?' he asked Farber. 'What do they have to say?'

'They want the prisoner taken back to Wewelsburg for study.'

Leitz could feel things slipping away from him, as the droning of the aircraft faded into the distance. He swallowed hard. 'To the castle itself?'

Farber nodded, not looking any more pleased than Leitz felt. 'They've had new generators installed to keep it secure, and forged special barriers.' He handed over the communiqué, which Leitz saw was personally signed by that charlatan Himmler.

'What do we do?' Farber asked, his voice quiet.

Leitz said nothing.

As Leitz and Farber stood there, a trio of indistinct figures smoothly descended through the ceiling behind them, silent and unnoticed.

They separated and moved into different areas of the café.

Leitz paid no heed to the colours of SS camouflage smocks which passed him by. Ordinary infantry soldiers under other men were facelessly uninteresting to him. He wondered absently which of them had left the front door open so that a draught could chill his back.

'If we return to Wewelsburg now, we'll never survive the debriefing,' Leitz said at length. 'Prepare the 232s. We'll simply have to go and find a new subject.'

'That could take some time,' Farber warned. 'And what if…' He looked noticeably paler. 'What if those things come back?'

Leitz considered the whole situation. If they failed to find another subject, well, he would still have three armoured cars and a clear route to neutral Switzerland. At least you could run from execution – in many ways he'd sooner face that than those… things in the fog again.

But it was his scientific curiosity that held him, that left him so frustrated that the subject was gone. He needed to understand it. If the creatures did come after another prisoner, let them attack Wewelsburg, and solve his problems for him.

Himmler could play at black magic at Wewelsburg until the cows came home, but Leitz had more sense. He hadn't spent years at university just to be led by the nose by a bunch of people who thought chanting in robes would help them conquer the world.

One of the three figures that had descended into the café passed two mortals discussing a piece of paper. Their human emotions were crude and loud.

It continued upstairs to where the Scholzen family's apartment had been turned into a little field medical station. There, it ignored the wounded men sitting around the living room, just as they ignored it.

It passed silently through the door to the bedroom. The dying were there, and the dying were the ones it had come to visit.

* * *

The ship had carried Sam and Galastel to a city set amid a verdant forest. It was an odd-looking structure – completely alien, and yet redolent of many different human architectural styles. Galastel told her it belonged to his own people, the Sidhe.

Dark spots caught her eye in the forest: scattered patches of painful decay. At first she thought they were simply some kind of fungus, something living on the trees. These things happened, and Sam wasn't one to query nature – it generally knew what it was doing.

On closer inspection, though, she realised that the decaying areas had radial lines stretching out from the central rotting core and little satellite patches around them… Like debris fields, around the image of an impact crater…

With sudden clarity, Sam realised that that was exactly what this was. These rotting patches were how the shells and bombs from the war affected the Sidhe's plane of residence that she could currently perceive. Presumably they had different effects on all the different levels that the Sidhe themselves could operate on. Perhaps they were patches of blinding light on one level, or bottomless pits on another…

Sam suspected that the list of possible perceptions was longer than the casualty list for the whole war, but she was willing to bet that none of them were good.

Like the forest, the city was suffering. Once-golden domes were now cracked and tarnished, and there was a rank smell in the air, that of poor sanitation and unhealthy people… Worse still, being a place of altered perceptions, it affected the emotions directly; this was a sad and dying place.

Sam couldn't quite catch her breath for a moment, as the woes of the population washed around her, and even the buildings wept.

The attacking aircraft were only Messerschmitt 110s; designed as fighters, they had a very limited load of light bombs. Nevertheless, it was enough to cut people down in the city centre with shrapnel and blast waves.

Some bolder soldiers opened fire at them from rooftops, but without any apparent success. Soldiers and the few remaining local civilians alike dived for shelter as explosions began to shake the buildings.

Bearclaw staggered slightly as the hospital shook, but didn't let go of the one-legged man he was helping down to the cellar. The Doctor was already returning from helping someone else down there. 'Need a hand?' the Doctor asked, taking the wounded man's other arm.

Bearclaw was glad to see him. 'No, but I'm grateful anyway. He's the last one from upstairs.'

They had crossed the lobby and almost reached the cellar door beside the desk, when the doors burst inward with the force of a blast. Plaster and wood swirled around the room and Bearclaw was slammed headlong into the desk, while the Doctor and the one-legged man were pitched across the floor.

The Doctor picked himself up. Bearclaw couldn't hear what he was saying over the noise of the bombs, but he could see the Doctor bending to check the man's pulse. Then he straightened and pulled Bearclaw to the cellar stairs.

Bearclaw tried to resist. 'But what about –'

'He took the brunt of the blast. He's dead. And so will you be if you take another knock like that.' He led Bearclaw down the stairs.

Dead? Bearclaw thought. What a damn stupid way to go. There was no meaning in it. No purpose. Just another one that he had jinxed and couldn't save when promised.

Was that all he was good for? Screwing up and getting unarmed people around him killed. What goddamned use was that? He'd had enough of his own failure. More than enough, in fact.

Audibly snarling, Bearclaw descended to the crowded cellar. It was filled with medics and patients trying to make themselves as comfortable as possible amid the boilers and washing machines and wine racks. He was there just long enough to pick up a Thompson, then turned to go back up. He barely saw the others in the cellar – just the aircraft he wanted to bring down.

He bumped physically into a body on the stairs, and took a moment to realise that it was the Doctor, blocking his way. 'No.' The Doctor's face was calm and mild, but unmoving, as if it was steel painted in flesh tones.

'I'm no good here,' Bearclaw growled. 'I should be out there fighting for this place.' He knew the Doctor was smart enough to understand that.

'Then they win. They weaken your resolve not to be pushed around. They make your choices for you.' He was advancing slowly, and Bearclaw found himself involuntarily stepping backward.

'You're just going to let them get away with killing that man?' Bearclaw demanded, shocked and disappointed at the Doctor's reaction.

'You're just going to desert all the others who need you, just to salve your pride in your ability to fight?' the Doctor countered. 'You're going to risk your life for a futile gesture of defiance that your enemy can't even see, let alone be harmed by, and in turn endanger these others who may depend on you? You're going to let your enemy draw you into betraying and abandoning your principles, your comrades and your friends?'

Bearclaw bumped up against a small table behind him, on which someone had set up a phonograph. He desperately wanted to argue, but he couldn't think of anything to say.

He wanted to punch the Doctor's lights out and go on up anyway.

He slammed the gun down on to the table, then, with a scream of rage, kicked the table over. Phonograph and record smashed on the stone floor, and he kicked the pieces away one by one into the darkness.

Gradually he felt eyes upon him, watching him. Bearclaw's fury subsided, dampened by guilt as he realised the nurses were watching his outburst. Guilt that was backed by shame as he recognised the look of fear on their faces.

'You seem troubled,' the Doctor said, holding out a china cup to Bearclaw with a smile. 'Tea?' he offered.

Bearclaw blinked and took the cup numbly, not asking when or how the Doctor had picked it up. He let the Doctor steer him to a couple of small beer kegs, on which they sat.

'I'm sorry, Doctor,' he said at length. 'I... It's just that sometimes I feel if I don't let it out something will burst in here.' He tapped his head. 'If you know what I mean.'

'Believe me, I do know exactly what you mean. Probably more than you can imagine. Perhaps it comes with age.'

'You don't look any older than me,' Bearclaw argued.

'Well... I'm a little more mature than my appearance suggests.'

'Sure you are,' said Bearclaw, sceptically. 'How old? Forty?' He certainly couldn't be much more than that.

'One thousand and eighteen,' said the Doctor, with a perfectly straight face. 'But they say life begins at fifteen hundred. Or they do now, anyway. Are you quite all right?'

'Fine,' Bearclaw said, choking slightly.

'It's interesting,' the Doctor went on. 'You know, for all humanity's violence, wherever I go, I still meet people who passionately want to hold back death. Who take great responsibility for it. Like Garcia, and you.'

'Me?'

The Doctor nodded. 'That's what's bothering you, isn't it? That you couldn't hold back death from the other men in the field. I think they call it "survivor guilt", don't they?'

Bearclaw shook his head. 'Maybe, I guess. I already lost my crew earlier… God knows that's bad enough. But what really gets me is the civilians, you know? Like your friend Sam.' The Doctor merely regarded him coolly. 'Not just because I survived and she didn't… It's my fault she was there at all… I gave her and a couple of GIs a lift in my jeep. If I hadn't, they might be prisoners somewhere else, but they… They wouldn't have been in that field.'

He could already feel tears forming. 'I said I'd get her home, you know? I said I'd get her home, and I got her killed instead.'

'No no no…' The Doctor shook his head. 'It was my fault for bringing her to this country in the first place. Her own fault for wanting to travel with me. Jochen Peiper's fault for not controlling his own men. The gunman's fault for shooting… Where does the blame end?'

'I don't know,' Bearclaw admitted.

'The best way to fix things,' the Doctor said, 'is to work out what's wrong, and to deal with it as best we can. If you waste time working out who to blame, then everything falls apart before you can fix it. And if we let that happen then Sam died in vain. And…' He hesitated, his voice not quite cracking. 'And I don't think either of us wants that. And neither would she.'

'So what do we do?' Bearclaw said, bitterly. 'Tell people not to shoot each other and hope they listen?'

'Something a little more practical.' The Doctor looked at the ceiling, but Bearclaw got the distinct impression that he was really seeing the stars far above. 'I think someone's goading one or both sides, interfering with the natural conclusion of the war.'

'You mean some other country that isn't involved?'

'No. I mean some other party. One not native to this world in this time.'

'Sure. Kachinas?'

'If you like.'

'I wish I had your calm,' Bearclaw admitted.

The Doctor sighed. 'I wish I wasn't so often right.'

Kovacs gazed at the pink ceiling of his room at the local brothel, wondering whether a bomb would come through it, and if he would sense it coming before it arrived.

He could have run out into the street and taken pot shots at the Luftwaffe, but he was smart enough to know that they were too high to be effectively threatened by small-arms fire. Or he could have run down into the cellar with everybody else, but that would have given the impression that he was scared. Screw that.

Besides, if a bomb did come down, he'd rather go quick and painless than be crushed and suffocated, buried under rubble in a weak cellar. Kovacs had never been afraid of death. Life just went on till it stopped. Death was the off switch. Why waste time wondering when it would be tripped?

He dug out his little black notebook from under the bed, deciding that this would be a good time to work out what he was owed by various customers and suppliers, both in terms of the catering goods he was black-marketeering, and the legitimate supplies his unit would need next time they went out into the field.

New black flaws were spreading across the walls nearby as Sam waited in a vaulted antechamber. Strangely, now that she recognised that this was just a place being hurt by the war, she found it much easier to deal with. There were more than enough examples of this sort of thing in her own time, and it was something she knew how to handle in her mind. It was something she knew how to hate and plead against.

She could hear a feast going on somewhere, too. Cheers and

laughter vied with clashing crockery and cutlery for the attention of her ears.

After a few minutes, Galastel seemed to wake from the fugue state he'd been in, and led Sam to a golden door. 'The Queen will see you now.' Before Sam could compose herself and think about how to behave in front of a Queen, she was through the doors – whether they had opened or not – and into a banqueting hall straight out of the Middle Ages.

No, she corrected herself. A banqueting hall straight out of some Hollywood art-house auteur's impression of the Middle Ages. Everything was clean and gleaming despite the dozens of people crowded around the long feast table.

Fuelless fires burned steadily, and the pots from which punch was being served never seemed to get any emptier. The people around were all like Galastel: quick, agile and somehow catlike in spite of their flowing hair and silk clothes.

At the head of the table, the Queen waited, and Sam noticed she wasn't eating or drinking with the others, though she was in the middle of pouring some drink for someone else. Sam frowned. Her eyes were certainly seeing something she somehow recognised as a queen, but her brain seemed incapable of really registering what it was.

All that she could really take in was that the Queen was beautiful and poised, and there was a melodious shimmer whenever she moved. For all the Queen's indefinite beauty, and for all that Sam was awed and quite flattered to be meeting her, she also made Sam wish she were anywhere but here. She couldn't say why.

'You are welcome, Samanthajones.'

'Pleased to meet you.'

'Perhaps. But I have bread here in my lap, and a flagon of fine wine. And, ere my subject returns you to your friends, you may rest and you may dine.'

Sam flushed, without quite knowing why. 'It rhymes,' she said, trying to find a neutral answer. 'Is it a traditional greeting?'

'Yes, but it also means what it says. This is a feast, so feel free to drink as deeply as you need.'

'Thank you,' said Sam, 'but…'

Galastel smiled. 'Are you thinking of human stories? That mortals who eat or drink in our realm can never leave? Or that a hundred years would pass in your world to a mere hour in ours? Or that we enslave unwary mortals who venture here?'

Sam hadn't been. She'd been more into the *Melody Maker* than the Mabinogion. But now he'd brought the subject up… 'You're going to tell me that those stories are just stories, right?'

'Stories are more than just stories. They're history that didn't quite happen – at least not yet. But the unwary remain only seven years, not one hundred.'

'I don't wish to offend you,' Sam said simply, 'but I suddenly feel a little wary.'

'Why?' the Queen asked. 'You need not fear. You have walked the paths of Time with the Evergreen Man, and are not constrained by them quite as much as other mortals. Besides…' She drew a hand between Sam's breasts and passed it over her hip and thigh – all the areas where Sam had noticed that new and different skin blended with her own. 'You share our blood now. You are our kin. And so you are not…' She visibly searched for the right word. 'You are not troubled by this place, or by anything in it.'

Sam heard Galastel's agreement beside her. 'A mortal human would not speak here, nor be able to eat or drink, but you may do so without fear. You have my word on that.'

'And mine,' the Queen said.

Sam nodded hesitantly. All right. Innocent until proven guilty, she reminded herself. The beings at the feast shifted aside, leaving a space for her.

She sat, and sipped the wine politely. She wasn't much of a drinker, but there didn't seem much choice. Besides, she got the feeling she had pushed her luck as it was.

The Queen watched her sit, only mildly disappointed. The girl wasn't worth any real effort, but there was no harm in making the offer. The Queen phased herself in such a way that Sam couldn't discern what was being said, and communicated with Galastel alone. 'She is adjusting?'

'Quite well, Majesty. She is not of us, but at least the Celestis do not have her.'

'Indeed… She lives, and the cycle continues. I will visit the Evergreen Man again and speak to him.'

'Only speak?' Galastel asked mildly.

'I do not imagine he will be so easily led a second time. Samanthajones must adjust to what has happened to her. Perhaps you should take her on another path, and show her the possibilities she is offered.'

It was a more subtle dismissal than she might have used, but no less a command of finality.

Wiesniewski and Garcia had finally found a moment in which to sit and brew some coffee. The populace of the cellar had settled after the Doctor had led Bearclaw aside, and it sounded like the bombing was dying off above.

'You got a family?' Wiesniewski asked.

Garcia shook his head. 'Just an ex who prefers the sin of divorce to so much as giving me the time of day. Probably just as well.'

'Sounds like you don't miss her.'

'Only 'cause I've learned to hit straight,' he scoffed. 'Bad joke, sorry. Though, God knows, there were times when I…'

Garcia trailed off. 'We were two teenagers who thought marriage would make us adults, and it didn't. I might be real clever, might have a medical degree, but that doesn't mean I can't be dumb half the time.'

Wiesniewski nodded and smiled. 'Being dumb's a basic human right. I always felt they should put it in the constitution that everybody's allowed to make an ass of himself from time to time.'

Garcia couldn't help but chuckle. 'Yeah, guarantee every citizen the right to be a dumb sonofabitch whenever he chooses.'

Galastel was waiting when Sam finished the meal. While she'd passed on the many small roasted animals being carved up and passed around, there had been more than enough vegetables and breads and buckwheat pancakes to fill her.

There was no fruit that she could see. Perhaps the trees were already too rotten.

'Are you well?' Galastel asked.

'Pretty good for a dead girl,' Sam admitted.

'Good. I have something to show you.'

'Yeah? As long as it's not puppies or etchings, I guess that's fine.'

'Come and see.' He stepped forward, and she followed. There was a sudden jarring sense of motion, and she was in a completely different place. She had been through transmats before, but this felt completely different. It was like simply being hurled from one place to another too fast to see anything in between.

She was still in a forest, but it was hard to tell if it was still the same one. There were half-glimpsed things all around that disappeared when she tried to look at them. If she focused too hard on something, she would find herself noticing not just its colour and texture, but tiny pieces of grit, and still tinier swirling particles that were both there and not there. Like molecules, or atoms almost...

Whatever they were, they were weird, and they were distracting. It was like looking at a Mandelbrot, she realised. Everything kept getting smaller and smaller, but their scale and patterns repeated, for layer upon layer until she began to feel dizzy and had to close her eyes.

'Is something wrong?' Galastel asked.

'No…' She grasped her head, in the hope of stopping it from spinning. 'Maybe it comes with the territory. I didn't think being dead would be so much like having stepped off a roller coaster and left my stomach behind.'

'You are not dead.'

'Hang on a minute. You said I was!'

'You were,' Galastel agreed. 'But not any more.'

Sam raised an eyebrow. 'Look… I don't know about you, but I was brought up to believe that death was a fairly permanent arrangement.'

The bombing had stopped, at last. The Doctor had taken gentle charge, making sure that everyone got back out of the cellar safely. Bearclaw had helped him. Solve what problems you can, the Doctor told himself.

He followed the others up to the hotel's ground floor, intending to make that visit to Lewis now – always assuming Lewis was still alive. He was surprised to find the lobby gloomy and empty despite the daylight. The doors that had been blown inward now opened only on to darkness.

It wasn't the darkness of mere night, but a starless velvet, like the inside of a shadow. The street was different too. There was no rubble on the main road – in fact it looked as if it had been swept clean. The alley to his left was jammed almost solid with thorns and briars. 'A bit of a giveaway,' the Doctor muttered.

He turned with a sigh, to find that a side street had opened up. It wound away tightly, making it impossible to see all the way along, and there were huge ferns where once there had been lampposts. The Doctor marched into the side street, until he found the single remaining street light.

It cast a leafy glow of sunlight in a glade, and there was a familiar figure leaning against it. 'I always did admire your sense of humour,' the Doctor told her as he approached. She was wearing the same dress, sprinkled with bells. The Doctor didn't need to count to know that there were fifty-nine of them. 'I was wondering when you'd come back.'

'You were expecting me?' The figure looked amused. 'For the most part, it is I who wait for others.'

'I'm afraid so. You don't catch me so easily this time,' he said apologetically. 'I wasn't expecting you yesterday – you bamboozled me. The same trick won't work twice.'

She gave him a radiant smile. Literally. 'I meant you no harm, Evergreen Man. I was simply enjoying a little game.'

'Mind games?'

She leaned forward. 'Everything's a game. Reality's just one of the players.'

'Some games aren't to my taste,' the Doctor told her.

She grinned. 'Not always. You have played before, many times.'

'You must be confusing me with someone else. Me, probably.'

She didn't seem put out by this apparent contradiction. 'Anything's possible, Evergreen Man.'

'I prefer to be called "Doctor". And I imagine I should think of something to call you… Titania, I suppose. It seems appropriate under the circumstances, and I doubt you would give me a real name to call you.'

'Titania,' she laughed, and it caused faint music to hang in the air. 'Like everything else in the universe, you change so much… Yet your heart remains the same.'

'Both of them,' the Doctor agreed.

'Everyone has one heart, Doctor. The body may have two, or none –' she pressed a finger to the centre of his chest – 'but everyone has one true heart.'

'Even the Leannain Sidhe?'

'Even me. And even the Lord of Time.'

The Doctor met her gaze with equanimity. 'There are many "Lords of Time" as you put it. I'm really nothing special.'

'There are many who *claim* Lordship over Time,' Titania corrected, 'but only one who behaves like a true Lord. Someday you'll make someone a fine husband.'

The Doctor looked a little embarrassed. 'Well, I –'

'I imagine that finding a soulmate can't be easy for the Lord of Time. These mortals age and die so quickly… You begin to get to know them, then suddenly they're a faded memory brought on by summer sunset.' She caressed his shoulder. 'It need not always be so.'

'Indeed?' said the Doctor, neutrally.

'Would it be so bad? We of the Sidhe have always had the best of relations with humans.'

The Doctor gently shifted to the side. 'I'm not human. Flattered, but not human.'

'Part of you is. That's enough.'

The Doctor gave a tight smile. '"That's debatable" would be more accurate.'

Galastel had brought Sam out into the countryside, and she felt strangely heavier now that she was back in a recognisable section of reality.

Although she recognised their surroundings as being a wood on a cold winter's night, she didn't immediately realise that it was the place where she had first arrived. Perhaps it was because of the slight differences that became apparent from this perspective, such as the balls of light that occasionally rose from the ground, and the eerily semisolid columns of shadow and darkness that stood here and there across the fields below.

Galastel didn't mention them, and she didn't want to ask, but she got the impression they were both natural and somehow watching her.

Despite the obvious snow and ice, she didn't feel the least bit cold. 'Look,' Galastel said, pointing to a bridge nearby. 'It's beginning.' Sure enough, the air began to quiver with a discordant resonance.

Suddenly, probing metallic tentacles slithered out of the air, and got a solid grip on reality. Then there was a triumphant bass note, with some very sinister undertones, and the tentacles levered a pulsating biomechanical crustacean out of a gap that didn't exist anyway.

The thing paused there, its fluid skin shifting and changing constantly as filaments stretched out to taste the air. It was certainly technological, but its fluidity of movement was strangely organic. To Sam, it looked like something Lovecraft and Giger might have designed after a bad hit.

Sam shivered. Whatever it was, perhaps it had something to do with what was harming the Sidhe, so she paid as close attention as her stomach could bear. Suddenly the fluid skin split, disgorging a figure. It was like watching someone step into a vertical sheet of calm water, but in reverse.

The shock of seeing that it was herself who emerged almost knocked her down. 'What –' She swallowed a couple of times, trying to ask the question she didn't want answered. 'That's never the TARDIS…?'

'Do you not recognise your own travelling carriage?' enquired Galastel. 'That of the Evergreen Man?'

'No, it's… Does it always look like that to you?'

'Should it not?' Galastel seemed baffled by her question.

'No! I mean, the outside's just, you know, a box.'

'Ah… To your limited perception, perhaps. Could a mere

box travel through time and space? Of course there must be more to it than you can perceive. Or at least more than you could perceive before now. There are many things that you can perceive now, if you wish, that you could not before. Places, the feeding creatures that swarm… Many things.'

As she watched, the Doctor emerged from the… well, from what she supposed she'd better accept was the TARDIS. Unlike herself or Fitz, he too looked strangely different: taller, more powerful, and somehow more real. It was like looking at a piece of TV or film where one person was in colour and the rest monochrome.

'The Evergreen Man,' declared Galastel. It was weird, Sam thought: she knew that she and Galastel should be visible from here, yet they still couldn't be seen.

'Is that what you call him?'

Galastel remained admirably inscrutable. 'It is who he is.'

'I never really looked at it that way. Couldn't we just go down now, and –'

'No. There are rules about such things. Even we cannot flout the rules.'

Sam thought about this. 'Are there rules about tweaking what people see and hear?'

'Rules,' Galastel confirmed, 'but it's not forbidden. Why?'

Sam grinned. This was more like it. 'There's somewhere else we have to go.'

Fitz had managed to find a crashed motorbike, whose dead rider was lying a few feet away, with a few more holes in him than he had been born with. Other bodies, both German and American, were scattered around.

There were a couple of dents in the bike, but nothing that Fitz couldn't fix with the tools and puncture repair kit that were in the pannier boxes. He had no idea whether there was any fuel left in it at all, but it started up when he tried it, and made good time on it. He had no idea where the hell he was going, of course, but he knew that west towards the Allied forces was probably a good idea. To that end he had ditched his looted uniform.

All in all, it made him feel just like Steve McQueen, except that Fitz was having enough trouble keeping the bike upright to even think about what would happen if he came to a fence blocking the road.

It was a moot point anyway, as the thing eventually ran out of fuel, and he was returned to moving on foot. It wasn't, he decided, much of a Christmas week, if the Doctor's theory about the date was right. He didn't remember the exact dates of this battle himself, but the calendar back at the Café Scholzen had shown December as the month.

His mood didn't improve when three men in dark green uniforms suddenly stepped out from behind the snow-encrusted trees, with rifles raised.

Even as he recognised the uniforms as American, Fitz's hands shot into the air. 'Don't shoot! Don't shoot!' He put on his best RADA accent. 'Sorry to give you chaps such a fright, but Jerry's right behind me…' He trailed off, suddenly realising what a bad idea that was if these men should happen to be more impostors.

The Americans hesitated. 'You're English?'

Fitz nodded. 'Working behind the lines. Eavesdropping, that sort of thing…'

'You got a name?'

Fitz knew that the words 'Fitz Kreiner' at this point probably wouldn't be a good idea, but didn't hesitate to answer. 'Bond,' he said. 'James Bond.'

Sam watched herself push her way into the spooky-looking house back in Lanzerath. It was well weird, being able to watch yourself doing something you remembered doing recently, and Sam had a momentary sensation of being unsure which of the two Sams was really her.

She saw her earlier self look around and shiver, and remembered that when she had first visited this house she had had the feeling of someone walking over her grave. She hadn't expected it to be herself. She hadn't expected it to be quite so literal, either.

Sam and Galastel watched the earlier Sam – the living Sam, she reminded herself with a shiver – try the telephone beside a large armchair.

When her earlier counterpart lifted the receiver, Sam could somehow see the fault: a downed line. It was as if some part of her mind had followed the telephone line until the break, and she swayed slightly at the sudden sensation.

Galastel caught her.

'Your perceptions of things will be different while you are with us.'

'What about if I return to my world?'

'Not so much, then.'

The Sam using the phone jumped as the door crashed open and Kovacs pointed a gun at her. There was a blur of drab-green uniforms as a couple of other men followed him in. 'Put the phone down, sister. Nice and slow.'

'It's dead,' Sam heard herself say.

'Put it down or so are you.'

'A "please" wouldn't have killed you, would it?' she demanded, recovering.

His expression faltered. 'You're a Brit? Who were you trying to call?'

'Nobody yet. I was just trying to get an open line to find some help. Not only do I not know where I am, but our transport was knocked into the river when the shelling hit the bridge down there.' She gestured in the direction of the TARDIS.

The soldiers exchanged glances. 'You said "our". How many of you are there?'

'Two others: the Doctor and an orderly. We got separated when our transport broke down on the bridge, and they're on the other side of the river.'

Kovacs hesitated. 'Civilians. Hoo-rah. Joe, get the field wire set up. I want a watch on the Losheim road.' He turned back to Sam. 'OK, so you say you're a Brit. What's your name?'

'Samantha Jones. Sam.'

As the earlier Sam spoke, Galastel moved in front of Kovacs, and now Sam got the confused impression of papers and passwords, curiosity and relief, as Kovacs's eyes unfocused for a moment.

Galastel stepped aside, and Kovacs recovered. 'Well, at least you're probably not a spy.'

'That makes a nice change,' the earlier Sam murmured. 'Usually people assume the opposite.'

Sam was astounded. She had known something was up when Kovacs had accepted her so readily, but she hadn't expected this. 'How the hell did you do that?' she asked Galastel.

'I let him perceive what was necessary for him to perceive. Your perceptions and ours are different, but related, and so we can –'

'Fudge things?'

'If you like. It's a defence mechanism, it helps us move through your world without hindrance or hostility. Even if we have contact with mortals, all we need do is have ourselves perceived as some harmless local, or an animal. Nothing of consequence. It's not difficult – even the feeding swarm do it, by instinct, to hide themselves.' He looked at Sam, the ghost of a smile on his pointed face. 'In time, you could learn this, too.'

Chapter Seven
The Art of War

Titania had walked the Doctor to the edge of the lake near her city. She had shown him the damage on the way. There had been no fooling of his perceptions this time. The Doctor had some concerns about getting back to Bastogne at roughly the time he left. He knew all of the old tales about how time ran differently here.

He also knew how time really worked, though. So long as his perceptions remained his own, he would have no problems getting back.

The Doctor could still feel Titania's eyes on him while he looked out over the lake. There was movement below the surface and he watched with interest. 'You keep following me around like a lost puppy,' he said suddenly. 'If there's something you want from me, why don't you just ask it?'

'It is not our way to seek help from others.'

'At least, not to come straight out and ask it?'

She didn't answer for what felt like several minutes, though he knew time had little meaning here. 'For the most part, when mortals make war, it does not affect us. We do not interfere with mortals. At least, not on a cultural or national level,' she added with the sound of a smile. 'But in this place the conflict is damaging us.'

The Doctor turned, to see that she had sat down on a worn and ancient piece of stone that hadn't been there a moment ago. 'How is that possible?' he asked softly.

'There is a breach, a tear in the veil that partitions the lands of Men from those of ours.'

'You mean something's causing dimensional instability in the region...?'

'I mean what I say, Evergreen Man.'

The Doctor came over and sat beside her. 'Then it's not you causing it?'

'No,' she replied, a little too quickly. 'Not us. Otherwise we would not have asked you for help. And we know you are compassionate enough to assist us.'

'That's a very big assumption to make.'

'Your friend said so.'

'My friend? Fitz?'

'Samantha.'

The Doctor remained motionless, and Titania kept her mask of inscrutability as she watched his surprise.

'Sam? You saw Sam?' His face darkened. 'She was here?'

'Yes.'

He hesitated. 'I was told she was dead.'

Titania appeared amused. 'No one dies here, unless I allow it. Your friend was brought here in time, and saved.'

'Sam's alive!' he exclaimed, delighted. 'Alive...' He swept Titania into his arms, and kissed her, but only on the cheek.

'That was very careful of you.'

The Doctor nodded quickly. '"But take one kiss of my blood-red lips, And sure of your body I will be", or so I'm told.'

'I'm sure you are.'

'Where is Sam?'

'On her way to where you are working with the humans. She will arrive shortly.'

'And the other humans you've taken from the battlefields and the hospitals?' He obviously hoped the sudden change of tack would surprise her, but it didn't work.

'They remain.'

'You can't just take them like that!'

'We can. They are on the brink of death, Doctor. We save them.'

The Doctor shook his head. 'By changing their natures?

That's what you do, isn't it?'

'It is our right,' Titania said icily. 'We are permitted to exact recompense from the mortals when they breach the truce that was reached.'

'A truce?'

'It was many generations ago, after the Sidhe and Men fought.'

'Titania, human civilisations are as mortal as their individuals. Whatever truce was signed, it's long since been lost to history.'

'I understand. That is why we do not punish their infractions of it. But we remember, and we stand by our vows, and our rights. Even the Lord of Time has no right to deprive us of our due.'

'These are living beings, with futures and –'

'They are taken at the moment of death!' Titania responded angrily. 'How can any of them have a future, other than that which we give them? We choose to take that compensation in kind. Those we take, we take body and soul; and they take the place of those we have lost. They have immortality, purpose and paradise.'

'Perhaps they don't all have what it takes to accept a completely alien world-view.'

'That is a problem with their limited thought,' she said simply.

'That,' the Doctor shouted, 'is a facet of their very nature!'

'Are you suggesting that death is preferable for them?' she challenged.

'That would be their choice! It's not up to you or me!' The Doctor visibly got a grip on himself. 'I'm just saying you should give the humans a choice. That was always the way it was done.'

'Ah,' Titania whispered sadly. 'That's true. But that was when we could move more openly, and approach mortals who were still hale and hearty, talk with them without being hunted by others. Now they kill so quickly that if we wait we lose everything.'

'Don't you care? Don't you care about human life at all?'

'We care about Life. Life endures. We care that there are mortals in their world; they endure.'

'But individual lives, Titania.' The Doctor took hold of her gently by the shoulders. 'Individual personae, and hopes, and dreams, and fears…'

Titania looked into his eyes. 'Yes, we care. We live and love and tell stories, as do humans. But we care about the life of humanity as a whole. Without them, we would be diminished. We would be alone.'

'Then show that you care,' the Doctor suggested. 'Offer a choice before taking them.'

Titania touched her cheek absently, at the spot where he had kissed her. 'Are you offering me a bargain?'

'Yes,' he replied after a moment. 'Do as I ask, and I will find a way to repair whatever dimensional problem is hurting both your people and the humans.'

She knew his mind of old, of course. He would have helped anyway, especially if the rift threatened humans.

'Agreed.'

And then she was gone, and he was standing in a bombed-out street in front of the hospital.

'You're trying to hide?' Titania asked once the Evergreen Man had left. 'There's no need.'

Oberon emerged from the trees, his wiry frame excited, and his grin just on the wrong side of manic. 'Is a consort supposed to openly watch his love courting another?' he asked.

'Courting?' she scoffed. 'I sought his help, not his love.'

'Perhaps that's what you tell yourself.'

'Is that what you seek from your pet mortal?'

Oberon laughed. 'My soul has always been complete. It needs nothing from others.'

'Then what?'

He hesitated, then wrapped an arm around her, his mind softly stroking hers. 'Taking our right. As we should.'

'We do take our right.'

'No.' He withdrew, irritated at her blindness. 'The humans no longer heed the terms of the truce –'

'Their civilisation is mortal. These are different humans –'

'Exactly! Ones who never agreed to the truce. Ones who we need not hide from. Ones who should be showing us our due respect.'

'And you expect to get that by interfering in their war?'

'If you really disapproved, you would stop me.'

'You know I can't do that!'

'Yes, I do,' he said happily. He came to her again. 'My Queen… I know that only I have the vision required to make things right between us and the mortal Men. That's why I am *Amadan na Briona*. You know that,' he added silkily, knowing just how to touch her mind to please her. 'So I will do this for you, because I know the laws constrain you from acting yourself.'

'More likely because you know they constrain me from stopping you.'

'That too,' he said quickly, with a grin.

Lewis had brought a new man in to take over security for the police station. He had been keen to find someone who wasn't gossiping about the oddities out there, and had finally found a suitably grizzled veteran with a platoon of men who had been attached to an artillery spotting unit.

Since their usual services were hardly needed in a besieged city, he had decided they would make an excellent defensive force for his headquarters. To that end, he and Sergeant Jeff Kovacs were currently supervising the installation of some anti-aircraft guns on the roof. There were two sets of .50-calibre quad guns that Kovacs had rescued from damaged half-tracks.

'The main thing,' Kovacs was saying, 'is to keep the planes from going over here. Artillery from outside we really can't do anything about, but they can't really see who's where from out there.'

'Good,' said Lewis. 'I don't want the Luftwaffe to disrupt my activities.' All things considered, he would rather make that the case by simply leaving the city. But he had waited too long, and now he was stuck here. 'If only it was so easy to stop the gossip,' he muttered.

'Gossip?' Kovacs echoed, in a tone that distinctly suggested such an activity was reserved for maiden aunts.

'The nonsense that's been going around about… weird stuff. You must have heard it. Things seen in the forest. Lights and shadows.'

Kovacs shook his head. 'Can't say I been listening. Sounds like people have got too much time on their hands.'

'Exactly,' Lewis said, pleased. Between Wiesniewski and what he'd been hearing from just about everyone at Garcia's hospital – he had people monitoring it, naturally – he was beginning to think the whole US Army had nothing better to do than chatter about things they shouldn't. Worse still, he couldn't tell them why they shouldn't without breaching more security regulations than he could count. It was the most frustrating situation he'd ever been in.

'Stories are stories,' said Kovacs. 'These guys are probably just reliving how they used to tell spook stories round the fire at summer camp. It's no big thing. It just helps them deal with what's going on in their heads. Besides, if I want to see things, I can always go get drunk.'

'Best way to do it,' Lewis agreed, readily. It was meant to be wise to find common ground with subordinates, though he'd rather he simply didn't have to deal with them.

'This looks secure enough,' Kovacs opined. 'The trick'll be to keep enough ammo on hand.'

'I'll see to that.' Lewis nodded to himself, or perhaps to his silent partner, whom he could feel at his shoulder. 'I could use a driver later. Meet me downstairs with a jeep at noon.'

'Yes, sir.'

Lewis ignored Kovacs's salute, and left.

He went back to his office, poured himself a whisky and sat back to flip through his private scrapbook. He took it on every posting. It was far too sensitive to leave lying around at home, or even in his office in Washington.

He turned straight to the photos surrounding a news clipping about a bar-room brawl at which the sailors involved had literally vanished into thin air. No one with half a brain had believed the story, of course, but Lewis knew better. The technology he had been experimenting with had been primitive, and he certainly hadn't expected knock-on effects like that to last for days. But those were the good days, he recalled. Being an army observer to a navy yard back in the States was infinitely preferable to being stuck in a frozen battlefield halfway round the world.

But as not all had gone well at Philly a year ago, he and the others had been lucky to escape with their jobs and ranks. The USS *Eldridge* had escaped, too, in a way – disappeared, anyway. Disintegrated by the strains of the energy field that was used on it, he deduced. Just like those sailors in that bar-room.

It had been a damned waste. The ship might not have been a good test bed, but she was good enough at her normal duties. And what an work of art she'd have been if the tests had worked out. He wouldn't be sitting in this Belgian dump now, that was for sure.

He felt the laugh before he heard it, and looked up to find the *Amadan* perched on the corner of his desk. As always he had a golden skin – not just tanned, but literally like liquid gold, glowing faintly.

'Why, Colonel,' the *Amadan* said mock-disapprovingly. 'Not busy with the affairs of running your army?'

'It's not my army,' Lewis reminded him. 'I'm just stuck here because I didn't get out quickly enough. Besides, I have the best mechanics hard at work on our project. There's not a lot I could do there other than get in the way.'

'Oh, I understand… But what a shame you don't see the fun there is in getting in the way.' The *Amadan* grinned magnificently. 'I know I would find it more fun if I could see you working to fulfil your part of our bargain,' he continued, with more of an edge in his voice. Lewis could imagine such an edge against his throat.

'I've finished the designs and schematics. Sergeant Kovacs will take me to view the finished test beds at noon.'

'Test beds? What curious phrases you humans use. You have such little poetry in your souls.' The *Amadan* snapped his fingers. 'That reminds me. Why didn't you tell me *he* was here?'

'He? Who?'

'The Evergreen Man – the Doctor.'

Lewis's ears pricked up. The *Amadan* knew of the Doctor? 'He's out of the way –'

'Fool!' the *Amadan* spat, then recovered himself. 'Still, what ought I to expect from a mortal.' He took Lewis's head in his hands, and for a horrible, fearful moment Lewis felt sure he was going to try to twist it off. Instead, he simply brought his face closer. They were almost close enough to kiss, and yet Lewis could feel no movement of breath from the *Amadan*'s nose or mouth. 'The Evergreen Man will interfere with us. It is what he does.'

'What do you mean by interfere? Attack us?'

'No. That, I could understand. But he will protest and take a moral stand. So boringly predictable – he just doesn't know how to enjoy himself. He feels the weight of the world on his shoulders but won't put his feet up and rest.'

'And what do you expect me to do?' Lewis asked.

The *Amadan*'s skin burned rather than glowed. 'I expect you to kill him.'

Bearclaw had returned from standing a shift on watch at one of the city's roads. He had hoped to thank the Doctor again, and now found him looking a little dazed in the street. 'Are you lost?' he asked.

'No,' the Doctor said, pinching the bridge of his nose and closing his eyes, as if trying to ward off a headache. 'Quite the opposite, in fact.' He jumped to his feet. 'It's time we sorted this mess out. I shall need to speak to Garcia and Wiesniewski…'

'Whatever it is,' Bearclaw said firmly, 'count me in, too. I owe you one.'

The Doctor shook his head. 'No, no one owes me –'

'*I* do.' Bearclaw wasn't going to let this one go. 'You Brits. I should probably introduce you to that secret agent, Bond, who just turned up. You'd get on like a house on fire.'

The Doctor looked up. 'Bond?'

'James Bond. We picked him up at –' He broke off as the Doctor laughed hard enough to need to steady himself with a hand on a bollard. 'Is something wrong?'

The Doctor recovered enough to shake his head with a wondering smile. 'Actually, I'd be very glad if you did bring him along. It sounds very much like I've made his acquaintance before…'

Fitz was in the back of an American half-track, wrapping himself around a hot coffee and wishing it was a large Scotch.

The top of the vehicle was open to the air – it was cold, but at least it wasn't raining.

Before he could react, the Doctor suddenly vaulted into the half-track from the street outside and hugged him briefly. 'Good to see you again! I was *so* worried!'

Fitz coughed, delighted but a little discomfited by this physical affection. 'No need to worry,' he said in his best *Dr No* Sean Connery. 'I was just doing my bit. Sorry I'm late.'

'I doubt you had much choice.'

'Actually,' Fitz admitted, 'I did. I had a stolen uniform and could have walked out of the German lines a couple of days ago.'

'Why didn't you get out when you could?' The Doctor sounded pleasantly surprised at Fitz's actions, but was looking at him approvingly. Fitz found himself feeling strangely pleased at that, but then told himself not to be. Surely the last person he wanted to impress was a nutty idealist with a martyr complex. Wasn't it?

'I saw something I thought you'd be interested in.' The Doctor, to his credit, looked suitably intrigued, and Fitz leaned in conspiratorially. 'There's a team of SS troops out there who aren't attached to the main attack. They've got a set of armoured cars, with these weird aerials on them.'

'"Weird" as in "anachronistic"?'

'Not exactly, I don't think. But weird as in too sophisticated to be just for radio or even radar. But they were definitely designed to detect something, and I think I know what.'

'Go on.'

It felt great to be the one explaining things to the Doctor for a change. He almost let himself slip into doing Andre Morell from *Quatermass*. 'They had a prisoner at Lanzerath, but he wasn't just kept in by bars. They had to wire up some electrical generators to keep him locked up. I'm not sure how that works, but it was something to do with generating a field, because the bars weren't actually electrified. I got him out, and when we escaped into the woods he vanished.'

'Ran off?'

'Vanished,' Fitz repeated firmly.

'Tell me about this "prisoner" you helped escape,' the Doctor said.

Fitz shivered in spite of himself. 'Weird bloke. If it was a bloke. I mean, I don't know what he was or why they were holding him, but I do know he wasn't human.' He broke off, reluctant to go any further than that.

The Doctor wasn't put off in the slightest. 'What do you think he was?'

'I dunno, you're the expert.'

The Doctor smiled. 'And you're my man in the field.'

'OK. I reckon they're elves.' There, he'd said it, and he'd belt anyone who hassled him about it. 'I mean, I know it sounds bloody daft, but I dunno what else they could be. Well, apart from aliens pretending to be elves, which I suppose is what they really are. But even that would amount to the same thing, wouldn't it?'

The Doctor started to speak, but Fitz cut him off and continued. Might as well be hung for a sheep as for a lamb. 'Yeah, I know, you don't believe in magic, elves, fairies or Santa Claus. But Leitz is conducting research into exploiting the abilities of Light and Dark Elves. Those are the words he used. All the methods of whoever they are fit some folk tales or other. I rescued one from Leitz's camp, and it fitted every story my old mum used to tell me. What else do you want?'

'Actually, Fitz,' the Doctor said, 'I was just about to say well done. For want of a better word, they are, as you say, elves.'

'But naturally you know a better word, I suppose?' The Doctor always did.

'Naturally. It would probably be just as accurate to call them psychomaterial constructs from a parallel evolutionary path.

But Sidhe will do well enough, since it's what they most commonly call themselves.'

Fitz opened and closed his mouth several times, like a goldfish. 'You mean I'm right?'

'One hundred per cent.'

'But that's ridiculous,' Fitz protested, aware of how typical this was. Even when *he* was giving the explanation, he couldn't really believe it. 'Push off, I can't be right. Elves can't really exist.'

'The next time you see one, tell him that.' The Doctor suddenly cocked his head. 'Leitz, did you say?'

'Yes. "*Sturmbannführer* Jurgen Leitz." Bit of a ponce if you ask me.'

The Doctor groaned and slapped himself on the forehead. 'That's what he said. Not "lights" but "Leitz". If I were this *Sturmbannführer* of yours I'd be worried. Lewis knows who he is, how far he's got, and has a local helper very much in the know.'

'One of the Sidhe?'

'Oh yes. A very particular one, I suspect. Oberon. The *Amadan na Briona*. The only one who could dare act so openly.'

Fitz had never heard that phrase before. 'What's so special about him?'

'Basically the Sidhe pay homage to the two great forces in the universe: chaos and order. Their Queen personifies order, but that means they need a personification of chaos, too. So he can do anything he likes, and not be held responsible for his actions, because it's part of nature. His nature.'

'What's to stop him just knocking off the Queen and taking over?'

'Because that's not part of his nature. Chaos and order can only coexist. You can't have one without the other, because you need the other to judge it against. To define it against, in fact.' The Doctor looked into the distance. 'The same basic conflict can be seen time and time again throughout the universe…'

'What about us?' said Fitz, not feeling terribly metaphysical in this freezing weather. 'We're not Sidhe; can't we hold him responsible?'

'Yes we can,' the Doctor agreed. 'Their laws don't apply to us, when they're confining themselves to our level of reality. Come on!'

Kovacs didn't mind driving Lewis around. It wasn't real soldiering, but then he wasn't bothered one way or the other about fighting Germans, anyway. So one duty was as good for killing time as another.

Lewis had got him to drive out to a large farm at the edge of town. There, just within the defences, was the biggest barn Kovacs had ever seen. Mind you, there hadn't been a lot of barns in Brownsville East, back in New York.

There were six Sherman tanks here – new ones, untouched by the dirt and dents of combat. Their dark-green paint was factory-new and unblemished. Kovacs had never seen a tank so clean outside an assembly plant itself, let alone half a dozen of them.

'Wait here,' Lewis said, his eyes bright with excitement. He looked like a kid on Christmas Morning, and Kovacs wondered what was so special about these Shermans. Then he noticed other differences, in addition to the fact that they were newer models with longer barrels and better-shaped armour. Strange circular plates hung down over the road wheels, but Kovacs couldn't guess what they were for. Since they just hung there on springs, they couldn't really be for extra protection in the way that a lot of German tanks had armoured skirts over their wheels.

Then there were the cables: thick, steel-ribbed ones that coiled around the hull and turret and connected to a large sealed box on the rear deck. Smaller cables branched off to attach on to those plates over the wheels. Kovacs was totally baffled: he'd never seen anything like it. The only thing he could think of would be that it might be for electrifying the outside of the tank, but what would be the point, even if you could do it without frying the crew inside?

As he inspected the Shermans, Lewis could be sure of at least one thing: Oberon could not come here. Not before the tanks' modifications were switched on, at least. Although Oberon was his friend, and had helped him, Lewis found – almost guiltily – that it was a relief not to have to worry about him showing up.

The crews were already waiting for him, so Lewis mounted the first tank.

'You can take the jeep back to headquarters,' he called across to Kovacs. 'I don't know how long this test is going to take.'

'Yes, sir,' Kovacs called back. With the speed of the jeep, he might still be able to collect some of his payments, he thought. Pleased with the idea, he drove the jeep back up the low hill into the town centre.

Kovacs absently glanced round on the brow of the hill, and was forced to stand on the jeep's brake to avoid crashing it out of pure shock. One of the Shermans below had not only revved up its engine, but was generating a strange electrical hum. The cables and wheel plates that had been added to it were glowing with a faint ochre light. Worst of all, it seemed to be fading.

The light rippled around it, turning the tank briefly to crystal-clear glass, through which he could see the building on the other side, and then it was gone altogether. Its tracks were still leaving indentations in the ground, but those too stopped after a few yards.

Kovacs sat there for several long minutes, just looking.

Garcia had attracted a certain amount of ribbing for the strength of his faith, but he dreaded to think how much laughter the Doctor's story would generate in the ranks. What was really odd was that Bearclaw, Wiesniewski and the new guy, Kreiner, were all listening in total seriousness, and had even exchanged notes.

'Elves and fairies?' he scoffed. 'I know it's Christmas, but that doesn't mean I expect Santa's little helpers to get involved in the war. Mind you, if the guy in the red suit wants to drop off some supplies to us, that'd be fine with me.'

The Doctor frowned. 'Believe me, you wouldn't want these people packing your Christmas parcels.'

'Doctor, I do like to think of myself as having an open mind, but –'

'"But but but but…" There's always a but, isn't there? Open minds are the best kind, but nature abhors a vacuum, so if you've got an open mind someone always tries to come along and put something in it.'

'But that is what you're saying, isn't it? That these creatures are what folklorists would call elves, or –'

'In a way,' the Doctor admitted. 'They're beings who exist in our space-time continuum, but out of phase with what we can perceive of it.'

'Out of phase? You mean like some sort of parallel world?'

'No no no. There *are* such things, of course, but this isn't one of them. Their world is your world. This is a single continuum that you and they share. It's just that they can perceive – and exist in – more of it than we can.'

'I don't understand. How can there be more of the world?'

The Doctor grabbed a piece of paper and a pencil, and drew a small circle. 'Imagine that circle is a two-dimensional being. It could move about anywhere on this paper, yes?' Garcia nodded. 'But it can't move vertically.' The Doctor waved a hand above the circle. 'It can't look up and see my hand, because it can't perceive the third spatial dimension.

'Now, Earth scientists will soon discover that the universe has more than four dimensions: in fact there are eleven at last count. That means the world has eleven dimensions instead of four. But life as you know it perceives only those four dimensions. You can't see the rest of it. The Sidhe, or whatever you want to call them, do perceive and exist in all eleven, and we are to them what our two-dimensional friend here –' he tapped the paper – 'is to us.'

'Hang on, though. The one we saw was humanoid. But the reports from Wiesniewski and the others are completely different – discarnate lights, shadows, movement… Are they humanoid or aren't they?'

'More than humanoid, perhaps.' The Doctor indicated the paper. 'If I put my hand through that, fingertips first, our two-dimensional friend would perceive it as four circles merging into a larger oval, with a fifth circle – my thumb – appearing to the side then merging with the rest…' Garcia nodded. 'But if I do this…' the Doctor slapped his palm down on the paper, fingers spread –

'Then it sees a hand…' Garcia finished thoughtfully.

'Or at least a hand shape, though there's more to the complete hand than it can see.'

'All right, so Bearclaw claims to have seen humanlike figures. But what about the things Wiesniewski saw? They weren't partial limbs –'

'You're still thinking in such limited terms. What the others saw could easily have been the kinetic energy of the Sidhe's movement, or their biodata reacting to the local environment, or any of a dozen other things.'

Garcia didn't understand a word of the Doctor's explanations. 'Then why appear as human here?'

'Well, as you saw, they've obviously adopted a different phase position –'

'No,' Garcia interrupted. 'I meant why? Out in the field they don't care whether their appearance fits in with the environment or the people around. But in here they take the trouble to "position" themselves as human-looking. They try to blend in. So why is that?'

The Doctor grinned. 'Excellent! A wonderful question, in fact. It's a pity I'm not sure of the answer. I mean, it could simply be a necessity to fit in with the environment, since these buildings are designed for human occupation. But my instincts tell me there must be more to it than that.'

'But if they're from Earth,' Garcia said, desperately trying to understand, 'surely they'd already be suited to the environment…'

The Doctor shook his head. 'Let me put it this way. Imagine Earth is a tower block. Each parallel world is a different floor. But each floor has eleven apartments, which correspond to the various dimensions or planes within that level. So, our perceptions keep us confined to apartments 1A to 1D, but the Sidhe have access to 1A through to 1K.'

'And would those parallel worlds have eleven dimensions, too?'

'If they're in a universe where the same physical laws apply, then yes, and they'd have their own parallel Sidhe as well.'

Garcia looked blank, trying to get it all straight in his mind. 'You said "your world"…' He hesitated, not wanting to upset the Doctor any more than he wanted to look foolish. 'You keep talking as if you're not one of us. Are you one of these Sidhe?'

'Oh, no, I'm afraid not. I'm just a normal guy from a different planet, that's all. A quaint little green one in a quiet neighbourhood,' he added.

Garcia just stared at him.

If he'd just heard what he thought he'd heard, then either he or the Doctor was a candidate for the nuthouse. Or, Garcia realised, the Doctor was bullshitting him to take his mind off the problems at hand. He couldn't really fault the guy for that. 'You picked a pretty crappy vacation spot.'

'A warzone…' the Doctor murmured softly. 'Where else is a Doctor most likely to be needed? I seem to end up in battlefields the way cigarette smoke is drawn to the only nonsmoker in a room.' He paused, then began to recite:

'*With an host of furious fancies*
Whereof I am commander,
With a burning spear,
And a horse of air,
To the wilderness I wander.

'*By a knight of ghosts and shadows*
I summoned am to tourney
Ten leagues beyond the wide world's end,
Methinks it is no journey.'

'Sounds like you,' said Fitz, casually. 'Don't recognise the poet; when was that written?'

'First published in *Giles Earle: His Booke*, in 1615, by that prolific writer "Anon". He's always been my favourite poet, you know.'

'So you didn't write it yourself, then?' Fitz teased, lightly.

Garcia decided it would be easier to ignore this little aside to the main conversation and steer things back to the matters in hand – whatever the hell they were. 'But come on, even if these beings existed, wouldn't there be some kind of evidence? Fossils or something?'

'Not necessarily. Tell me: how long has *Homo sapiens* been around?' Garcia shrugged, and the Doctor continued. 'The accepted figure's about half a million years, though it's really nearer six. Now… Recorded history of *Homo sapiens* goes back only ten thousand years or so. So what was happening in the rest of that time?'

Garcia opened and closed his mouth silently, trying to grasp the idea. 'Dinosaurs?' he said finally. 'No, sorry that was silly… I don't know. What was it then?'

The Doctor smiled. 'Lots of things. Things that have left race memories in humanity's collective unconscious. And those memories are what produces religion and folklore, to try to explain half-forgotten shadows in the psyche.'

'Like the Sidhe.'

'Intriguing, isn't it? A race dimensionally out of phase but still sharing your planet with you.'

'And getting caught in the crossfire of this war,' Fitz added.

'Yes. Either by accident or design. I think accident, though at least one of them seems to be taking advantage of the situation for his own ends. We'll have to deal with him too. What we're going to need is –' The Doctor stopped, as a column of whirling light suddenly extruded itself into the lobby. The whirlwind resolved itself into a few glowing embers which orbited each other, merging and pulsing.

'Damn,' a female voice said, sounding like something half heard from another part of the building, 'I'll never get the hang of this if I live to be a hundred.'

The Doctor blinked. 'Sam?'

'Hang on, I think I'm supposed to –' The lights disappeared, and a young blonde woman was standing in the middle of the room. Garcia's hand fumbled for the arm of a chair, and sat down without taking his eyes off her. It wasn't that she was attractive – though she was – but that she had seemed to be an invisibly thin line that had turned round and become solid. Behind her, a faintly glowing figure had also appeared.

Maybe he'd got a whiff of some ether or something…

* * *

Lewis didn't feel at all uncomfortable sitting in the back of Leitz's command truck. He had brought the same number of guards as Leitz, and their vehicles were about equally matched. He had nothing to fear from a double-cross.

Besides, nothing had gone wrong in their previous meetings.

'I don't suppose you'd care to share a few of the battle plans with us, Jurgen?' Lewis asked casually in English. 'Just for old times' sake?'

'Oh, come now, Allen, you know I can't do that. It would look bad if ever it got out. Not like discussing the *Elfenhaft*. Besides, you and I both know that this offensive cannot last. Already it is beginning to crumble, and soon you will push our forces back.' Lewis nodded. That was true enough. 'The important thing is to prove that the *Elfenhaft*'s home, this... *Marchenland*, is something worthy of exploiting in future military development. It will give the forces of the West a huge advantage when they eventually face the Russians.'

'If it can be proved that it can be exploited practically.'

'Exactly.' Leitz took a sip of his cognac. 'Which is why I'm sending a Panzer squadron – a couple of Tigers, maybe ten Mark IVs – to meet your forces. If the battle can be manoeuvred into *Marchenland*, then we know it is a suitable subject for development after the war.'

Chapter Eight
Natural History

The Doctor and Fitz had both hugged Sam. God, it was good to be held again.

'I've had enough of losing you,' the Doctor said. 'More than enough. We were told you were dead. There were enough witnesses.'

'Apparently the Sidhe patched me up. Being seen with you has been a good thing, just for a change. They seem to like you.'

'You mean they want to keep on my good side so I'll help them,' the Doctor said, gently.

Sam nodded. 'I've been there. I mean, here. Well, wherever they live I've been, and the damage is appalling. It's like a warzone there as well as here.'

'Who's your friend over there, trying to cloud our minds?' Fitz looked around, clearly realising that the Sidhe had disappeared from his vision.

'The only bit I caught was something like Galastel.' Sam turned to look at him, hovering discreetly by the far wall, and smiled. 'He's not really bothered what we call him.'

The Doctor tapped his chin as if in thought. 'Hmm. "Radiant hope".'

'What?'

'You said you called him Galastel. It means "radiant hope". Didn't you know?'

Sam shook her head. 'I just caught a snatch of what he told me; it doesn't really mean anything.'

'All names mean something; it's what gives them their power.' He smiled reassuringly. 'It's probably a race memory, like speaking in tongues. You humans have been dealing with these beings for all of your species' existence.'

'We have?'

'What else are fairy tales? Not the sanitised ones of your century, but the old tales, of the little people, and the changelings…'

'The whats?' Sam asked.

'Don't you know what a changeling is?'

'No, I never saw much of *Deep Space Nine* – Dad was always watching the news.'

The Doctor paused to look at her. 'I sometimes despair for the state of education in your decade,' he said finally. 'People used to believe that fairies – or elves, leprechauns, whatever – would steal away a healthy human baby and leave one of theirs, or a half-breed, in its place. A changeling, in other words.'

'Some kind of genetic experiments?' Sam wondered aloud. 'Cross-fertilisation?'

'Possibly. Or it could just be human paranoia after coincidental side effects. Like I say, humans and the Sidhe have been in contact with each other for a very, very long time.'

Titania could sense her Oberon returning. He didn't announce himself, of course: just phased himself into her private sanctum, in breach of all etiquette. He knew there was nothing she would do.

'Harridan!' he snapped. 'Witch! Adulteress!'

'Is something wrong?' she responded mildly.

'Apart from my consort attempting to seduce members of other races?'

A familiar argument. 'I was merely –'

'Playing games, yes.' He scoffed. 'Games are fun, but old games are so dull. I much prefer new ones.'

'And I do not. There is a tradition that must be upheld.'

'That you must uphold,' he corrected. 'The only tradition I

must uphold is rather different.'

'As you never cease to remind me,' she answered wearily. How wonderful it would be to not have to endure his excesses any more. 'Stop pretending to be something other than a fool, and admit you're simply jealous.'

'Jealous?' He seemed to think about this. 'And what if I am?'

'Your position as my consort is a political one, not a spiritual one. It should not matter to the *Amadan na Briona* if I take a thousand mortal lovers.'

'Should? Should not? What do I care about should and should not? I feel what I feel. You "should not" be paying such attention to the Evergreen Man. You know he will never return your affections.'

'What makes you think you know anything of him? I enjoy such challenges most of all.'

'I'm not blind and I'm not stupid.' He turned on his heel expansively. 'So I thought I'd give him something more… pleasant to trouble himself with.'

'Pleasant?'

'Well, he enjoys challenges too. Adventures, threats to life and limb…'

'What have you done?'

Oberon remained smugly silent. 'That would be telling,' he said finally.

Oberon watched her leave, irritated that she was ignoring his feelings. He was her counterpart, and he enjoyed it. The Evergreen Man was, however powerful and near-immortal, an outsider. An interloper, in fact. Only one person could be the *Amadan na Briona*, to be so freed of duties and responsibilities. He would never surrender the position to anyone else.

Leitz instructed Farber to leave the armoured cars' engines

running when he returned to Lanzerath. All he had to do was collect a few files and schematics, and then he'd be ready to meet Lewis's force at the Eifel.

They'd have to put on a good show of fighting, of course, but the important thing was that both of them had enough information about the Sidhe's ability to phase in and out of the world that they could construct equipment to allow men to do the same.

And, he decided, to hell with Himmler and his cronies at Wewelsburg. There simply weren't enough raw materials to make use of the *Elfenhaft* to win this war, so he wanted only to make sure he had the chance to win the next one, when the West fought the Russians, as he was sure they would.

He glanced absently at the gowned medic on his way through the Café Scholzen, but paid him no mind, until he realised that the man was wearing a mask and cap in the middle of the mess area.

'Excuse me,' Leitz said slowly. He had the suspicion that it was the traitor, Kreiner, and drew his gun. 'Take off your mask.'

The man turned as if looking for an exit, but a couple of off-duty soldiers had noticed his suspicious actions, and were drifting over. While the ersatz medic was distracted, Leitz snatched the mask away from his face.

All he got was an impression of triangular jaw and flattened ears, before a sweeping arm knocked him sprawling across the floor, as the blurry figure solidified. As everyone reacted to this, the creature darted towards the door, ripping it clean off. Even while frozen with shock, one part of Leitz's mind still realised that it hadn't needed to do that. It had demonstrated such preternatural strength only in order to distract them.

Leitz's first shot exploded bloodlessly into the creature's elbow in a puff of yellow light. By the time Leitz had shot him twice more, the other men in the room had lifted their guns, and opened fire.

None of it had any effect, though Leitz could see some of the shots hit the wall on the far side. His theory was correct, then, that these creatures could phase themselves into and out of solidity, unless they were held to one phase by an electrical field.

Farber had the initiative to start driving after the fugitive immediately, and the armoured car was following it towards the woods outside the village.

Breathlessly, Leitz followed his men through the woods. Knowing what he was stalking didn't make him feel any happier. It was far too easy to imagine that he had got things the wrong way round, and that it was he and his men who were being stalked.

Every pool of blackness could harbour one of the creatures that had attacked Lanzerath earlier, or could be a literal pool that would drag him to his death. The shadows cast by the moonlight seemed to be watching him, too, with a simmering intelligence.

He told himself his imagination was running away with him – but who was to say that the creatures weren't causing that too? The one he had captured earlier had certainly displayed an ability to affect the mind, by hiding its true appearance. Perhaps they were out there, all around, deliberately inducing hallucinations.

Abruptly, one of his men screamed and fell, prompting several bursts of gunfire above his body. Leitz silenced the gunfire, and rolled the body over. The man was clearly dead, green bile oozing from the corner of his mouth. A tiny dart was embedded in his neck.

Leitz cursed. The dart was small and delicate, like a scale model of an arrow. Poisoned, no doubt. It occurred to him that such a toxin was worth getting a sample of, but, by the time he reached for the feathered portion of the miniature arrow, it had disappeared.

He cursed again. At this rate he would have nothing to show to the occult Circle at Wewelsburg, nor anything with which to bargain his way to the West after the war.

The engines of the armoured car roared, and it crashed through the undergrowth, sideswiping the creature, which suddenly became visible.

Manifestly terrified, one of the soldiers opened fire with a Schmeisser. With the steel of the armoured car trapping it, the creature couldn't phase out to let the bullets pass through it harmlessly. Pale blood exploded from the creature, and it dropped to the ground.

Leitz whirled round to face the killer. 'Put him under arrest,' he shouted to another soldier. These creatures had to be captured alive for research; what use was a dead one?

Nevertheless, there was one thing Leitz could learn from the corpse, and that was what the things really looked like. Somehow the live ones, even in captivity, managed to be vague and indistinct. Even if you saw them, they looked different every time, and he knew that somehow they were affecting their captors' perceptions.

In death, however, there was no pretence, and so Leitz was slightly cheered as he knelt to examine it.

He almost immediately drew back in disgust.

It was even less human than he had imagined.

'They killed one of us?' Oberon exploded. Like all the Sidhe in the Clan, he had sensed what had happened.

'It happens.' Titania reminded him

'Not while I am *Amadan na Briona*.' Between Lewis's ignoring Oberon's advice to get rid of the Doctor, and Titania's flirting with the Lord of Time like a mortal girl, Oberon was beginning to wonder if the fates were arranging this to spite him. 'When Men kill any of our number, they declare war. I shall have the Black Dogs released.' That would also slow down the Evergreen Man, he thought, pleased. Since Lewis had not taken his advice to kill the Doctor, he would be punished too, when the Black Dogs attacked his men.

'You have no right to do this without my authority!' Titania protested.

'I have every right. It's my place to do what is felt, and what is desired by our people. Are you going to try to hold me responsible for that?'

Titania swallowed her fury. He was right. He was the Chaos, the outsider, unconstrained by any semblance of Order, so not even she could hold him to account for what he did. How could you demand that irresponsibility be responsible?

He laughed. 'You're beautiful when you're angry: isn't that what the mortals say to flatter one another?'

Lewis sat in horror as the *Amadan* told him what he was doing.

'But what about my men? They had no part in this.' This bargain was getting more costly all the time.

'Your men, your men, your men…' the voice mocked.

The *Amadan* appeared, then, pulling Lewis around in his chair. 'They're only mortals. Normally not worth bothering with. I care not whether they live or die. But…' His face split into a bleak grin, baring needle-sharp teeth. 'They have killed one of our number.'

'The Germans killed one of you. A different mortal… clan.' He hoped that would placate the *Amadan*. If he understood that the humans had tribes and clans as the Sidhe did, perhaps he would focus his wrath on the other side.

'Mortals are mortals,' Oberon spat. 'You're not defined clans: your blood mixes. You yourself have the blood of your current enemies. You're all the same to us.'

* * *

The Doctor had brought Sam into Garcia's office. 'Are you all right?'

'I'm living and breathing, aren't I?'

'That's not what I asked.'

'I know. I'm... not sure.' She hesitated, not feeling comfortable with the idea of showing him the different skin she had acquired. 'I think that when I came back they changed me. I have some of their flesh as part of me.'

The Doctor nodded. 'It's what they do.'

'What am I, then?' she demanded. 'Am I one of us or am I one of them?' She bit off whatever she was going to say next, and shook her head. 'Or am I just a... changeling?'

The Doctor sighed, and put his arm around her. 'Sam Sam Sam Sam Sam... You're what you've always been – one of you. The only one of you, just as unique as everyone else.'

'But these changes they've made... These alterations... Doctor, I've been put through so many bloody transformations and transfigurations I've no idea who the hell Sam Jones ever was!'

The Doctor took a step back, and pushed his hands in his pockets. 'Sam... Ironic though it is, change is the one and only constant in the universe... And certainly nothing new to you. Do you know how many of your cells are being renewed all the time? Even if you sat in a room doing nothing for a whole year, you'd still technically be a different person at the end of the year than you were at the beginning.'

'Whatever. I'm still just a changeling...'

'No.' A slow smile spread across his face. 'No... From the description you gave, I'd say that you were given a little physical nudge in the right direction, but that you're still you. The closest thing I can think of is that you've... well, regenerated.'.

'What?'

'Oh yes. Some damaged cells rebuilt, your biodata somewhat

spliced together… You may have a little Sidhe DNA in you now, but you're still you. You're actually quite fortunate, Sam. You change only from today onward. It's different for a Time Lord. Changes that affect one of my people can affect his past as easily as they affect his present and future. A Time Lord's biodata isn't just a linear structure like your basic DNA. It can change retrospectively and retroactively.'

Sam stared at him. 'You mean it can affect not just who and what you are and will be, but who and what you *were*?'

'Yes.' The Doctor smiled. 'Confusing, isn't it?'

'You mean what you are has been changed? Like me?' She frowned. 'You lost a part of yourself, or gained a new side?'

'Depends on one's mood, doesn't it?' the Doctor replied. 'It's a "half full or half empty" kind of question. Now I'm half human and you're half human…' It seemed rather fitting, somehow. 'Does that mean we gained something, or lost something?'

'I hope it means gained,' said Sam.

'That's what I hoped you'd say. Funny thing, regeneration.'

'So… does that mean you could even change sex? Regenerate into a woman? I mean, how would that work?'

The Doctor paused thoughtfully. 'I'll explain later.'

Jeff Kovacs had downed a whole bottle of Jack Daniels at his regular seat in the brothel's bar, and it hadn't stopped him from seeing that damn Sherman shimmer and vanish, over and over.

What the hell had that been about? Was that what Lewis had been referring to when he talked about gossip? The damnedest thing of all was that he couldn't even blame it on combat strain. He had seen it first when everything was calm.

Still, this was war, and Lewis was into developing new things to win it, and Kovacs knew it wasn't unreasonable to assume that the invisible tank was – however far-fetched a comic-book idea it might be – some kind of new secret weapon.

No, what really got to Kovacs was some of the things Lewis had murmured to himself when he got back. If Kovacs didn't know better, he would have thought it sounded like Lewis had been meeting with the Nazis.

That opened a whole new can of worms.

And so he had eventually found himself here, on the doorstep of the hotel that Garcia had turned into a hospital. Kovacs wasn't exactly ready to trust Garcia, but the guy had kept his word about not turning him in, so maybe he was OK.

Garcia eventually arrived, and looked as surprised to see Kovacs as Kovacs felt to be here. 'Something I can help you with?' Garcia asked.

'Look…' Kovacs said, and trailed off. It wasn't going to be easy to say this. He had been trained and brought up to respect his superiors. 'It's Colonel Lewis. I think he's been having secret meetings with the Germans.'

Garcia stared at him. 'Why tell me?'

'I didn't know who else to talk to. I can't take it up through channels in case it gets back to him.'

'Do you know who he's been meeting? Peiper, or…?'

Kovacs shook his head. 'Some guy called Leitz, I think. Not sure how high up he is.'

'Leitz?' an oddly dressed civilian in the corner echoed. He smiled. 'Interesting. Come back at dawn, Sergeant. I think we may have some things to discuss.'

'Why not now?'

The man smiled, not unkindly. 'Because I think it's best that you're sober for all this…'

Bearclaw and Wiesniewski had found the time to get something to eat. Neither of them could remember his last hot meal.

'Be nice to get home to the kids,' Bearclaw declared

'Never met my kid yet; she'll be about a month old, and I haven't rotated back Stateside since before Normandy,' said Wiesniewski, sighing.

'Doesn't it bother you that you've not seen her yet?

'Yeah,' Wiesniewski declared. 'But I figure it's probably easier for her – if I get killed, she'll never know to miss me. Better for her that way.' He shivered theatrically. 'I dread to think what sort of father I'll make.' He had never really been able to imagine himself bringing up kids. It just didn't seem like him. But, now that he had one, he found that there were things he was looking forward to. Seeing his daughter's face when she opened her Christmas presents. Teaching her to read. Things like that. 'I ain't much of a role-model, am I?'

'Let her be the judge of that,' Bearclaw said.

Lewis was examining some aerial photographs of the site on the Eifel that he had agreed for a battleground with Leitz. The *Amadan* had been particularly happy with the choice, and for some reason that no longer cheered Lewis.

'Checking on the progress of the war?' a voice asked. It was a mild English voice, undoubtedly the Doctor's. Lewis looked up, surprised, to see the Doctor leaning on the doorjamb. Lewis was taken aback, and listened out for any word from the *Amadan*, but there was no hint of him in the room.

Lewis smiled in a rather sickly way. The last thing he wanted to do was face the Doctor alone. They weren't enemies, of course, but he had the sort of eyes that suggested he wouldn't approve of some of the things Lewis was up to. Many years navigating through funding committees to get appropriations for his work had taught Lewis that skill of judgement. It was more or less second nature by now.

The Doctor strode forward, and leaned on the desk. His brow furrowed as he peered deeper into Lewis's eyes. 'I see such light in there – so much brightness and love of life,' he said, in a surprised but encouraging tone. 'Why do you pretend otherwise?'

Lewis gathered himself quickly, telling himself that the Doctor was talking nonsense, trying to snow him. 'There's no pretence here. These are my… portfolio. Samples of my work.'

'Portfolio?'

'The battlefield is my canvas, Doctor. These photographs depict my work there. My art.'

'Oh, art?' The Doctor glanced down at the pictures. 'Not very good, is it? Violence, pain, injury. The sort of art a five-year-old could do. Where is he?'

Lewis was caught unawares by the sudden change of subject. 'What? Who?'

'I imagine for the sake of consistency that I ought to call him Oberon. I don't doubt for a moment that he's the one who's been leading you along your merry path since last October. None of the others would be so reckless.'

'Other what?' Lewis asked stiffly, feeling rather like a rabbit caught in the glare of a truck's headlights.

'The other people involved in this battle,' the Doctor said easily. 'You know, the ones who aren't human. The Sidhe.' The Doctor straightened, and walked around the room with a slow and deliberate pace. Lewis wasn't going to let it get under his skin, of course. Even when the Doctor insisted on stopping right in front of his slide projector.

The Doctor was still standing between it and the screen, blocking the projection. Lewis's protest died before it could make a sound, as he realised that, although the Doctor was standing right in front of the beam, the screen behind him was as bright and unblemished as it would be if he wasn't there.

The Doctor wasn't casting a shadow. None at all.

'I was beginning to wonder if you'd see it through your blindness,' the Doctor said.

'But… You…'

The Doctor smiled benevolently. 'Odd, isn't it? Still, it's just one of these things that separate sentient individuals – Kovacs has got no hair on his head, I've got no shadow...' The smile faded, just for a moment, and Lewis recoiled from the power that suddenly flashed in those pale-blue eyes. 'And you've got no qualms about dealing with the enemy. Either of them.'

Lewis knew he should be calling for guards to arrest the Doctor. He knew he should get rid of him as quickly as possible. Despite that, he found himself unable to make a sound. His conscience, perhaps, had finally outflanked him.

'I don't imagine,' the Doctor went on, 'that your superiors would necessarily believe me if I told them that you were making deals with the Sidhe. But they would believe any photos I showed them of you secretly meeting with *Sturmbannführer* Leitz of the SS. I doubt they'd like that very much either, would they?'

'No,' Lewis squeaked. He began to recover slightly. That the Doctor was still talking at all suggested that he had some sort of deal in mind. That gave Lewis some leverage. 'I don't expect you to believe that I'm not a traitor –'

'Oh, on the contrary. I don't doubt for a moment that you and Leitz are both trying to outbluff each other. I also know that when the war ends, the Allies will have a policy of keeping key Nazi scientists for themselves. Who am I to argue?' The Doctor sat on the corner of Lewis's desk. 'But the men in this town... They might like to argue. To a fairly permanent sort of result, I'd imagine.'

'Unless?' Lewis asked. If the Doctor was simply going to turn him in, he'd have done it, not waste time with all these threats. The bastard was too clever by half.

'Some of my equipment is lost. I need to retrieve it.'

'That's all?'

'That's all. I need a few men, a way out through the siege in safety, and preferably some kind of engineering vehicle. A bridging tank.'

Lewis could hardly believe his luck. The *Amadan* wanted rid of this guy, and so did Lewis. And now he came asking to go out to certain doom. Lewis had no reason to stop him, but he wasn't going to send out any equipment with them to be wasted. 'You can have Kovacs; he's experienced. I'll arrange for maps and intelligence reports. But no vehicles; we can't afford them.'

The Doctor considered this. 'All right.'

'Doctor,' Lewis said, quietly. 'The shadow... what happened?'

The Doctor's face softened a little. 'I'm not sure,' he confessed. 'One more aspect of a loss that's either already happened or is to come, I should think.' He advanced on Lewis. The projector light made his skin seem sickly and pale. 'You should look to your own losses, Lewis,' he said.

Sam and Galastel were out behind enemy lines again. Although Sam knew that she couldn't be seen by mortal men, at least not while with Galastel, she didn't feel any safer.

These men, after all, had killed her.

She knew that the best way to conquer her fears and troubles was to face them, but she hadn't expected to feel quite so calm about it. She was doing what she felt she had to, and that was that. She wasn't running away, or following another's lead: she had identified the problem and was getting on with it.

The problem in this case being why did the Schnee Eifel have a breach in reality. It hadn't taken long to persuade Galastel to take her out to do some detective work. Now she wished fervently she hadn't bothered.

Several months ago, on Earth in 1963, she had seen the horror caused by a flood of parasitic beings that fed invisibly on humans. They were harmless in themselves, but hideously overwhelming.

Sam tried not to throw up, as all the revulsion she had felt for the Beast before came rushing back. There was a tremendous glowing crack in the sky, running along the Eifel for miles. And churning in the midst of it all was a spawning ground, streamers of Bealsch energy signatures flowing up and down, dissipating to the sides as the unfortunate creatures were torn apart by dimensional shift beyond their capacity to withstand.

'The Beast,' she murmured.

'You know these creatures?' Galastel asked, surprised.

'Yes. Come on. Let's go and tell the Doctor.' Forgetting herself, she turned to start walking back to Bastogne, but then reality shifted around her and she was back in the hospital.

'Where did you go?' the Doctor asked, hurrying in.

'Yeah,' Fitz agreed, 'you'll turn back into a pumpkin if you keep going out this late. Without me, anyway.'

Sam didn't smile. 'I went out to see what was causing the tear between us and the Sidhe. It's what Galastel calls the Bealsch. The Beast. From 1963.'

'The Beast?' the Doctor echoed.

'Oh yes,' she said. Her hands were still shaking. 'Mind you, the tear's not exactly good for them either. Some kind of anomaly, it must be. They're attracted to it, and as they keep breeding, and more fall in, the crack widens – but the pressures at the edges kill them.'

'Good,' said Fitz. 'Can't we just kill them all and seal the thing up?'

The Doctor looked dismayed at him. 'Even if that *were* an acceptable solution, it wouldn't work. The rift would still be open.'

'Exactly,' said Sam. 'Somehow we have to close the rift. Those Bealsch trapped inside will be killed, but the others will be freed.'

'Yeah,' Fitz said sourly, turning away in disgust. 'And we all know what happens to them then. They get my mum killed.'

Chapter Nine
The Best Form of Defence

The night passed slowly, and Fitz was on the prowl looking for some breakfast when he ran into Garcia in the hotel's kitchen. 'Are you another one of them?' Garcia asked.

'One of what?'

'That's what I'd like to know.' Fitz saw that there were a couple of empty red-wine bottles on the worktop. Uh-huh. That explained a lot.

'Sam, it seems, has been... hybridised. By some creatures that aren't part of God's scheme.' Garcia shook his head. 'And as for the Doctor... I was brought up to believe that God created man on Earth in his own image. The Doctor has the same image but it seems he isn't from this Earth... And as for where these Sidhe fit in... What are they? Angels or demons?'

Fitz had never been much of a churchgoer. He'd gone with his mum as a kid, but the services were just on too early on a Sunday – he always enjoyed a good kip after a Saturday night out. 'I dunno either. But... Earth's just another word for dirt, soil... Maybe God created all of it, on every planet.' He had no idea whether that would make any sense to Garcia. He would've told the guy to stop being such a boring sod, but the Doctor's influence seemed to be rubbing off on him. He didn't want to offend someone whose help they would need to get the TARDIS back.

'Good answer,' Garcia murmured. 'Doesn't explain the Sidhe, though.'

Fitz shrugged. 'Maybe they're just people too.'

Garcia smiled. 'Thanks.' He stood, and stretched. 'I'd better go. I think the Doctor needs me to help out.'

Fitz watched him go. 'That was easy... He *must* have been pissed.'

* * *

Jeff Kovacs was sitting alone in the brothel. The local girls were too sensible to come to work while under fire, so the only thing he'd been caressing over the past night was a bottle of Jack he'd been keeping under the bar for times like this.

At least his arrangement with the locals meant he could get some sleep here while off duty. Even if that was all he was getting, it was still an improvement on being bunked with a dozen other guys from the division in some stinking hole. How they envied him… Only the free handouts kept them in line. Still, he guessed accommodation was a big deal to them. The furniture here might be a bit rococo and dusty, but at least it was soft and reasonably private.

He knew that the rest of the men appreciated his absence, anyway. Their spirits would be more buoyed by his trusting them to look after themselves for a night without his breathing down their necks all the time. Sometimes you had to cut them some slack.

He was almost dozing off on the reclining chair in the Madam's little office, when he heard someone come in the front door. He could tell it was a GI from the sound of the boots; whoever it was was going to be severely disappointed. Sighing, Kovacs stood and went out into the bar area. 'Oh, it's you.'

'I'm afraid so,' Captain Garcia agreed. 'Nice little billet.'

'It has its moments. You come to make good on our little deal?'

Garcia nodded. 'A few of us have a little excursion planned, and we need an experienced combat man to get us through the lines.'

'Yeah?' Kovacs was immediately interested. Although some reinforcements had arrived, he didn't much like being stuck in a city under siege.

'Up to the Schnee Eifel.'

Kovacs almost laughed at the absurdity of it. 'What, just walk through the German lines into their new territory, and waltz back up the Skyline Drive? How many units are we talking about here?'

'One. You, me, the Doctor and his aide, Bearclaw and Wiesniewski.'

'Six of us? What the hell do you think six of us can do up there, even if you could get there in one piece?'

'Solve a problem.'

'Try cutting your wrists – it'll solve your problems just as well and a hell of a lot faster.' He made to leave, rather than listen to any more of this nonsense.

Garcia caught the door with his heel, and slammed it before Kovacs could leave. 'I don't think you're quite following me, Sergeant,' he said. 'You owe me a favour, and I'm here to collect.'

Kovacs blinked. 'A favour….?'

'You remember what we discussed about your… entrepreneurial activities? I let it slide, in return for some recompense yet to be decided. Well I'm calling it in.'

'That's your idea of payback? To lead five men Christ knows where behind the lines? Haven't you noticed we're under siege?'

'That's my choice. Look, we got two civilians, two walking wounded, and a medic – me. We need a good combat vet, and since you're conveniently familiar with the people in question and know some of what's going on…'

'As well as owing you a favour,' Kovacs finished.

'That's right.'

'Great plan,' Kovacs agreed finally. 'Suicidally reckless, but predictable. When do we go?'

'Dawn, like the Doctor said. What will you need?'

'Need?' Kovacs sighed. 'I need a bottle of Jack, I need a night in a real bed, and I need to get laid before I forget what it feels like. But, if you're offering supplies for this mission of yours, I want six Thompsons, two boxes of hand grenades, enough rations and ammo to last a field party two or three days… And a sit-rep about Noville.'

'You ain't gonna be selling this stuff, are you?'

'No, I ain't selling them,' Kovacs said. 'Smart ass,' he added under his breath.

Sam was marking the details of the rift on an intelligence photo of the Eifel. 'Closing the rift will stop the damage to the world we were in?'

'Yes,' Galastel confirmed. 'It's unfortunate that our home is in such a vulnerable place.'

'Your home is here? But I thought you were nomadic…'

'We are.'

'Then you have many homes?'

'Just one, but it is always here.'

'Then you take it with you?' Elven tortoises; there was an image for you.

'No.' He sighed, and Sam got the impression that he was feeling the way she might feel if she tried to explain the theory of relativity to a goldfish. He pointed at the ground between his feet. 'This is here.'

'OK…'

He walked a couple of yards, then did the same thing. 'This is here.'

'Ah,' Sam understood. 'Wherever you are is "here".'

'All is here, Samanthajones. There is only one here. Between the first ato-second after the world began, and the last ato-second before its final electron fades. That is Here.'

Kovacs had finally joined them, and been informed of their rather strange allies. To Garcia's immense surprise, it didn't faze him at all. 'Elves,' he had muttered. 'What the hell else will they think of?' And the Doctor had said Kovacs ought to be sober for this. Yeah, right.

He went over to Galastel. 'I don't know if you are who you claim to be, and I don't want to know. All I want to know is what's in it for me.'

Galastel seemed disappointed. 'How human.' He tossed a pouch, which jingled when Kovacs caught it. 'Pure gold. And ten more bags when we are done.'

Kovacs weighed it thoughtfully, and tossed it back. 'I'm not a mercenary. Not in that way. These guys tell me you can take people anywhere instantly.'

'That is so.'

'Can you take me to the front line in the Pacific theatre?'

'You wish to go to another battlefield?' Kovacs nodded. 'That can be done. May I ask why?'

'You may, but you'd be wasting your breath.' Kovacs turned back to the others. 'OK, I'm in.'

'To business,' the Doctor said loudly. 'To close the rift I'm going to need some equipment from my transport, my TARDIS. What we really need to get the TARDIS out of the river is something with a lot of horsepower. A bridging tank, or something of that sort.'

Kovacs shook his head. 'You heard what Lewis said: no dice. He isn't going to even ask McAuliffe, and even if he did, McAuliffe can't spare any. No, you're gonna have to rely on something else…'

Wiesniewski scratched his head. 'A shame nobody's got some tanks to spare.'

'Except the Germans,' Fitz said drily. Everyone looked at him.

'What did you say?' the Doctor asked.

'I said "except the Germans". They've got enough Panzers out there to –' Fitz's eyes widened as he began to suspect what the Doctor was thinking. 'Now wait a minute, I didn't mean –'

'Why, that's perfect!' the Doctor gave a broad grin. 'The ideal solution: plenty of horsepower. It wouldn't interfere with the defence of Bastogne, and –' He broke off and started rooting through the maps and charts, tossing rejected ones aside. He clapped a hand on Wiesniewski's shoulder. 'We'd want to go northeast… Where can we find some suitable German tanks?'

'Just about anywhere,' Wiesniewski said. He put his finger to a spot on the map. 'But if we're leaving to the northeast there's some heavy action going down in Noville. Panthers, Tigers, assault guns, you name it.'

Kovacs shook his head wonderingly. 'Jesus Christ, you aren't seriously listening to this crap? This guy's gonna get you all killed!' He snatched the map back from under Wiesniewski's fingertip.

Bearclaw shrugged. 'What do you think we should do? Wait until the SS get here and shoot us all in another field? It looks to me like we're getting killed anyway, so we might as well at least choose how we want to go.'

Kovacs gave him a 'watch it' look. 'All I'm saying is that none of you have to go anywhere, especially not to get involved with some freakin' elves or pixies, or whatever the hell line of crap this guy's been spinning you.'

'Listen to me,' the Doctor said sharply. 'The Sidhe are an intelligent and dangerous energy-based life form with whom you share your planet. Deal with it.' He turned away, angrily. 'Besides, you agreed.'

'Yeah, I agreed to go, but that doesn't mean I think these guys should be risking their skins as well.'

'We all feel the same way,' Bearclaw pointed out.

'Believe me,' the Doctor said, 'I'd be much happier if this wasn't going to endanger any of you.' He rolled up the map. 'Sam, you and Galastel liaise with Titania if necessary, and keep a watch on the Eifel for German activity. The two of you should be able to go unhindered if you're out of phase. The rest of us have to get to Noville on foot.'

Noville was a smaller provincial town outside Bastogne.

Galastel and some other Sidhe had helped out by making the Doctor's party unnoticed by the Germans, but that stopped when they reached the centre of town.

'We can go no further,' Galastel said. 'There's too much iron here. It would make us vulnerable.'

'That iron is sadly necessary,' the Doctor replied. 'You and Sam get up to the Eifel. We'll join you soon enough.'

'Fare you well, Evergreen Man,' Galastel said with a nod. He vanished.

The Doctor and his five human companions were now skulking at a junction just outside Noville's cobbled market area. The Doctor peered around the corner. There were three tanks flanking the roadblock. All of them had sloping front armour quite unlike the usual German tanks, and two of them were larger, with oversized turrets. 'A Panther and two King Tigers,' the Doctor said. 'We could take one of those.'

'The Panther,' Bearclaw suggested. 'It's faster and more reliable.'

Kovacs looked at the pair of them. 'Are you out of your goddam mind? There are three of them, remember. And it ain't just the crew of the one we want, either. How the hell are we supposed to off the two King Tigers, when we got no air support and no armour?'

Fitz spoke up. 'We've enough grenades to –'

Kovacs rounded on him. 'Hey, who died and made you Ike? None of us are John freakin' Wayne. If you're about to suggest we climb up and drop a couple of pineapples through the commander's hatch, I'll shoot you in the head right now. This is the real world we're dealing with here.'

Fitz had been about to suggest exactly that, but suddenly felt about two inches tall. He didn't bother to answer.

'I suppose you're gonna tell me you've got some crazy idea how to pull this off?' Kovacs asked the Doctor.

'Haven't the foggiest,' the Doctor admitted cheerily. 'But I'm sure I will have by the time we get down there.'

Bearclaw held Fitz back a moment as they began to spread out. 'Don't let the sarge get you down. I think it's his subtle way of telling us he loves us.'

'More like his subtle way of telling us he wants to be thought of as a hard man,' Fitz retorted. 'Like he's the only one who's been screwed up by this bloody war,' he added with feeling.

Bearclaw shook his head. 'He's pissed because he *really* wants to kill Japs, not Krauts. Kovacs was a weapons instructor until half his family got caught in the bombing of Pearl. Then he volunteered for combat duty, hoping he'd be sent to the Pacific. Instead they sent him to North Africa, then Sicily… Eventually he ended up here.'

Fitz sighed. 'And eventually a hard man like him will only end up six feet under.'

This hadn't been quite what the Doctor had in mind, but it was too late for second thoughts now. He just hoped the others had got to the positions they had discussed, as the Panther advanced along the road. The trio had split up, the two King Tigers taking other roads on whatever patrol route they were following.

With a deep breath, and reminding himself that this kind of thing almost always worked, the Doctor stepped out into the middle of the road in front of the Panther. 'Excuse me,' he called out. 'I'm an Allied spy. Could I have your attention for a moment?'

Even through the armour, the Doctor could hear the exclamations of the crew. He hurled himself forward and under the tank, just as the machine gun in its nose opened fire. He crawled frantically along the length of the tank's underside as its engine roared back into life. If the driver thought to turn the tank on its axis, the Doctor would be smeared across the road.

The driver evidently didn't think. In a couple of seconds, the

Doctor was through, and the Panther had stopped right where he wanted it.

Wiesniewski leapt from a broken wall, landing on the narrow stretch of steel deck in front of the Panther's turret.

Lying flat across the radio operator's hatch, he stretched an arm down to shove his .45 in through the driver's vision slit, and pulled the trigger as fast as he could. Something warm and wet splashed on to his hand, and Wiesniewski could feel the hatch under his midriff try to open. The crewman inside had Wiesniewski's weight to deal with, and he was not for moving. There was a clang from above as the tank's commander opened his hatch to see what was going on. Bearclaw, clinging to the roof of a clock tower on the corner of the marketplace, worked the bolt of his rifle. The Panther's commander was so large in his scope that he could make out the *Untersturmführer*'s rank pips on his collar.

The man had clambered out of the hatch, and was moving on all fours across the roof of the turret, with pistol in hand. Bearclaw could also see that Wiesniewski was stuck under the main gun.

He couldn't tell whether this tank commander was one of those who had taken part in the massacre, but to be honest he didn't give a damn. All he did care about was that he had one of the bastards in his sights, and none of them were innocent.

He caught himself in time, almost firing at the wrong moment. He was mad at the Krauts, yes, but he knew that if he really wanted to hurt them he had to do it right. He had a job to do. It'd hurt them well enough.

Wiesniewski tried to turn, but didn't want to either stick his head to the left of the main gun, or drop over the bulge below the radio man's hatch, since there were machine guns fixed in both positions.

He managed to twist his head around just far enough to see the tank's commander appear above the gun mantelet. Wiesniewski knew he could never bring his pistol to bear on the officer from here.

The officer's forehead exploded just the briefest instant before the shot rang out. His body, still wearing a surprised expression on the remains of its face, slumped and then tumbled down the front of the tank, crashing painfully into Wiesniewski on the way. The impact knocked him free, and they both fell into the wet road. The radio man didn't fire, and Wiesniewski figured that he must have held back for fear of hitting his own superior.

Kovacs now emerged from hiding in a doorway, and clambered up on to the Panther. One man, then another, emerged from the hatch, and Kovacs shot them both. That left one man, whom Wiesniewski shot through the radio man's hatch. He wasn't comfortable with this way of doing things – there was no guarantee that the tank crewmen were even personally armed. But the world was in enough trouble as it was, without letting Lewis, Leitz or Oberon ruin it further.

Wiesniewski had done what he had to do, and that was enough.

The interior of the Panther stank of cordite, oil and unwashed men. It also smelled like someone had crapped themselves, but Fitz didn't want to bring that up in case it turned out to be himself.

Fitz concentrated on bracing himself so as not to let his head bounce into any solid metal objects – a tricky proposition, considering how many boxes, turnwheels and other obstacles filled the interior of the tank. He wasn't sure why he had expected the inside to be as smooth as the outside, but he had.

The Doctor ducked down and squeezed himself into the driver's seat.

'Bit violent for you, all this, isn't it, Doctor?' Fitz asked mildly.

The Doctor stared at him. 'Yes,' he concluded, after a while. 'I suppose I'm looking at the greater picture… and the devil's in the detail. You know what we do is necessary.'

There was a coldness in the Doctor's tone that made Fitz uneasy. Do I? Fitz wondered. You don't sound too sure yourself.

As the Doctor brought the engine to life he looked round at the others. 'Unless one of you knows how…?' Everyone shook their head.

Kovacs propped himself up on the commander's seat with a sigh. 'OK, Doc, all yours. Bearclaw, you're gunner. Kreiner, you're loader –'

'What?'

'Put the shells in the gun,' Kovacs said, with exaggerated patience. 'Pointed end to the front.' Who needed to waste taxpayers' money on weeks of training? Being scared out your wits made anyone a great student. 'Wiesniewski, take that machine gun beside the Doctor.' It didn't seem to bother Wiesniewski that he was being ordered around by a subordinate. Fitz supposed that experience must outrank rank.

'What about me?' Garcia asked.

'Keep an eye out behind us, just in case.'

The radio buzzed suddenly. Everybody looked at it, reluctant to touch the machine. What would be worse: remaining silent, or being recognised as imposters?

It kept buzzing insistently. Fitz couldn't stand it any longer, and reached out – and the noise stopped, the instant before he could lift the handset.

'Get us out of here, Doc,' Kovacs instructed. 'I think we're going to have company soon.'

* * *

187

Without warning, the wall of one terraced house burst outward in a cloud of dust and bricks. A leviathan lumbered unsteadily out of the destruction, like a chick tumbling from an eggshell. It had a sloping front like the Panther they were in, but was much larger. Steel skirts protected the tops of the wheels and tracks, while the vaguely diamond-shaped turret narrowed to a small square at the front. The fiddly details were lost to Fitz, because his eyes had developed a horrible fixation on the biggest gun he had ever seen.

It was stretched out from that small square front of the turret, and seemed to be pointed right between his eyes.

'Sweet Jesus,' he breathed, in a very small voice in case it heard him.

'Yeah,' Kovacs agreed. 'King Tiger. We're screwed.' He grinned down at Fitz and Bearclaw. 'Armour-piercing; lock and load.'

'I thought you said we were screwed.'

'If someone's gonna kill me, I want the bastard to feel it was more trouble than it was worth, not enjoy it. You got a problem with that?'

'Only with the getting-killed part,' Fitz said plaintively.

'What's the matter – you wanna live for ever?'

'I dunno yet,' said Fitz. 'Ask me again in five hundred years.'

Kovacs laughed; the first genuine sound of mirth Fitz had heard him make. 'Oh hell. We better stay alive! Guy as smart as that just has to be saved.'

With that, Bearclaw fired the Panther's gun.

The shell hit the King Tiger square on, and the blast momentarily blotted out all view of it. 'Yippee-ki-a...' Fitz's elated voice died as the smoke and dust cleared. Though a few flames licked ineffectually at its hull, the King Tiger shook itself free of the remains of the wall, and turned its turret to aim at them.

The Doctor pushed and pulled at the steering levers frantically. 'I hate driving stick-shift...' The Panther lurched and turned, then darted backwards just as the King Tiger fired. There was a bone-shaking crash like being in an earthquake, and Fitz thought the ceiling was falling in, though the shell explosion came from somewhere off to the right. He realised the Doctor had reversed into a building, chunks of which had collapsed on top of them.

'Jesus! How do we kill it?' Fitz gasped.

'Even a Tiger has its Achilles' heel –' the Doctor began.

'But,' Kovacs interrupted, 'in this case its his Achilles' ass. If we want to be the ones who get out of this neighbourhood in one piece, we gotta get behind him and hit him right in the butt.'

Another shell burst in the place where the Panther had been, as the Doctor sent it careening through a terraced house.

The King Tiger spun around with a strange and massive agility, and rumbled down the next street.

'Where are we going?' Garcia asked.

'To find the second King Tiger,' the Doctor said cheerily. Fitz got the terrifying impression that he was actually enjoying this in some way.

'The other one?' everybody in the Panther exclaimed.

'Trust me. And hope I judge this right.'

The Panther slammed through another wall, cutting across the path of a King Tiger. The first King Tiger was coming up behind that, and its gunner fired instinctively.

The Doctor, however, had judged things perfectly. The shot hit the rear of the second King Tiger, which was jerked sideways by the blast. In flames, and its crew not knowing why they were being fired upon, it returned fire. Bearclaw joined in, and both tanks pounded the first King Tiger.

The front armour was strong enough to not breach, and the Doctor called 'The steeple!' Fitz saw that the King Tiger they were fighting had backed into the corner of a small chapel.

Bearclaw fired at the building's steeple. Fitz almost burned his hand against the ejecting shell case as he loaded a second round almost before the first had time to hit its target.

Both shells burst in rapid succession against the base of the steeple. Smoke and dust billowed around it like exhaust from a rocket launch, but the steeple toppled sideways rather than rising into the air. It slumped down across the King Tiger with an indescribable noise, and Fitz wondered if the tank could have survived even that.

Out of the viewing port, he could see the visible part of the enemy tank's turret attempt to turn its gun on them. There was too much stone resting on the front deck, and the barrel couldn't shift it aside. The King Tiger's engine revved, and it started trying to pull itself free of the collapsed steeple.

'Try not to kill them,' the Doctor suggested, with something unspoken belying the softness of his tone.

'Not kill them?' Kovacs asked incredulously. 'They're Nazis in that tank!'

'Aim for the tracks.'

Bearclaw fired, the shell exploding against the King Tiger's frontmost wheel, and sending smashed track links flying away. He fired again, this time clipping the track on the other side. 'They ain't going nowhere now.'

'Good.' The Doctor gunned the Panther's engine, and reversed out of the square. Through the viewport, Fitz could see the driver's hatch of the King Tiger – the only hatch still free – open, and men start to emerge. They looked very unsteady on their feet, and it was obvious that they were in no condition to fight any more.

The second King Tiger was now burning merrily, and men were jumping from that too. Fitz would have given a bottle of single-malt Scotch to eavesdrop on what the two crews would have to say to each other.

Once they were outside of town, Fitz managed to contort

himself enough to tap the Doctor on the shoulder. 'Stop the tank.'

The Doctor did so, and Fitz levered himself out and dropped to the roadside. He grabbed a handful of mud, and climbed back up to smear it on the '4' until there appeared to be just a '1' left. Then he climbed over to repeat the action on the other side of the turret.

'What are you doing?' Garcia asked.

Fitz tapped the side of his long nose. 'Unless the crew of that other tank were blind, they probably noticed our number. That means they'll be telling the first other Germans they meet that tank 421 is in enemy hands. This way anyone looking for us will hopefully see the number as 121, and ignore us.'

Lewis couldn't believe the strength in Oberon's arms as the *Amadan* threw him across the room. The Sidhe might be as light as a feather, but he was as strong as an ox. 'You fool!' Oberon snarled. 'Why did you not do as I ordered? Why did you not kill the Doctor?'

'I have done,' Lewis insisted, strangely forgetting to be angry. He knew he should be for some reason, and knew that Oberon must be interfering with his perceptions again, but somehow couldn't put the two things together. 'Just in a roundabout sort of way.'

'Roundabout? So circular it comes back to not having happened.' Oberon perched on the corner of Lewis's desk, and helped him up. 'What exactly did you do?'

'The Doctor wanted to walk headlong into enemy lines. I gave him a map to lead him into a German ambush.' He was quite proud of his ingenuity.

'Idiot. The Evergreen Man has walked the paths through a thousand wars. He will clear this one unscathed.' Oberon put on a mock-thoughtful air. 'Still, perhaps it doesn't matter. After all, it's only your plans he will ruin.'

That drew Lewis's attention. 'What do you mean, my plans?'

'The Evergreen Man is, as we speak, on his way to close the rift that will make the passage of your new war machines into our realm easier. If he closes it, you will have to start again, and may never succeed.'

Lewis stared at him. 'We have to go there and stop him.'

'*You* have to,' Oberon corrected him.

'You're not coming?'

'Eventually. But first I must know how he intends to close the rift.'

'How will you find that out?'

Oberon smiled. 'I'll ask those who know.'

Chapter Ten
No Friendlies

Fitz and Kovacs sat on the ruined bridge, watching as the others attached some steel cables from the Panther to the TARDIS.

Kovacs had found a hip-flask of Jack Daniels in his gear, and Fitz had found a new streak of laziness. Well, he was knackered after all the running about he'd been doing.

'Shouldn't you be down there helping them?' Kovacs asked.

'Both of us should, but I guess we have the same problem.'

'Which is?'

'We're too smart to waste our efforts on manual labour.'

Kovacs grinned. 'A man after my own heart. Best way to live. Of course out here...'

'You think about dying?' Fitz shrugged. 'I suppose that's a stupid question; out here if you thought about that all the time you'd go nuts.'

'Hell, half of us are nuts anyway.' Kovacs gave a cynical and distant smile. 'Actually I got my death all planned already: of exhaustion in a whorehouse, aged about a hundred and fifty. That saves me from having to worry about it.' He took a slug of Jack, and passed the bottle back to Fitz.

'It must be bloody handy to not worry...'

'It probably is, but I wouldn't know.' He nodded towards the others. 'I still got these assholes to worry about. I gotta get them all back home in one piece.'

'So they can kill Japs?' It had slipped out before Fitz even realised he was going to say. How much of the booze had he had, anyway?

Kovacs's face darkened, but then he shrugged off the mood. 'So they can get back to their lives.' The expression that masked him slipped, and he looked both haunted and driven.

'I wanna kill Japs, but that don't mean I want to put their lives on the line as well. Already lost enough people to them, so why risk anyone else but myself?'

'You can't win a war on your own.'

Kovacs was silent for quite a long time. 'Depends what war you're fighting. The one outside, or the one within.'

Sam stood on the deck of the ship that had taken her across the lake earlier, when she had first visited the Sidhe levels – at least, she assumed it was the same ship; she could see one or two thoroughly identical ones across the waters. She got the uncomfortable feeling that if she looked closely enough at them she'd see herself, either on the previous journey or this one.

Galastel leaned on the wooden rail beside her, as the crew lowered a stone anchor into the water. It didn't splash, and didn't create any ripples at all. 'A fine day,' Galastel said.

'It always seems to be fine here.'

'Naturally. We wish it to be so, and so it is.' He toyed with the bodkin that hung at his belt. It was far too small to be called a knife, let alone a sword, though he wore it as one.

'Are you sure your people want to do this?'

'Samanthajones… The Queen says we are to protect you and your friends from harm. We cannot do that if we are not there.'

'But this isn't your fight.'

'No,' Galastel agreed, 'but the Rift is our problem. It merely allows mortals to move, but it kills us. And although the battle is not ours, one of us is involved. We must… moderate the effects he would cause.'

'But not just stop him doing anything?'

'The Queen is risking her position just by allowing this. If it became felt that allowing our presence here was in some way an act towards holding Oberon responsible for his actions… She would have to be replaced.'

'There's another Queen?'

'No. There's only one Queen. But she has many aspects,' he added cryptically. 'In any case, we are where we have to be.' Galastel nodded to a small knot of Sidhe gathered amidships, and sang to them. At once, they began to vault over the side, dropping into the blue below.

Sam heard no splashes, and no water seemed to be displaced, yet they vanished smoothly into it. She didn't relish the idea of trying it herself. Especially given that the view through the water looked more like the view from a plane at high altitude.

'Don't fear,' Galastel said. He took her hand and led her to step on to the rail. 'This is the quickest way. No harm will come to you, while I carry you.'

He wasn't holding her, so Sam assumed his presence was enough to 'carry' her. She must be mad, trusting him, she thought. By the time that had gone through her mind, they had both stepped forward.

There was a sudden coolness, and then they were in the forest, standing on the roadside under the invisible glow of the Rift.

Garcia put a hand on the rear edge of the turret to steady himself as the Panther rumbled back up the riverbank. He was curious to see what vehicle the Doctor wanted to recover.

To his astonishment, it wasn't a vehicle at all, but a police telephone booth similar to the kind he'd seen in London before his unit was sent to the front. It gouged a large furrow in the snow and mud as the Panther dragged it on to dry land.

'This is it?' he asked the Doctor, who was standing to one side, rubbing his hands with glee.

'This is it. Just an old Type Forty TARDIS, but she's home to me.'

Garcia, not for the first time, wondered if the Doctor was

entirely sane, especially when he unlocked the police box and stepped inside, shutting the door behind him.

Kovacs jumped down from the Panther's turret and regarded this… TARDIS dubiously. He turned to Fitz. 'OK, we've got your equipment – whatever the hell you call that – but how do we transport it to the Eifel? I mean, it's a good fifteen or twenty miles south, through the German columns.'

'We are in a German tank,' Fitz pointed out. 'So long as we keep low in the hatches, nobody can tell we're not its crew.'

Kovacs shook his head. 'We'd have to get out at some point – fuelling, checkpoints, that sort of thing. And then there's the language barrier…'

'That's not a problem,' Fitz said, hesitantly. 'I can talk German.' At least, they'll hear it as that, he thought.

There was a sudden rushing sound. The GIs looked panicked, but Fitz recognised the sound of the TARDIS's drives. He turned to see what the Doctor was up to, but instead of the TARDIS on the riverbank he found himself looking at the wall of the little garage space that used to house the Doctor's VW Beetle before it was melted down. The Panther's sides were jammed solid against the walls.

As the soldiers looked around in awe and bafflement, the Doctor hurried into the room.

'Getting through the German lines to the Eifel isn't going to be a problem,' he grinned.

'What the hell's happened?' Kovacs demanded, looking half terrified and half in wonderment. He touched the wall suspiciously, as if he was afraid his hand would go right through it.

'You know that police box we just pulled out of the river?' the Doctor asked mildly.

'Yeah…'

'Well, now we're inside it.'

Kovacs looked momentarily fazed, for once. 'Inside? But this place is huge!'

'Yes. The interior dimensions transcend the outer one,' the Doctor explained.

'I may be just a dumb old grunt,' Kovacs said slowly, 'but you're not going to tell me any human beings made this. Not in a million years.'

'You're right, I'm not going to tell you that, because if I did I'd be lying.' The Doctor rubbed his hands together. 'I don't know about you, but I could use a bite to eat. "An army marches on its stomach," and all that.'

'Do we have time for R and R?' Bearclaw asked dubiously.

'We want to be at our best, don't we?' The Doctor rubbed his stomach. 'Besides we can have our council of war at the same time.'

Oberon watched their efforts to recover the Doctor's TARDIS with interest. He knew of the Evergreen Man's mode of transport, of course.

It was always possible the Doctor merely wanted to recover it to leave later, but Oberon doubted that was all there was to it. If the Doctor planned to interfere with Oberon's own interference, then perhaps this machine was a part of it.

Unlike the Sidhe, other races needed to use mechanisms to walk through time, since they had no natural affinity with it. Perhaps, then, the Doctor sought something in the past or future?

They were all gathered in the kitchen Fitz had found earlier. The soldiers were tucking in to unhealthy fry-ups, and even the Doctor seemed to be not immune to the charms of greasy cooking. Fitz remembered not to offer Sam a bacon buttie when she came in, though.

'Titania's got a contingency plan, so at least the few of us here won't be alone,' Sam said.

'Good,' the Doctor said, finishing off his lunch and licking the grease off his fingers. 'Down to business. We have to find some way of repairing the damage the Beast and the war have caused...'

'Wouldn't destroying this Beast do the same job?' said Fitz.

'We can't.'

'Right, sure we can't.' Fitz grumbled. 'I know. They're like ants or termites, just doing what they do. But... if you get termites in your house you call in the exterminators.'

The Doctor shook his head. 'You know we can't interfere with our own subjective past.' His voice softened. 'No matter how wonderful it would be to save your mother. The Beast leave of their own accord. I can't risk disrupting causality...'

'What's the hurry here, anyway?' Kovacs asked.

'Three things,' the Doctor explained. 'First the dimensions have to be separated to stop damage being caused to both levels of reality. Second, this colony of the Beast are trapped and just making things worse. Third, the *Amadan na Briona* has been helping Lewis build some rather special tanks, which could easily be here by dusk.'

'The ones I saw? Some kind of camouflage field, making tanks invisible?'

The Doctor shook his head. 'I should think it goes rather further than that. I imagine that what Lewis wants, and has been given, is a way to move those tanks out of phase altogether, so they can move in a completely different level of reality before phasing back into this one.'

'Like the Sidhe?' asked Garcia.

'Exactly.'

'Then... The tanks would be travelling through the Sidhe's realm,' Bearclaw concluded.

The Doctor nodded. 'Yes. And the build-up of forces here is already causing problems in the Sidhe world.'

'Because iron is dangerous to them –' began Garcia.

'Yes, yes, exactly,' said the Doctor, apparently losing patience. 'The damage an engagement of any size out of phase would cause could be incalculable. The Sidhe would, of course blame humanity.'

'But it's the *Amadan*'s fault!' protested Fitz.

The Doctor looked at Fitz. 'The *Amadan* is paving the way. Chaos is his thing. It's still the human war that will be blamed for the catastrophe. There could be open aggression between man and Sidhe.'

'But they're just elves – primitives. What could they do against human technology?' Garcia asked.

'Primitive?' the Doctor echoed. 'The Sidhe? Oh, they're "primitive" all right: they like music and arts, they have royal courts, they live and love… Primitive!' He shook his head. 'They have a sufficiently advanced knowledge of quantum homeostatics to re-edit Sam's biodata. They can phase themselves in and out of your perceptions. They can go anywhere on Earth, no matter the walls or security. They can walk through time and interact with your past, change your attitudes and experiences…. And if the worse comes to the worst they're experts at poison and assassination. Those are your "primitives".'

'And they don't like iron.'

'No… Electromagnetism-based lifestyles come at a price.'

'Oh, every time,' deadpanned Fitz.

Garcia frowned. 'So how do they do all that?'

'Magic,' the Doctor said simply.

'Don't insult my intelligence, Doctor. This is the twentieth century; surely you don't believe in magic.'

'Well, let me put it this way: I can call it "magic", with all the nice feelings of wonderment that that word inspires; or I can waste your time with half an hour of technobabble that you could never possibly understand a word of anyway. Which would you prefer?'

Garcia thought about this, then nodded lamely. 'OK, magic it is.'

'Good, because I don't think we've got half an hour to waste. I know how we can close the breach.' That got everyone's attention. 'We need the TARDIS's relative dimensional stabiliser, and a large metallic mass to act as a focus. Both the rift and its cause are electromagnetic in nature, so, if we can realign the dimensions on to a... well, in effect a circuit-breaker, the rift should implode into the metallic mass, and seal up.'

'That'll stop Lewis's tanks?'

'Yes, I think so. It's possible to phase them all the way into the Sidhe range of realities on their own, but it would take far more electrical power than they can possibly generate independently. So he must be relying on the Rift to ease the way through.'

'Can't the TARDIS transfer us into the levels the Sidhe originate from?' Fitz asked.

The Doctor shook his head. 'It could support their environment inside, but trying to exist inside and out in all the levels would be beyond its design limits. If I tried to stretch the TARDIS that far, she'd almost certainly lose dimensional cohesion.'

'And that would be bad?'

'Profoundly,' the Doctor confirmed. 'Imagine all of your senses each being trapped in a different room, and your body having been simultaneously hanged, drawn and quartered.'

'I'll try not to, if you don't mind.' Fitz knew he inevitably would now, probably when he least wanted to, like while preparing breakfast. He wondered if the Doctor knew what effect his throwaway lines could have on people.

Sam tapped her foot on the floor. 'Wait a minute,' she said. 'All you need is a large metallic mass, right?'

'Yes.'

'So why not just use *this* tank? It'd be better than sending it back to the war, and I don't think much of it as a souvenir, either.'

'Fifty tons of steel isn't enough.'

'Then why didn't you take a bigger tank?'

'Like a King Tiger, you mean?' he asked. Sam nodded. The Doctor shook his head. 'Seventy tons of steel isn't enough either.'

This was exasperating, even for Fitz. 'Then how much do we need?'

The Doctor frowned, and started counting on his fingers. 'About two thousand tons ought to do it,' he said casually.

'Two thousand? That's, what...?' Fitz did some quick mental calculations of his own. 'Forty tanks! How are we supposed to get forty tanks together?'

'Well,' the Doctor admitted, 'there are a couple of hundred of them knocking around at the moment, but I doubt we could gather so many in one place. Besides, we've then got to get them into the rift.'

'Then where...?'

'From Lewis.'

'But you said using tanks isn't practicable. And he'd never agree to it. So how do you expect to get any equipment out of him?'

The Doctor merely smiled. 'That would be telling.'

The TARDIS had materialised under the Rift, at a road junction atop the Skyline Drive. Kovacs emerged first, and couldn't help glancing up. He knew the Rift the Doctor had told them about must be right here, but he saw no sign of it. Other, perhaps, than a few stray shadows in the woods on either side of the road.

Garcia, Wiesniewski, and Bearclaw followed him out, the Doctor bringing up the rear. 'Remember. The Sidhe will meet you here at any moment. I need you to prevent either Lewis or Leitz from getting tanks into the Rift. Preferably through persuasion, but I doubt that'll really be practical.'

'You know what they say, Doc,' Kovacs replied coolly, 'you can get further with a kind word and a two by four, than you can with a kind word.'

'Well, try the kind words first. I'd better get going; I have something to collect. Good luck, and stay in one piece.'

'You too,' Garcia told him firmly.

The Doctor merely smiled, and vanished back inside the TARDIS, which faded into thin air with a strange, rasping, groaning sound. 'I wonder if he's really going to fix things,' Kovacs muttered, 'or just showing more sense than us.'

'He'll keep his word,' Bearclaw told him in no uncertain terms.

'Yeah, if you say so.' Totally unconvinced, Kovacs leaned against a tree and rubbed his eyes with one hand. 'What the hell do you think you're doing, Jeff?' he asked himself softly. 'Since when did you put your life on the line for someone who isn't one of your boys?' He sighed. 'Since they got to thinking that a Hero was more than just a New York sandwich…'

He could really use a drink right now, but if he got drunk now he probably wouldn't be sober before the Doctor and Garcia decided it was time to move out. And Kovacs had to get them all home safely. Only then could he go to the Pacific theatre and kill Japs.

He opened his eyes again after a moment. 'OK. Where are these Sidhe who were supposed to meet us?'

'Right here,' a cheerful female voice said, stepping out of the trees. Shadows shifted behind her, and Kovacs got the impression of well-hidden men in there. Not wearing camouflaged gear, just very hard to see.

Easier to recognise was the speaker, though Kovacs still

doubted his eyesight. It was Sam. 'Wait a minute. How the hell did you get back here? We just left you in there.' He pointed to where the TARDIS had been, recalling too late that it was no longer there.

'Where?'

'In the TARDIS,' Bearclaw said, sounding as baffled as Kovacs felt. 'You joined us back at the bridge.'

Sam shook her head, looking worried. 'No,' she said. 'I didn't. Whoever's in there, it's not me.'

Kovacs knew that everybody was thinking of their favourite curse-word. 'Well, there's nothing we can do about that. For right now, we'll just have to set up a perimeter around this junction.'

A lithe and dangerous-looking figure with white hair emerged from the shadows behind Sam. 'My people have already taken up positions on all four roads. We can deal with humans on foot, by clouding their minds and making them walk in circles so that they never arrive here. Those in vehicles, however, we cannot approach. You will have to deal with them.'

'Oh, joy,' Kovacs opined. 'You can at least warn us when they get here?'

'Of course.'

'Good.' He pointed down one road to the south. 'Most likely the Germans will have to come along from that direction. I want you to post a couple of your people there, a couple of miles along.' He pointed to the western road. 'Lewis'll be coming that way. Same arrangement: a couple of your people a couple of miles along that road. When your people see tanks on the way, they're to pull back and let us know. Got that?'

'I understand,' the white-haired figure agreed, melting away into the afternoon shadows.

'OK,' Sam said. 'So what are we doing while Galastel and the other Sidhe are watching our backs?'

Kovacs smiled lopsidedly. 'Becoming lumberjacks.'

A few miles away, Leitz signalled his column to halt on the road towards the Eifel. His three armoured cars were flanked by a couple of Tigers and half a dozen half-tracks full of troops.

He spread out a map on the top of his armoured car's turret, as Farber climbed up to join him. 'This is where we divide our forces,' Leitz told him. 'Position the Tigers in this copse, ready to approach the rest of us if needed. I want a defensive perimeter around this area on the Eifel.'

Leitz had drawn a circle on the map, enclosing all the points at which the detection equipment in his armoured cars had registered Elven activity. Lines drawn between them all crossed through a central point in the southern half of the Schnee Eifel, at a crossroads on the road the Americans had nicknamed the Skyline Drive. 'According to Lewis, the Americans will try to take and hold this area.'

'And we have to stop them?' Farber asked.

'No. We let them in, then enclose them, and make sure they never get out.'

'It would be easier just to mine the road here, and –'

'Easier, but not as useful in the long term. We – and here I speak for Wewelsburg also –' he lied – 'want to test whether a battle can be fought inside the *Marchenland*, the Sidhe realm. So, we let the Americans go there, then we follow them in and destroy them. If the experiment is successful, then we know we can engage enemy forces from there in such a way as to leave undamaged those resources in the areas they occupy. Then we can move in and take the spoils.'

Sweating despite the cold weather, Sam and the four men had been using their entrenching tools to cut down trees a mile along both the southern and western roads. The fallen trees had been stretched across the road, braced by those that had been left standing. Large tanks like Tigers would be able to roll over them, but any half-tracks or armoured cars would be held up, at least for a short time.

Even a short time was better than none at all.

Kovacs had also strung some grenades about ten feet off the road, a few yards on the far side of the fallen trees. Their pins were pulled, and the safety levers held on by thread tied to one end of the fallen trees. If someone tried to push a tree aside, anyone waiting in an open-topped half-track, or sitting out of the hatch of a tank turret, was in for a nasty surprise. Sam hadn't been happy about it, but Kovacs had overruled her.

Now Kovacs and Bearclaw withdrew into the undergrowth just within the boundary of the southern roadblock, while Garcia and Wiesniewski were positioned to watch the western approach. None of them had any illusions about how well two men, even with Sidhe help, could hold up an armoured column.

The Doctor had a time machine, so surely he would have the sense to come back to a point as soon after he left as possible? Kovacs hoped so, anyway. Just as much as he hoped the shadowy presences around him were on his side.

Back at the crossroads, Sam paced nervously, watched by a calm Galastel. 'Be at peace,' he suggested. 'What happens, will happen.'

'That's not very reassuring.'

'The Evergreen Man will do what is necessary.'

Sam grimaced. 'I'm the one who should be telling you that.' She was the one who should be doing something, anyway. Not sitting waiting for news.

'You probably will,' he said enigmatically.

'They – we – are so outnumbered.'

'Numbers mean little in such things,' Galastel said. 'Heart

matters. Soul matters. Those things have infinite capacity. Numbers are finite, and therefore nothing.'

He solidified, and she knew he had discovered something.

'They are here,' he announced. 'Leitz is approaching the south road.'

Kovacs had received the same news, and was now alert. He could hear tank engines and tracks in the distance, but the only sign of life so far was a small patrol of maybe half a dozen camouflaged SS troops, who were examining the roadblock.

Kovacs cursed again. He didn't want them to discover the grenade trap, but nor did he want them to trigger it. Not before there was a better target.

There was only one thing to do. Pressing himself against a tree-trunk, Kovacs opened fire with his Tommy gun. One of the SS troops fell, but the rest ducked under cover, and started laying fire down the road.

'What's happening?' Leitz demanded as his column halted. If the elves had returned, some ought to be taken alive.

A Waffen-SS corporal on foot saluted. 'The Americans. They've set up a roadblock about a mile from the crossroads. We need armour support.'

'How many Americans?'

'I don't know, but they're on both sides of the road, and have us pinned down.'

Leitz considered this. 'Send the two Tigers to flank them and run northeast through the woods to the crossroads. We'll charge them directly.'

Lewis sat in the turret of a modified Sherman, studying the roadblock of fallen trees. Surely the Germans would have gone for something more sophisticated, like concrete tank traps, or mines, or antitank guns?

No, this must be the Doctor's work.

He looked around carefully, and spotted the grenades strung above. He was surprised, horrified, but also harboured a faint sense of admiration. Who'd have thought the Doctor had such a devious trap in him?

'Button up,' he ordered, sinking into the turret and closing the hatch.

Garcia was curiously glad that Lewis had decided to take cover. He didn't want to be responsible for killing any American soldiers. Hell, he was a doctor – he didn't want to kill anybody.

The trap was better here anyway, as the southern side of the road fell away in a steep cutting, leaving the Shermans even less room for manoeuvre.

The leading Sherman nudged the fallen tree, and detonated the grenades. They exploded harmlessly above the tanks' steel.

The modifications made to the Shermans were less well protected, however. The strange electrical box on the first one exploded in a shower of sparks, while the second fizzled, and began to ripple, neither quite here nor there. It remained unmoving, preventing the four Shermans behind it from continuing along the road.

'What the hell is that?' Wiesniewski muttered. Garcia didn't have much of an answer. 'I wonder if it's hurting the Sidhe.'

'No,' Galastel's voice said in his ear. 'The mechanism is merely damaged. With such weak forces they can only break through at the centre of the rift.'

'The crossroads,' Wiesniewski said thoughtfully.

The first Sherman halted, even though the road was clear. Lewis and his crew were hastily disembarking, and opening the toolboxes that were also affixed to the sides of the tank.

'They must need repairs to continue,' Garcia said. 'Maybe this is our chance.'

'To do what?' Wiesniewski asked. 'I sure as hell can't open fire on our boys. Can you?'

'No, that's not what I was thinking,' Garcia said. He turned to the Sidhe. 'Galastel, if we can get the crews of those tanks away from them, can your people cloud their perceptions enough to lead them out of harm's way?'

'Easily,' Galastel said. 'If they leave the road and enter the woods…'

Garcia felt more at home suddenly. He would save some more lives here, not take them. If nothing else, those men would be able to fight the Germans later.

'Come on,' he said. 'Let's go and do our stuff.'

Bearclaw ducked behind a tree as the air filled with flying lead. More SS troops had reinforced the originals, and now a half-track was approaching the roadblock.

He realised with a mixture of fear and annoyance that he was too close to the trap they'd set – the shrapnel from the grenades would catch him too. He turned to run for a safe place, and found himself face to face with a German soldier.

Bearclaw was sure he was dead. He had survived the massacre, just to die alone like this. It wasn't fair.

Then the German stiffened and fell, and Bearclaw saw a tiny dart embedded in his neck. It was like a clothyard arrowshaft, but scaled down immensely. He sensed the area from which it had come, and directed a smile of thanks. All he could see there was some dead wood shifting in the breeze.

Behind him, the Hanomag rammed the barrier, and the grenades exploded. Yells and screams came from the half-track, as it careened off the road, its driver obviously incapacitated. It had knocked the roadblock aside, however, and armoured cars were approaching the gap. Bearclaw straightened. It was time to go.

* * *

Kovacs was in a clearing on the other side of the road. The Sidhe might have been keeping any footsoldiers out of the woods, but they weren't doing much about the ones who were accompanying the vehicles.

Several Germans had him pinned down in a small snow-filled depression, and he had begun to suspect that they might have figured out that they were just facing two men. Hell, maybe just one, if Bearclaw had been taken out.

He saw more SS helmets moving along the roadside ditch, and loosed a burst at them. They went down, but he thought they had dived rather than fallen.

Kovacs's nostrils were filled with the scent of hot metal from an overused gun, and he could barely hear himself think over the sound of shooting, but he just managed to hear the movement behind him. Someone had outflanked him.

Kovacs whirled round, but his Thompson was empty, and he had no spare magazines left. He swung the gun into the German's stomach. Winded, the man doubled over, and Kovacs smashed the butt of the Thompson over his head.

Kovacs drew his backup automatic, and saw that the German had a Luger stuck in his belt. He took that too. 'This is getting personal,' he muttered to himself.

Wiesniewski crept around the back of the last Sherman in Lewis's column, and climbed on to the rear deck. He rapped softly on the turret hatch. 'Hey, open up.'

The hatch cracked open about an inch, and an eye and a pistol muzzle peered out at him. When the owner of both saw an American soldier, he emerged more fully. 'What's up?'

Wiesniewski hoped he could make this convincing. He should be able to; it was more or less true. 'I need you and your boys to get out of this Ronson, and get into the woods.'

'What the hell for?' Wiesniewski winced, hoping Lewis's own crew up at the front wouldn't hear.

'Because you ain't here for whatever reason you think you are. You're here because Lewis has made a deal with the Krauts.' The tank commander started to protest, but then looked into Wiesniewski's eyes, and must have seen something there that silenced him. 'There's an SS colonel called Leitz, who's coming up the other road. Lewis has arranged to meet him at the crossroads.'

'Bullshit.'

'Look,' Wiesniewski said. He brandished his Tommy gun. 'If I was a German, I'd just shoot you, right? But I'm not, so I'm telling you something you need to know.'

The tank commander hesitated. 'OK... I guess you've got me on that one. And we can't move the tanks anyway until the front ones are repaired.'

'Right.'

Bearclaw got back to the crossroads, thoroughly out of breath. 'They're through the roadblock,' he told Sam.

'That's not your only concern,' a worried-looking Galastel said as he reappeared from co-ordinating his people. 'We have perhaps a hundred humans trapped in circles in the woods, but one of your tribes has sent two vehicles through the woods. We cannot approach them, and they are heading directly here.'

'Take us there,' Sam said immediately. Now maybe she could do something useful. Galastel grabbed both their arms, and suddenly the three of them were in the woods, about a hundred yards from what Sam recognised as two German tanks.

'Tigers,' Bearclaw said. 'Leitz is smarter than Lewis; I'll give him that. But we three can't hold them alone. Unless...'

'What?' Sam asked.

'The best way to stop Lewis's tanks would be to blow them to hell, right?'

Sam paused, clenching her fists. 'I guess. Given the circumstances.'

Bearclaw grinned. 'So if we gave these Tigers some nice American tanks to shoot at…'

Lewis heard a commotion from the rear of the column, and walked back to see what was happening. For some reason, the crews of the remaining four Shermans had dismounted, and were walking into the woods on one side of the road. There, the shadows enveloped them.

Stranger still, there were two newcomers watching him – Garcia and Wiesniewski. 'Traitors!' he yelled, and ran towards them.

Garcia ran, Wiesniewski held his ground.

'Sir! Sir!' he yelled urgently. 'I have to talk to you! We're no traitors!'

Lewis paused, still aiming his gun. He doubted the man could say anything to convince him.

Garcia ran. Perhaps he could use this opportunity to circle round, and get the rest of Lewis's crew to safety. Then they could think of some way to get rid of the tanks. Damage their engines, perhaps.

Before he could do any of this, he saw that Lewis's crew had taken it upon themselves to go and see what was happening. Once off the road, they would be taken.

He spotted Sam and Bearclaw running down the road from the direction of the crossroads. 'What's up?'

'The Germans have broken through,' Sam told him, 'and there are two Tigers cutting through the woods down there.' She pointed to the floor of the cutting on the other side of the road.

'Damn. Then we're –'

'In luck,' Bearclaw finished for him.

'In luck?' But surely the Germans would cut them off?

'We need something to destroy these Shermans, don't we? If

we go down and attract those Tigers' attention, we can draw them over here.'

Garcia nodded. It was crazy, but what wasn't crazy around here?

'All right,' Sam said, 'I'll make sure the crews are kept safe.'

'Yeah,' Garcia agreed. 'You do that. Then go find Kovacs and Wiesniewski, and tell them what we're up to – if they're still alive.'

'And if not?' Sam asked.

'Then you and Galastel get the hell out of here.'

To Wiesniewski's relief, Lewis had lowered his gun. He was a US officer, after all. He had to listen to listen to what Wiesniewski had to say.

The two men walked into the woods, Wiesniewski leading the way.

He had to make Lewis understand, somehow.

So what if Wiesniewski got cashiered; at least his family wouldn't have to worry. He might even see his daughter sooner on account of this.

Lewis followed him into the little clearing. 'Traitor!'

'Sir,' Wiesniewski said. 'I know how this looks, but you're being led into a trap, and I had to –' Something exploded into his chest, and he felt himself stumble, suddenly light-headed.

It wasn't until he fell to his knees that he even realised Lewis had shot him. He couldn't believe it; surely even a nut like Lewis had more morals than that. Didn't he?

Everybody dies alone, he realised suddenly. It didn't really matter whether it was a lonely alley or a bed in a deserted ward, or even a field in the thick of battle. Once people couldn't hear you anymore, and ignored you as no longer a threat, then you were alone under the open sky; small and afraid, the futility of your life naked and exposed to any passing gods.

The last thing Wiesniewski noticed was that Lewis had turned away, and not even stayed to watch him die.

Chapter Eleven
All the Time in the World

'What now?' Fitz asked the Doctor in the TARDIS.

'Now we beat the *Amadan* at his own game.'

'Not magic again?'

'That's simply a word humans use for arts they don't understand. Magic is the software system which operates reality. Sometimes it's formed by rudimentary technology; sometimes it's inherent. It's all the same thing. People tell each other that magic doesn't exist, and that there's only science; but really they're two words for the same thing.'

'I can think of a useful two words to say to you,' grumbled Fitz.

Bearclaw could think of better places to be than in freezing woods listening to two Tiger tanks rumbling towards him. There were huge crashes deeper in the woods, as the Tigers pushed down trees that they didn't have room to go around.

Even here, where the Tigers were far enough away to still look tiny, snow was being shaken loose from the deadwood all around.

For about the hundredth time, Bearclaw breathlessly checked the action on his Thompson. He felt as if his lungs were simply too small for all the air he needed. In his head he knew it was fear, but his heart wasn't listening. It didn't need to, because it knew he was doing the right thing. The only thing he could do, in fact.

He glanced across at Garcia a few yards away. The medic looked as sick with fear as Bearclaw felt, but he knew the reverse wasn't true. As if to prove him right, Garcia glanced round, and seemed to draw strength from Bearclaw's apparent calm. He felt a little better for being able to boost Garcia's confidence.

'You ready?' he asked.

Garcia hesitated before answering. 'No,' he admitted finally. 'You?'

Bearclaw smiled. 'No.' It wasn't really possible to feel ready for something like this. They exchanged a look, and Bearclaw knew that Garcia understood that too. You just had to go for it anyway.

By now the Tigers were close enough to hit with a thrown baseball as they churned through the snow. Bearclaw hefted a grenade, and pulled the pin. He threw it at the lead Tiger, and heard it clang against the hull a moment before it exploded to one side.

Garcia then leaned out from the side of a tree, and fired a burst. Bearclaw did likewise, this time aiming at the second Tiger.

The lead tank paused, its turret purring round. It was terrifying looking down the barrel of an 88mm cannon, but Bearclaw knew that no tank crew would be stupid enough to waste valuable shells on two lone footsoldiers.

The machine gun set beside the cannon opened fire instead, but Bearclaw and Garcia had already taken cover. There was no more sound for a moment, and Bearclaw began to wonder if maybe the tank crews had decided that two men weren't worth bothering with. Then he heard the blast of another grenade, and knew that Garcia had regained their attention.

He turned, pausing long enough to fire off a few rounds at the tanks, but not long enough to let them get a bead on him. It didn't matter how inaccurate his own shooting was – the bullets couldn't harm the tanks anyway – he just needed to get their attention. Now the Tigers' engines roared, and he knew he had it.

The trick now was to stay just out of killing range, but close enough to lead them towards the west road. It shouldn't be too difficult, Bearclaw reasoned, since the rough ground was hampering the Tigers. There was no danger of them catching up to the two men.

The TARDIS had materialised, much to Fitz's horror, at the Philadelphia navy yard. From a convenient vantage point, the Doctor sipped some tea as they watched a medium-sized destroyer in the docks. 'There we are,' he said. 'Just over two thousand tons.'

'You can't steal the ship from the Philadelphia Experiment!' Sam protested. 'It's famous.'

'Famous for disappearing, isn't it?' the Doctor pointed out reasonably.

'Well, yes… But…' Sam didn't actually quite know what to say. 'That's not the point! What happens to the ship when the rift closes?'

'It'll be buried under the Eifel.'

'That'll confuse the hell out of Tony Robinson if ever they do a *Time Team* here.'

'If she means it's going to play havoc with future archaeologists,' Fitz said, 'she's damn right.'

'Oh, I can think of at least one who'd see the funny side,' smiled the Doctor. But then it was time to move, as the ship began to glow.

Leitz was glad to see that the gunfire had died down. Sitting comfortably, half out of the turret of his SdKfz 232, he doubted that the fierce battle had been a sign that Lewis had betrayed him.

The American colonel would have to have put on a show for the benefit of his subordinates, so that they wouldn't know about the private deal between the two of them. It was also possible that lone pockets of isolated resistance still remained behind the new lines. Perhaps a few soldiers, cut off from their units.

Whoever they were, they were no longer firing at the impromptu roadblock. Leitz ordered his driver to halt for a moment to survey the situation. There was still no sign of Lewis's Shermans, and the fallen trees were pushed far enough to the side that his 232 could get past easily.

To his right, a dented Hanomag was listing in the roadside ditch, a couple of bodies draped over the side. The rest of its occupants must have spread out on foot in the woods to either side.

'Go ahead,' he told the driver.

As the first of three armoured cars approached, Kovacs tensed. He was crouched down in the abandoned Hanomag, and the three-man armoured car looked like just the sort of thing he'd been waiting for.

As it passed, Kovacs sprang up, firing both his Colt and the Luger at a couple of footsoldiers who were walking beside it. They fell, and the *Sturmbannführer* in the 232's turret – from the circumstances, Kovacs figured it could only be Leitz – turned in astonishment.

Before Leitz could pull a gun, Kovacs had planted a foot on the edge of the Hanomag's side, and launched himself across the gap between vehicles. It wasn't easy at his age, and he knew he'd better hit the mark; if he fell he doubted he'd be able to get up again.

He slammed into the rear deck of the 232, and damn near slid right off. Luckily he managed to wrap an arm round one of the supports for that big clothes-rack antenna. All the same, he lost his moment as well as his captured Luger, and Leitz managed to draw a gun.

Kovacs fired blind as Leitz leaned out to bring his own pistol to bear. The shot caught Leitz in the shoulder, and he lost his balance, tumbling from the turret with a yell. Kovacs didn't stop to see whether he was dead or not, but squeezed up under the antenna to drop into the turret.

He let the driver live for now, but shot the other man, and kicked him out the side door that was set into the main hull. Then he put his gun to the back of the driver's head. 'Turn this thing around.'

'What?'

'Turn this thing around or you're dead.'

The driver was sweating with fear, Kovacs saw. It didn't take another order to convince him. He stopped the 232 and made a surprisingly smooth three-point turn. 'Good boy,' Kovacs breathed. 'Now get going.'

'Towards them?' the driver asked in surprise, indicating the other two 232s, which now loomed in the vision-slit.

'That's right. Never played chicken?'

Kovacs prodded the driver's neck with the gun muzzle to reinforce the order. Gulping noisily, the driver started the armoured car moving.

'Step on it,' Kovacs urged. 'As fast as this heap will go.'

The driver complied, sending the eight and a half ton car hurtling towards its fellows at fifty miles per hour. There was a scream and a wet thud, and Kovacs realised with a mixture of horror and pleasure that they had just run over Leitz.

By the way the driver's knuckles had whitened on the steering column with fear, Kovacs knew he'd be the chicken, and turn away first. He couldn't risk it. He grabbed the back of the driver's collar, so that the man wouldn't fall sideways and pull the car off course when Kovacs shot him in the head.

The man didn't. Ignoring the blood that spattered his hands, Kovacs released the body slowly, making sure he kept the car on course. He then ducked back, and dived headlong out the open side door.

As Kovacs thudded into the ground and rolled into the roadside ditch, the 232 sped on. The other drivers had realised the danger too late, and tried to dodge aside. But the lifeless car simply smashed into both.

The careering car went up on one side, a couple of wheels flying off, while slamming one of the other 232s to a complete halt. Then it exploded, scattering burning fuel across the crash site. None of the other cars were in any condition to continue – they were mangled, with shattered axles and dead or screaming crew.

Kovacs wanted to get up and get the hell out of the way, but he couldn't. His body didn't want to know. At least he was still breathing, which was more than he could say for the red and black mess that used to be Leitz, a few dozen yards along the road.

Kovacs hoped that maybe the Germans would think he was dead too. At least the Sidhe could pick off the survivors. It didn't matter about the remaining half-tracks, or even the Tigers. They couldn't enter the Rift.

Patton had said that no poor dumb bastard ever won a war by dying for his country; that you win wars by making the other poor dumb bastard die for his. He'd had the wrong end of the stick, Kovacs admitted. Poor dumb bastards like himself won wars by staying alive for their country, and keeping their men alive for their country too.

Of course, it helped if you had something to believe in.

Kovacs had another war to believe in. And as soon as the Sidhe reached him, he was going there.

The TARDIS materialised a little more quietly than usual, on the deck of the USS *Eldridge*.

Outside the TARDIS, the sea and sky were a jumble of colours and tastes and sounds. The deck the Doctor, Fitz and Sam stood on wavered like a desert mirage, and fragments of speech and music drifted, just barely on the fringes of hearing.

It was uncomfortably warm, and the tonalities produced by the unfelt winds were dizzying.

'Groovy,' Fitz said approvingly. 'This place would give Lennon and McCartney headaches.' He half expected the Doctor to be very blasé and shrug it all off as just another storm.

'It probably would,' the Doctor agreed, looking out at the unreality of it all with the expression of a small child on his first visit to Santa's grotto. 'Magnificent, isn't it?'

That was one way of putting it. 'Where is this anyway? I thought we were supposed to be in Philadelphia.' Fitz had the distinct impression that the jumbled universe above was looking down at him, reminding him how small he really was.

'We are,' said the Doctor, 'but this ship has been dephased. Right now we're out of phase with Earth's reality ourselves.'

'You said the TARDIS couldn't do that,' Sam pointed out.

'I said the TARDIS couldn't give a full reach over the entirety of the Sidhe domain. This ship has been dephased by very primitive technology, so it's just on the borderline of reality. That's why there's so much interference out there. Well within the TARDIS's limitations, though.'

Maybe, thought Fitz. But not within the crew's limitations. Some of them were frozen in screams, others radiating streams of pain as visible energy. It looked as if their bodies were on fire. Some of them were contorted grotesquely, a few even literally beside themselves, somehow duplicated in time.

'Jesus Christ! This is...'

'Loss of dimensional cohesion, you see. We're all right walking around when the ship is fixed at one phase, but during transition, anyone not protected by a stabiliser and a dimensional osmosis dampener has got severe problems.'

'Then they're all dead?'

The Doctor shook his head. 'Far worse. Remember what I said about the senses and being hanged, drawn and quartered?'

Fitz shuddered. 'Can't we do anything for them? I mean, anything's better than this, surely?'

The Doctor shook his head. 'In this state we can't do anything that would affect them. Look.' By way of demonstration, he waved a hand clean through the nearest crewman, who showed no sign of even having noticed.

The Doctor locked the TARDIS door, then unlocked it again, with a strange flick of the wrist. 'Come on, you two, I'll need some help to carry things.'

'Why did you lock it first, then?' Fitz followed him in, Sam bringing up the rear, but instead of the usual converted-monastery console room, he found himself in a relatively small and cramped white room. Indented circles were set in rows in the walls, and a smaller metallic hexagonal console was set on the floor.

'Because,' the Doctor said, 'entering *this* console room through the front doors is easier than walking through three miles of corridor to get here.'

Instead of the interlocking console and ceiling rotors that Fitz was familiar with, this console simply had a cylindrical column, filled with plasticky-looking tubes. Industrial type dials and switches were set on to the white and steel panels. The Doctor had already got his sonic screwdriver to work, and was pulling off one of the console panels.

He laid it carefully to one side, then disassembled another panel further round, and started digging out odd-looking pieces of scientific junk from the heart of the console. He worked rather like a pagan priest casting horoscopes from sheep's entrails, Fitz thought.

'There we go!' the Doctor exclaimed finally, holding aloft a complex piece of crystalline electronics. 'A spare RDS.'

'Lucky you had a spare,' Sam said, rather sarcastically.

'Actually, all TARDIS consoles have them.' He gathered up the two console panels, and some of the other technological viscera, and dumped them in Fitz's arms. They were heavier than they looked, and Fitz gasped at the weight. The Doctor, meanwhile, pocketed the stabiliser, and lifted a selection of the tubelike instruments out from the time rotor. Carrying them, and the remaining bits and pieces that had fallen from the ill-balanced pile Fitz held, the Doctor left. 'Come on!' he shouted. 'No time to waste!'

The sparse wood led back to the steep cutting that bordered the road where Lewis's tanks were halted. Both Garcia and Bearclaw hared out across the open ground. The cold was really stinging Garcia's lungs, and he wondered how Bearclaw kept up the pace. Would he ever have such a level of fitness himself?

Abruptly, the ground ahead of them exploded into steam and shrapnel, and they flung themselves backwards. Looking up, Garcia could see the rounded turret of one of Lewis's Shermans, and Lewis and a couple of his loyal troopers trying to get a clear shot at them.

Garcia grimaced, and hurried Bearclaw to a point directly under the troops, out of their line of fire. Propping himself against the rock that supported the promontory on which the tank stood, Garcia at least had the chance to catch his breath. 'Flares?' he suggested after a moment.

Bearclaw shook his head. 'I've got a couple of smoke grenades.'

'For all we know,' Garcia said doubtfully, frowning, 'that just might make the Germans think the Shermans are out of action.'

'You got a better idea?'

Garcia didn't bother to reply. They both knew what his answer would be.

Lewis fired again as he registered a flicker of movement at

another part of the ledge below. More traitors. They were down there somewhere.

There was a massive explosion to his right, and then another to his left. Lewis ducked under the Sherman, even though part of his mind knew that if those had been fragmentation grenades he would already be hit.

He never saw the Tigers that were rumbling through the trees, but he turned just in time to see the smoke marking the positions of those tanks flanking him. They hadn't yet got into position to enter the Sidhe realm, and now they never would.

The last Sherman split apart with a thunderclap, a wall of fire billowing outwards and engulfing the few men around it.

Garcia and Bearclaw hurled themselves back down the cutting as soon as they had tossed the smokers up on to the road. They lost their footing in seconds, and tumbled headlong back down the slope.

A good job, as it turned out, as the nearby Tigers' guns boomed, and shells slammed into the Shermans. Explosions hurled chunks of shrapnel out from the stalled tanks and off the edge of the road.

Bearclaw yelled out, only half in fear, but half in exhilaration. The feeling of sliding through the air was thoroughly enjoyable, and he could almost forget the imminent impact with the ground.

The bone-crushing impact he had expected never occurred. Instead, he slapped into a wet heap of snow, where the slope became more gentle, and tumbled uncontrollably downhill. He managed to catch brief glimpses of Garcia sliding and tumbling a few feet away.

Garcia and Bearclaw flung themselves flat as the phasing Shermans were torn apart in a series of blazing fireballs on the plateau above. They were certainly earning their 'Ronson' nickname today. Chunks of burning shrapnel hissed into the snow all around.

Bearclaw could hear little else over his own ragged breathing. A plume of smoke was billowing from the plateau, and steam was rising into the air from what looked like a thousand little craters all over the slope. He concentrated on settling his breathing, as the Tigers fired a last few shots up at the road.

The Tigers paused, then rumbled around on their axes and resumed their previous course towards the crossroads.

Bearclaw didn't really care so much now. Duty was done. None of the tanks could enter the other world.

The whole exterior of the USS *Eldridge* was festooned with thick insulated degaussing cables. At junctions, dials and meters were set up, with wirerecorders preserving the measurements for posterity. Not that anyone would ever get a chance to see them, Fitz reflected.

A faint green glow, like the phosphorescence of rotting meat, bled out of the cables, along with a straining hum that pulsed steadily.

The Doctor, Sam, and Fitz followed the cables inside, and below decks to the engine room. There, large electrical switchboards crowded the already-cramped area. The noise was deafening, with both the hangover-like pounding of the engines, and the magnified pulsing of the cables.

'How long have we got before the ship reverts to normal space, or disappears off to somewhere else entirely?' Fitz asked.

'I've no idea.' The Doctor put down his cargo of TARDIS components, and bent to examine a central set of dials and recording apparatus. 'Time is out of synch here.'

Quickly, he started connecting the TARDIS components to a large addition at the centre of the engine room. Though built of the sort of resistors and transformers that Fitz recognised, it glowed with that same eerie green air. It didn't take long for the Doctor to make his adjustments.

'What exactly will this do?' Sam asked.

'Allow us to remotely position the ship in the Rift and switch off the phase inversion field from the TARDIS. Much more sensible than doing it manually in here. That *would* be somewhat suicidal.' He peered at a junction for the second set of cables, which accompanied the main ones around the ship. 'Interesting, there seem to be two sets of coils here. One setting up the phase inversion field, and the other rendering the hull geomantically neutral...'

'Geo-what neutral?' Fitz asked.

'The Sidhe are vulnerable to ferric metal, remember? One of these coils is demagnetising the hull, trying to keep the ship non-ferrous. In this context that can only be so that it's possible for Sidhe to board her.'

'What, so it was done before it ended up here?' Fitz said.

The Doctor nodded. 'Must've been.'

'Then it's safe to assume we can expect company before too long?'

'Yes.'

'But this is a year earlier than where we were,' Fitz protested. 'Any Sidhe we meet won't know why we're here yet...'

'Not necessarily. They have an intuitive relationship with time. Remember what Sam said about Galastel taking her back several days, to when we arrived? Oberon isn't a fool; there's always the danger that he might work out what we're up to, and follow us back.'

'Oh, I don't think that'll be necessary,' Sam said nastily. The Doctor and Fitz looked at her, realisation dawning. This wasn't Sam. Their perceptions had been altered, Fitz realised. They'd been made to see Sam; hear Sam's voice saying the sort of things Sam'd say. Clever. But this was Oberon; lean, mean, catlike.

'I thought as much,' the Doctor said. Fitz suspected he was lying through his teeth, but you could never tell with the Doctor. 'Couldn't resist the chance to have a go at me, could you?'

'Titania needs no other consort.'

The Doctor looked as surprised as Fitz. 'Is that what this is about? Jealousy?'

'No,' Oberon admitted. 'But I do have my position as *Amadan na Briona* to protect.'

'You have a funny idea of how to go about it, then,' the Doctor said dismissively. 'Interfering in human affairs, risking a war between your people and theirs…'

'And the problem with that is…?' Oberon laughed. 'Mortals fight and die all the time. Why shouldn't I enjoy it?'

'Enjoyment doesn't seem motive enough,' the Doctor said, motioning behind his back for Fitz to head back up on deck. At the same time, he stalked to one side, drawing Oberon away from the TARDIS components. 'What's in it for you?' the Doctor demanded. 'I may only be the Evergreen Man, and not as well-up on your people as I should be, but I can't understand how you can possibly hope to profit from turning this war to your own ends.'

'Of course you can't,' Oberon said dismissively. 'You're small, and narrow-minded. You can't see what freedom really is.'

'Then tell me,' the Doctor demanded. 'Tell me what you hope to gain.'

'Gain?' Oberon echoed. 'I have everything I could ever want. Why should I need anything else?'

'But then…' The Doctor paused. 'You know, I was assuming that you were aiming for some plan, some goal. But you're not, are you? You're just doing this because you can. You've got nothing to gain, and nothing to lose.' But then his eyes narrowed. 'Or have you?' he murmured under his breath. 'Perhaps I'm looking at this from the wrong angle…'

He started ascending the companionway back up to the deck. 'The other Sidhe won't stand for this! Do you really want to alienate yourself from them?'

Oberon laughed. 'You may know us, Evergreen Man, but you do not understand us, or you would never speak so foolishly.' He swaggered up after the Doctor. 'No one from any clan will speak ill against me. I am Chaos, to Titania's Order. It's my existence to be chaotic, random, dangerous.' He pretended to think about it. 'In fact, it's my moral duty to do absolutely anything I feel like, and not worry about the consequences! You should try it sometime,' he added, 'it's very liberating.'

'I'm liberated enough.' By now, the Doctor had led Oberon back out on to the quarterdeck. Without warning, he moved back and slammed the bulkhead door closed behind the *Amadan*, pulling the small wires away from it. Oberon recoiled from the door immediately. Now he couldn't get back into the engine room – the door was no longer neutral. He was trapped outside with the Doctor and Fitz.

'Nice one,' Fitz thought.

'Stop this!' The *Amadan* lunged for the Doctor, drawing a dagger of pure malice from the air.

'Fitz, get back to the TARDIS.' The Doctor tossed the key to him. 'I left a note –' He broke off to throw his coat around Oberon's arm, trapping the dagger under the cloth.

Fitz didn't need to be told twice. But, he thought, that note had better be some instructions on how to close the Rift.

The *Amadan* was stronger than he appeared, and it took all of the Doctor's strength just to force his arm away. But that overbalanced Oberon, and the Doctor took the opportunity to swing him around, slamming him against the wall. Oberon must have guessed his move in time, as he phased himself through the wall at the moment of impact, and it was the Doctor who crashed painfully into the steel.

He dropped to his knees, shaking his head in the hope that it would clear the ringing in his ears. He managed to recover just in time to dodge Oberon's next lunge, and caught the Sidhe's arm again. He rapped sharply on the back of Oberon's wrist, and the dagger clattered across the deck, fetching up against one of the junction boxes.

The Doctor hesitated, thoughts swirling through his mind, and then hurled himself towards the dagger. His fingers closed round the hilt just as Oberon pulled him back by his collar.

'No more games, Time Lord,' the *Amadan* hissed in his ear. 'This ends now.'

Steeling himself, the Doctor rammed the dagger into the nearest degaussing cable, where it entered a socket on the junction box.

The energy discharge blew him backwards, and blasted Oberon clear across the deck. Sidhe and Time Lord both rolled and thrashed where they fell, contorted with agony.

'No,' Oberon snarled. 'You mustn't.' He started to rise, and the Doctor forced himself to his knees. He couldn't allow Oberon to reach him before he got back to the cable.

The Doctor grabbed the cable in his left hand, and took a deep breath before touching the hilt of the dagger again. Pain coursed through him as if every nerve was on fire, but he managed to hold on long enough to rip the dagger upwards, severing the cable and breaking the circuit of which it was a part.

Even as the Doctor fell backward, screaming, he could sense the electrical energy snaking across the ship's hull. The junction box exploded in sparks, and brief flickers of lightning wrapped themselves around the superstructure.

Oberon screamed, a high and warbling screech, chillingly like the sound of a child in agony. 'No!' The Doctor half expected the insane Sidhe to attack him again, but no assault came. It had worked.

Fighting to dismiss the burning that coursed through his bones and teeth, the Doctor rose, and looked for Oberon. The *Amadan na Briona* was quivering, rooted to the spot, and sheathed in lightning. It looked almost as if the little rivulets of blue fire were consciously trying to enter and possess him through any available pores.

'Release me!' he demanded.

'I can't.'

'I can change,' Oberon managed to say through gritted teeth. 'I can undo what has been done…'

'No, you can't. That suggestion is just more proof that you could never change. Besides, I didn't say I wouldn't get you out – I said I couldn't. With the degaussing loop off-line, the steel will have its normal effect on your kind. You can't move, can't phase out, can't communicate… And enough exposure will kill you. If it's any consolation, you won't be here long enough for the latter.' The Doctor retrieved his coat from the deck, and pulled it on.

'No?' Oberon whispered hopefully.

'No. The ship will phase back into normal space soon, and close the rift.'

'But I am trapped here. When the rift collapses…'

'You'll lose dimensional cohesion, and anything that's left will be crushed when the rift collapses in on itself.'

'Make it stop!'

'It's too late for that,' the Doctor said sadly. 'You see, you've lived so long, able to do anything and not be held responsible by others. Absolutely anything. But what about holding *yourself* responsible? I think that's what you hoped to gain from meddling in the war. I think you wanted the only thing you didn't have – a limit. You risked the destruction of your own world and the humans, just to see how far you could go before you were stopped.' The Doctor shook his head. 'Well, now you know.'

'No! Help me!'

'I can't,' the Doctor told him simply.

'Please,' Oberon screeched. 'Please, Evergreen Man. I'll be good…'

The Doctor turned on his heel. He'd made the same promise, once, himself.

Fitz was relieved to see that the note was exactly what he hoped, telling him which controls to work on the console. How long was he supposed to wait before following the instructions? Or did the Doctor mean to sacrifice himself by having Fitz do the honours immediately? How could he –

As he hovered in indecision, the Doctor ran into the console room, and started pulling on the controls. Fitz sighed with relief.

'Hang on,' the Doctor said, without commenting on whether Fitz had done the right thing or not.

The TARDIS faded from the *Eldridge*'s deck, chased by a heart-rending scream from Oberon.

Then, as the Doctor's additions to the engine room became active, the sky changed, and the crewmen faded away like dying echoes.

The churning forces of reality tugged at Oberon, tearing him apart in eleven directions at once. Every fibre of his being was ripped asunder, his whole existence peeled away layer by layer. With a last heart-rending scream, the *Amadan na Briona* flared out of existence.

A dull boom sundered the sky over the Ardennes. Vibration lifted the snow off the ground in a single massive sheet for just a moment, then a series of shock waves rippled out, shaking snow loose from the branches, and causing men to duck and stagger as they fought to keep their balance.

* * *

Garcia and Bearclaw had made it back to the crossroads, noting the smoke from the burning armoured cars.

Garcia paused, somehow knowing in his heart that this was a sign that the Doctor had succeeded. He couldn't see or hear any physical difference, but he felt it all the same. That Oz factor the Doctor had mentioned before seemed to be gone. That was the only rationale he could think of.

'There's Kovacs,' Bearclaw pointed out. They went over, Garcia feeling rather worried again. Kovacs was lying by the roadside, unmoving.

As they approached, however, Garcia could see that he was watching them with a vague smile. 'Are you hurt?'

Kovacs shook his head. 'Nothing a few drinks wouldn't cure. Just dead beat.'

Garcia nodded, and looked around him, his heart heavy. He was a healer. His duty was to all the wounded around here – Sidhe, allies – even the Germans. There was one struggling weakly nearby.

Garcia went over to the German and examined him. 'Well, you'll probably sit out the war in a prison camp, but at least you'll live –'

Garcia felt the breath leave his body, as if he'd been winded by a heavy punch. He looked down. Between himself and the wounded man, the hilt of a bayonet was protruding from Garcia's solar plexus.

He stared at it, unable, for a moment, to comprehend how it had got there. The truth hit him at the same time as the pain did – a relentless cold burning that was spreading out from the blade.

His medical knowledge was suddenly a curse. One part of his mind calmly told him that the blade had missed his heart, but that it had gone through the liver and one kidney. Intellectually he knew that blood and bile were flooding his torso, but the only thing he found himself able to consciously think was to wonder, 'Why?'

He hadn't even realised he'd spoken the word aloud. He had been trying to help this man; the fight was over. Why had he done it? Why –

'No!' Bearclaw screamed.

Without Garcia's help, the German would clearly die now. But though the German was wounded, dying, and now unarmed, Bearclaw emptied a pistol into his head anyway, screaming out his rage.

Sam and Galastel passed through the woods around the crossroads unseen. They'd dragged soldiers from wreckage, and Galastel had soothed the injured. There was no sign of the burning Rift, or of the Beast within it.

They were still bristling all over the people, of course.

'That's enough,' Sam told Galastel. 'Too many bad memories. Take me back. Back down to human levels.'

At least when constrained by human limitations of perception, she couldn't see the Beast. That alone was worth it.

'You're sure?' Galastel asked. 'You would turn your back on these powers. You would be… human?'

Sam nodded. 'It's who I am. Who I know.' She found herself smiling as she spoke. 'It's who I want to be.'

Kovacs, Bearclaw, Galastel and Sam gathered round the TARDIS as it arrived in a small clearing near the crossroads.

'It's done.' Galastel said when the Doctor and Fitz emerged.

'It damn well better be,' Kovacs growled. 'It cost enough.'

'It *is* done,' the Doctor confirmed, turning to Galastel. 'The Rift is closed. The humans' war shouldn't damage you any more.'

'And the *Amadan na Briona*?'

'I imagine Titania will have found a new one by now.'

Titania was radiant in every respect when she returned to the forest. The battle had moved on, leaving the survivors to lick their wounds.

'Thank you,' she told the Doctor.

'Don't mention it.'

'For someone who cares so much about others, and would sacrifice so much, you are so alone.' She passed a hand absently through the tabletop. 'Why is that? You have friends in a thousand worlds and a thousand eras, yet you choose to go on alone. It seems odd, to those of us who need companionship to survive.'

The Doctor tapped the spot on the table, where her hand had passed through. He looked disappointed that he couldn't pull off the same trick. 'I choose it because I can. That's what choices are for; it's what free will is for.'

'That's not an answer.'

'No, it isn't really, is it? But I'm not sure what answer I could give you, other than it's who I am. Maybe that's all that matters. And what's your excuse?'

'I'm not alone.'

'Ah… You have courtiers and attendants and guards who will die for you… But you're still alone. And being alone in a crowd is the worst form of loneliness. I think that's the difference between us.' He tapped his chest. 'There's a little part of all my friends in here. They're always with me; and in the same way, I imagine, I'm always with them.' He hesitated, as if searching for the right words, then leaned in close to her ear. 'My path often crosses those that wander from the light, and I find myself in places where shadows cast themselves freely. Others walk those paths, too, but only from one place to another. No matter how many get to where they're going, there will always be someone else who needs a fellow traveller on the road through the shadows. And it's a road that winds and will never end.'

'But someone has to be there,' she said understandingly.

'Yes. And that's not what I want, or what I do…'

'It's who you are,' she said softly. He didn't answer.

The Doctor returned to the TARDIS long after he'd left it, hands pushed deep in his pockets. Sam watched him approach on the scanner screen, and sighed. The brooding alien coming back to his insignificant humans.

He came through the door and beamed at her. 'Well, it's been quite an adventure, but –'

'Take me home,' she said simply.

The Doctor stopped in his tracks and stared at her. She flushed very slightly as she realised Fitz was staring at her too. He looked a little hurt, perhaps because she hadn't discussed this with him first before saying anything.

'Why?' Fitz asked. 'Why now?'

Sam shrugged. 'I think… I think I finally learned it's time to stop running.'

'I've always said exercise was bad for you,' Fitz said, deadpan, but Sam held up a hand, silently asking him to let her finish.

'You know what I mean. I don't need to do this anymore.'

'It's not…' Fitz fiddled with his jacket nervously. 'It's not because you and me…'

'No,' Sam said quickly. 'No, not at all, don't be silly. It's just…' She sighed again. 'I don't need to follow someone else to know who I am, now. I feel like I've been pulled apart and put back together again – literally – more times than anyone should have to put up with… And yet it's like you said, Doctor. Whatever I've been through, I'm still me – the only me – when I come out the other side. I'm Sam Jones… and I don't think I really need to be anyone's assistant anymore. If someone needs my help, I can give it. I know that now.'

She checked to make sure the Doctor wasn't making puppy-dog eyes at her or something, but no, he was still just staring at her. The old sod, why couldn't he just react or something?

In the silence, she carried on, her voice a little more plaintive. 'You said to me, remember, when Fitz first came on board. You said that sometimes we all had to make choices. That's what makes us ourselves, doesn't it? The choices we make?' She listened to herself, still asking him questions, still wanting his approval, even now. Still he could do this to her. 'I am... I'm myself, who I ought to be.' She smiled. 'Might be the best thing I've learned from you.'

Fitz nodded, regarded her evenly, then turned and headed towards his room. 'You heard her, Doctor,' he said. 'She's made her choice. Set sail for 1997.'

The door closed behind him with a gentle click. Sam took a deep breath and a step nearer the Doctor. 'The next time we land on Earth,' she said, 'if it's around the time we first met up, I'm getting off.' She paused again, still waiting for some kind of reaction. 'OK?'

When the Doctor's answer came it was to flick an array of switches on the console and to yank the big brass take-off lever down in its housing. 'OK', he said.

PRESENTING

ALL-NEW AUDIO DRAMAS

Big Finish Productions is proud to present all-new *Doctor Who* adventures on audio!

Featuring original music and sound-effects, these full-cast plays are available on double cassette in high street stores, and on limited-edition double CD from Forbidden Planet and other good specialist stores, or via mail order.

The adventures begin with
THE SIRENS OF TIME

A four-part story by Nicholas Briggs.
Starring **Peter Davison, Colin Baker** and **Sylvester McCoy**.

The Fifth, Sixth and Seventh Doctors, together for the first time!

Gallifrey is in a state of crisis, facing destruction at the hands of an overwhelming enemy. And the Doctor is involved, in three different incarnations – each caught up in a deadly adventure, scattered across time and space. The web of time is threatened – and someone wants the Doctor dead.

The three incarnations of the Doctor must join together to set time back on the right track – but in doing so, will they unleash a still greater threat?

If you wish to order the CD version, please photocopy this form or provide all the details on paper if you do not with to damage this book. Delivery within 28 days of release. Send to: PO Box 1127, Maidenhead, Berkshire. SL6 3LN.
Big Finish Hotline 01628 828283

Please send me [ ] copies of *The Sirens of Time* @ £13.99 (£15.50 non-UK orders) – price inclusive of postage and packing. Payment can be accepted by credit card or by personal cheques, payable to Big Finish Productions Ltd.

Name...

Address..

Postcode..

VISA/Mastercard number...

Expiry date...Signature..

For more details visit our website at **http://www.doctorwho.co.uk**

EIGHT DOCTOR BOOKS

DOCTOR WHO: THE NOVEL OF THE FILM *by Gary Russell*
ISBN 0 563 38000 4
THE EIGHT DOCTORS *by Terrance Dicks* ISBN 0 563 40563 5
VAMPIRE SCIENCE *by Jonathan Blum and Kate Orman*
ISBN 0 563 40566 X
THE BODYSNATCHERS *by Mark Morris* ISBN 0 563 40568 6
GENOCIDE *by Paul Leonard* ISBN 0 563 40572 4
WAR OF THE DALEKS *by John Peel* ISBN 0 563 40573 2
ALIEN BODIES *by Lawrence Miles* ISBN 0 563 40577 5
KURSAAL *by Peter Anghelides* ISBN 0 563 40578 3
OPTION LOCK *by Justin Richards* ISBN 0 563 40583 X
LONGEST DAY *by Michael Collier* ISBN 0 563 40581 3
LEGACY OF THE DALEKS *by John Peel* ISBN 0 563 40574 0
DREAMSTONE MOON *by Paul Leonard* ISBN 0 563 40585 6
SEEING I *by Jonathan Blum and Kate Orman*
ISBN 0 563 40586 4
PLACEBO EFFECT *by Gary Russell* ISBN 0 563 40587 2
VANDERDEKEN'S CHILDREN *by Christopher Bulis*
ISBN 0 563 40590 2
THE SCARLET EMPRESS *by Paul Magrs* ISBN 0 563 40595 3
THE JANUS CONJUNCTION *by Trevor Baxendale*
ISBN 0 563 40599 6
BELTEMPEST *by Jim Mortimore* ISBN 0 563 40593 7
THE FACE-EATER *by Simon Messingham* ISBN 0 563 55569 6
THE TAINT *by Michael Collier* ISBN 0 563 55568 8
DEMONTAGE *by Justin Richards* ISBN 0 563 55572 6
REVOLUTION MAN *by Paul Leonard* ISBN 0 563 55570 X
DOMINION *by Nick Walters* ISBN 0 563 55574 2
UNNATURAL HISTORY *by Jonathan Blum and Kate Orman*
ISBN 0 563 55576 9

OTHER BBC DOCTOR WHO BOOKS

SHORT STORY COLLECTIONS

SHORT TRIPS *ed. Stephen Cole* ISBN 0 563 40560 0
MORE SHORT TRIPS *ed. Stephen Cole* ISBN 0 563 55565 3

NON-FICTION

THE BOOK OF LISTS *by Justin Richards and Andrew Martin*
ISBN 0 563 40569 4
A BOOK OF MONSTERS *by David J. Howe*
ISBN 0 563 40562 7
THE TELEVISION COMPANION *by David J. Howe and*
Stephen James Walker ISBN 0 563 40588 0
FROM A TO Z *by Gary Gillatt* ISBN 0 563 40589 9